CHARGER

Steel Valley Chains MC

C.M. DANKS

Copyright © 2021 C.M. Danks
Charger
All rights reserved.

All rights reserved. No part of this book may be reproduced in any manner without written permission of the copyright owner except for the use of quotations in a book review.

This is a work of fiction. Names, characters, places, and incidents are the product of the author's imagination or used fictitiously. Any resemblance to actual persons, living or dead, events, or locales is entirely coincidental.

Edited by KAT PAGAN
Cover Designed by WICKED OWL DESIGNS
Formatted by WICKED OWL DESIGNS

ISBN 978-1-7362807-3-7

SYNOPSIS

Jules

He was my shield from the outside world. My best friend. My protector. The boy next door, who promised he would never hurt me, never abandon me. But he did leave, and he crushed my already shredded heart in the process. I can't forgive him, and yet... it was always him; it will always be *him*. Until every last star burns out.

Charger

I promised her all the stars in the sky. And then, I ran. I ran because I was hurt. I ran because I was afraid. Because I was a coward. And now? Now, she's back. The girl next door with the gorgeous smile and eyes that make me weak. But I'm not the same boy I was in high school. That boy is gone. My name is Charger now and I roll with the Steel Valley Chains MC. And while I can never be that guy for her again, I just cannot let any other man touch her either. Because it has been, and will always be, *her*. Until every last star burns out.

Please Note:

Some of the content found in *Charger* is not suitable for persons under the age of eighteen. This book contains the use of strong language, sexual content, and mild violence.

SPOTIFY PLAYLIST

Find it under: Charger or C.M. Danks
https://open.spotify.com/playlist/45TadIcywSWasH7A0dzYCJ?si=SlOQLUZLQRqWHbtH8isGxg

I'd Rather See Your Star Explode, Slaves
Like a Stone, Audioslave
Blank Space, Taylor Swift
Wrecking Ball, Miley Cyrus
Wonderwall, Oasis
Guiding Light, Foy Vance
Mean, Taylor Swift
I Miss You, Blink-182
I Will Follow You into the Dark, Death Cab for Cutie
Can't Hold Us, Macklemore & Ryan Lewis
Everything, Lifehouse
Arcade, Duncan Laurence
Alone, I Prevail

Popular Monster, Falling In Reverse
Don't Stop Believin', Journey
Girlfriend, Avril Lavigne
Stupify, Disturbed
Talk to a Friend, Slaves
You Broke Me First, Conor Maynard
For You, All That Remains
Memory, Dead by April
Blood, Breaking Benjamin

Surrender, Natalie Taylor
Hurricane, I Prevail
All I Want, Olivia Rodrigo
Wherever You Will Go, The Calling
Ohio Is For Lovers, Hawthorne Heights
Fire Up the Night, New Medicine
Rise Above It, I Prevail & Justin Stone
NBK, Niykee Heaton
Boys Like You, Anna Clendening
Puzzle Pieces, Framing Hanley
There For You, Flyleaf
The Enemy, I Prevail
Here With You, Sick Puppies

C.M. Danks

CHAPTER ONE

Six Years Ago

Jules

Have you ever had that one best friend who completed your whole world, made everything make sense? That person you always wanted to be around. Who made you feel safe, made you feel like no matter what, they would always be there for you? The one you could always count on.

I have. In fact, I still do.

The door to the kitchen flies open, the sounds of screeches from their shoes filling the room.

"Go long!" My brother calls out to Zach, whose tall, lean, muscular frame towers over us.

He's waving his arms in the air, signaling for the football, and I'm incredibly thankful for his old, ratty, shrunken t-shirt that he likes to work out in. It rides up while his sweatpants hang low enough to show the subtle V-shape of his torso. Yeah, you can say I stole a glance or two, but who wouldn't? Zach's a work of art. He's always been hot, but lately he's been really, really hot.

When he glances over at me, I quickly divert my eyes to a less interesting plate of food sitting in front of me. My heart skips a beat, followed by a warmness that floods my cheeks.

Knowing my mother, her patience for an airborne football in the house is about a zero. Not because she's uptight, but because she doesn't want her home in chaos.

One… two…

"Garrett Patrick, I think not. You boys know better than to throw a football inside, please."

My father grunts behind his newspaper, reaching for a piece of toast. It's not even eight a.m. and my dad's annoyance level is at a limit.

"Come on, mom, we weren't going to actually throw it."

"Yeah, you know us, Mrs. T, we would never try to cause harm to your beautiful home." Zach moves swiftly, planting a kiss on my mom's cheek while trying to butter her up.

"Uh-huh, grab a plate and get some breakfast before you three are late for school." My mom scoops up some of her delicious cheesy scrambled eggs, setting them on a plate. "And are you two going like that? You boys smell."

I can't help but crack up, letting out an unattractive snort.

"Oh, you think that's funny, Specs?"

I have to laugh to myself because Zach likes to call me that, a lot. It's like his own personal pet name for me. Actually, scratch that, I don't think "Specs" qualifies as any type of pet name.

He throws his sweaty, muscular (more so than I remember) arm around my shoulders. His embrace is warm and comforting. And I can't help but melt at his touch.

"Ew, Zach, gross." But I don't find myself pushing him away. Maybe it's the sick fact that his post-workout scent is actually a turn on. Or maybe because he's ever so smoothly making circles with his thumb on the bare skin of my arm. With each motion, it's like a shock through my body.

"Whatcha reading?" He nods his head toward the book I've been scanning between breakfast bites.

"Our summer reading assignments. You know, the ones Mr. Applewood assigned to us and the ones that he *always* likes to drill us on the first day about."

"Shit, I forgot about those."

"Language!" My dad's aggravated voice carries over from the other side of his paper.

"I kind of forgot about those too," Garrett adds.

My mother rolls her eyes as she slides a plate in front of Garrett. "Good way to start off your first day of senior year, guys."

"Mom, you know Coach would just pass us anyway, so it's no big deal," Garrett tries to reassure our worried mother.

It's true—even though both my brother and Zach are straight A students on their own, Coach Russel would never let them fail. Not when they're our school's best football players and my brother's riding on a full football scholarship for college. He has dreams of making it into the pros and if he wanted to, he could do it. Being the star quarterback is one thing, but being one of the best in his age range is another. Zach, on the other hand, never talks about football like my brother does. To be honest, I am not really sure it's what he wants to do after we graduate. I'm not even sure it's what he wants to do now.

"I don't think you should be relying on a free pass from your coach." She warns him. "We taught you better than that."

"Just saying," Garrett mumbles around a bite of his food.

CHARGER

With Zach's arm still around my shoulders, I start to come undone. How long is he going to keep his arm around me? It's starting to feel warmer in here as the heat flows through me.

Over the last couple of years, my feelings for Zach have started to change. I no longer see him as just the boy next door, or my and my brother's best friend. No, he is becoming more than that. The way his body has gotten harder, sexier with lean muscle. The way his voice has become gruffer, husky sounding. The way his dirty blond hair is always longer on top and shorter on the sides, making his bangs forever falling in front of his sky-blue eyes. Let's not forget the way he can make me laugh or how we can hangout for hours, just being ourselves. The hot as hell senior football star with a bad boy attitude. And enter senior me, who's never had a boyfriend before, a plain Jane, and is crushing on her best friend. A best friend who we all knew since we were like ten.

"All right, I better run home to shower." Zach leans closer to me. His breath tickles my skin. "Since your mom says I smell." He smirks and I give him a shove.

"You do smell. And if you two make me late on the first day, I'll murder you both while you sleep."

"I don't think you have to worry, sis. He wants to be on time so he can make out with Samantha before first period."

I mentally eye roll at the mention of Sam. She and Zach have been going out since last year. I'm not sure why because honestly, she sucks. She's bitchy, hates me, and is a cheerleader with a preppy attitude. Zach might be popular, but he's not an asshole by any means. We all hate seeing him with her. Especially me, but that is for different reasons. He doesn't know the way I feel about him and I won't dare tell him. One, I don't want to ruin the friendship we have. And two, I can almost guess he doesn't feel the same. With my average face, average body, and not to mention the oh so not sexy glasses I wear, the only thing I have going for me is my Italian skin complexion and dark, thick hair. Other than that, I would probably average a five if I'm lucky.

Zach ignores the comment about Sam as he's walking out the door. "I'll be done in ten minutes. Beep when you're outside," he tells my brother. "Bye, Mr. and Mrs. T."

My brother looks over at me and starts mouthing a countdown. I know why he's counting down and I try my hardest to stifle a laugh. Our mother is so predictable.

"Garrett, will you please go shower, now. What kind of first impression are you trying to make?" We both break out into laughter and I swear milk almost comes out of my nose. We know what the other is thinking all the time—must be the twin thing.

★★★

Garrett drives us to school and "Like a Stone" by Audioslave is blaring through the car's speakers. I scoot forward from the back seat, placing both my hands on their headrests. "So, guys, what are my chances that people will not remember the *you know what* incident from last year?"

"Um, I would say your chances are good?" Zach glances to the left at my brother.

"Why did you say it like it was a question?"

Zach twists his body enough to be able to see me. "It's been like three months, so I doubt that anyone will remember or even care. Not saying the view wasn't nice to look at though." He gives me a playful wink, but I know he's only joking. He's only ever just joking with me. I plop back into my seat with a sigh.

"That's my sister. Don't be fuckin' nasty. You're my dude, but I won't hesitate to break your face." Garrett punches Zach's shoulder.

"Fuck, I'm kidding." But his sly grin holds something deeper.

Weird.

We pull up to the high school and students are everywhere. Some, I recognize but some are definitely new freshman meat. Those poor guys don't know what they are in for. Students can be mean, especially to a freshman. Scratch that, all of high school is mean.

I toss my long black hair into a pony, nudge my glasses up the bridge of my nose, and grab my bag. The boys are already walking ahead of me when Sam does her prissy skip over to Zach. She wraps her bony arms around his neck and kisses him like she's marking her territory. I honestly don't blame her. He's probably one of the hottest guys in school, with his sexy hair and those eyes. Every girl wants to throw herself at him.

Garrett nudges me with his elbow. We smirk at each other because Sam is still locking lips with Zach. I might be wearing a smile, but the kiss sends knives through my chest. He pulls away first, but she's still attached to him like a lost puppy.

"Hi, Garrett." She smiles then looks over at me. "Julianna," she says with a permanent resting bitch face. I'm not exactly sure why she feels threatened by me. It's not like Zach and I have anything going on.

C.M. Danks

"*Samantha*," I emphasize her name with a fake-ass smile right back. Oh yeah, I could keep this up all day. Bring it on, bitch.

"How was your break, *Julianna*? Did you finally get a boyfriend or did you just hang out with mine all summer?"

"I just hung out with yours. But thanks for asking." No one has ever tested my patience more than she does. She's playing a game she can't win. I'm practically with Zach every day, not that it's a competition.

Sam and I know that our hate for each other is mutual and so do the boys. So, when we have our little cat fights, they just let us go. Garrett stands there unamused, but Zach looks like he's fully enjoying it. He's probably loving the fact that two girls are fighting over him. Although, I wouldn't say I'm fighting over him, just standing my ground. It's not like I'm jealous of her being with him or anything.

Total lie.

With every kiss and touch I have to witness, my stomach drops.

"Pathetic." She flips her hair and we all walk inside the school. The only thing that's pathetic is her pair of knock-off Louis Vuitton shoes.

The smell is still the same as we walk inside. Schools have the same smell, books and pencils. There are posters everywhere, already hyping up the first pep rally and bonfire.

After we find our lockers, Garrett wastes no time in taping pictures up of half-naked women. "I'm so proud that you're my brother." Sarcasm drips from my tongue.

"Get used to it, sis."

After struggling with my lock, like I do every year, I finally get it to open. There, hanging on the inside, are a pair of lace thong panties. A wave of nausea washes through me and humiliation burns my face.

"Oh my God."

"What?" Garrett asks, without taking his attention away from his porn stars.

"Remember how I asked you guys if they forgot about my incident last year?"

"Yeah, why?"

"They didn't forget."

Garrett turns to witness the laced-up joke hanging inside, and laughter erupts from behind us. Josh, along with his two buddies, points in my direction.

Right before the end of junior year, I slipped on someone's spilled drink in the hallway. Not only did I fall, but I split my pants open, showcasing the lovely granny panties I was wearing that day. It was not my fault that it was between washes and I had no other choice. My guess, the reason for the lace thong was to tell me to go buy some sexy underwear. I, in fact, do not wear granny panties. But now half the school thinks I do, and of course, Josh was in the hallway at that exact moment when it happened. Nothing else was worth talking about? They had to resort to my humiliation as entertainment.

I hate high school.

"Douchebag. Just ignore him, Jules." Garrett scowls at Josh with a look that says, "Mess with my sister again and I'll kill you." I'm trying to act like it doesn't bother me, but unfortunately, all I want to do is crawl inside my locker, hoping it swallows me whole.

I groan at the same time a tall, shadowed silhouette appears behind me.

C.M. Danks

"What's going on?" Zach's body is like having a barrier standing between me and the enemy. It's safe, reassuring, and makes me feel invincible. Unstoppable.

"Nothing," I'm quick to deny. "Josh is just being an asshole."

"Was that him?" Turning my body enough to see Zach point to the thong, I try to think of an excuse. When I don't answer, he aggressively rips the underwear from my locker and stalks over to Josh with his circle of friends.

"Oh fuck," Garrett says out loud exactly what I am thinking. He's pissed and we both see it.

Zach shoves the underwear into Josh's chest, sending him flying back into the lockers behind him. At the sound of clanking metal, students stop what they're doing.

"Think this is funny, asshole?" Zach stands over him by at least a foot. The vein in his temple is pulsating and his breathing is deep, heavy.

"Dude, chill out. It was just a joke." Josh raises his hands up in defense.

"Do something like that again and I'll punch your fucking teeth out."

The hallway is dead silent as students gather around, watching the scene unfold. Sam is standing with her arms crossed at her chest, glaring at me. Obviously, she's bitter because her boyfriend just showed up like a knight in shining armor and came to my rescue. I didn't need him to come to my rescue. If it's not my brother, it's him saving me. I could have handled it on my own. I don't need saving. But I have to admit, seeing Zach run to my defense doesn't exactly suck.

He finally backs off from Josh, connecting eyes with me just before walking away with Sam under his arm. I

CHARGER

remember when we were ten and some sixth-grade boy pushed me, typical of course. Zach chased him down and kicked him in his shin. My lips curve up into a smile at the memory. But it fades when I glare at Josh, who's fixing his shirt. It looks like he wants to say something to me, but he doesn't. I avert my attention to my locker and Garrett goes back to rearranging his porn stars.

"Okay, what the hell was that?" Lisa jogs over to me while hugging her books to her chest. "Oh, hey, Garrett, nice pictures," she teases and he slams his locker shut.

"Don't be jealous, Lisa. I'd be glad to hang pictures of you inside my locker if you wanna pose for me."

"Um, hello. I'm standing right here." I wave my hand in the air, completely grossed out. Garrett throws Lisa a playful smile and walks to his first class. Her eyes follow him down the hallway until he turns the corner. "Can you please stop ogling my brother in front of me? It's weird."

"Sorry, but it absolutely cannot be helped. Not when your brother's that hot." I flick her arm. "I just came over to make sure you were okay. Josh can be a real asshole sometimes."

Lisa is my other best friend and I probably wouldn't have been able to survive high school without her. Sure, hanging out with Zach and Garrett is great, but a girl needs her girlfriends.

"Yeah, I'm fine, except for the permanent humiliation that is forever scarred into me."

"Well, I think Zach took care of that for you." She smiles. "Speaking of, did you see the way Sam has been peeing on him everywhere? Bitch looks like a worried hooker in church." We bust out laughing, walking to first period together.

C.M. Danks

★★★

When we get home, Zach and Garrett are already down the street throwing the football, and my mother's in the kitchen tossing the salad for dinner. I wrap my arms around her waist and rest my cheek on her back, startling her from the sneak attack.

"Sweetheart, everything okay? How did the first day go?"

"Will you let me drop out?"

"Uh-oh." She takes off her apron then guides me to the coffee bar chair. "What happened?"

I slouch down with my chin in my hand. "Just some jerk at school."

"Is everything okay, Jules?" She places a motherly hand on top of mine.

"Yeah, Zach took care of it, so I don't think he'll be bothering me again."

Her face goes from an angry "no one messes with my child look" to a smile. "I'm glad you have *Zach* and your brother to look out for you." The way she says Zach's name is odd. "You wanna help me with dinner?"

"Do I have a choice?"

"You always have a choice, Julianna, remember that." She gets up and reties her apron. "Just not in this case. Grab those potatoes over there and start peeling them, please." Without protest, I get up, grab a potato, and start peeling.

"Julianna Taccarelli, you're going to make a good housewife someday." Zach leans against the doorway. A sly

CHARGER

grin creeps up his perfectly handsome face. My mom is smiling, pretending to not pay attention.

"I'll have you know, *Zachary*." I give him a stern sounding voice. "I'm going to be a successful business woman one day, not a housewife. No offense, mom." It's not that I don't look up to my mom. She's incredibly strong — raising a family and taking care of a home is no joke. But it's just not in my cards.

"None taken." She continues prepping dinner.

"I don't doubt that. I don't doubt that for one second." His words run through me. He always holds me on this pedestal. Higher than anyone else.

After dinner is ready, we all sit around the table, including Zach. He spends more time at our house than his own. He never talks about his home life and we don't ask much. His dad is never home and his mom is always drinking from what Garrett tells me. It has to be sad to live in a household like that. Growing up, I guess we were lucky to have a family like this one.

"Wanna pass those mashed potatoes, Specs?" Zach's hand hovers out, waiting for me to deliver them. "I'm curious if your housewife skills are actually any good." My dad gives him a raised eyebrow and I try with all my might to throw my napkin at Zach, but fail. Zach laughs and all I can do is smile.

C.M. Danks

CHAPTER TWO

Jules

While waiting for the boys' practice to end, I sit on the bleachers sketching the football field in front of me, since we all car pool together. Garrett's my ride home and Zach is his, so on the days they have practice, I wait for them.

The hot Ohio sun is beating down on me; it'll likely be one of the last eighty-degree days for the year, considering it's September. I close my eyes for a second, soaking in the sun. I already feel the sweat trickling down from my neck to my chest where my tank top doesn't cover. I lean back, placing my elbows on the bleacher seat behind me—just letting my mind drift and wander about after graduation. I like where we are all at right now, being best friends, being together all the time. But it's sad, knowing that we're probably going our separate ways. Knowing that my brother is going to become some star football player one day. Hopefully I'll get to open up a restaurant or some kind of business. Zach, I'm not sure exactly what he wants to do after graduation. It's funny, for someone I'm so close to, he's so guarded with his life.

CHARGER

I open my eyes, falling right into Zach's line of sight. He's standing on the sidelines, watching me. His eyes trail down my chest, then back up, holding my stare for a second before turning away. The way he eyes my body like that has my stomach all fluttery. I want more of it. Was it crazy to think there was something seductive in his eyes? Something desirable even.

I have to admit Zach in his uniform is not a terrible sight either. He definitely knows how to wear a pair of football pants. Why are sports uniforms so damn sexy anyway?

"Look out!" Someone shouts from the right, but it's too late to brace for what's coming. A quick thud of pain bounces off my head.

"Ow, what the hell?" The ball hits me right on the side of my head. Luckily, I catch myself before toppling off the side of the bleacher seats.

"Shit, sorry. Are you okay?"

There's a dull sting from being smacked with a soccer ball lingering on my forehead, but I guess I'm fine. "Yeah, I think so." I look up to one of my senior classmen, Tommy Stevenson. He's part of the soccer team and apparently has one hell of a kick.

"My bad. I tried to warn you, but obviously not in time." He flashes me an apologetic smile.

"It's okay. I've been told I have a hard head," I joke as I run my finger over my right temple.

He chuckles. "I'm Tommy. I feel like an ass because I don't know your name."

I'm not surprised he doesn't know my name. I'm not exactly "Miss Popular" and I don't see guys looking my way very often. So, I'll give him a pass, even if I did sit next to him in homeroom all of last year.

C.M. Danks

"I'm Jules. You know, the girl who ripped her pants last year."

Smooth, Jules, real smooth. You didn't need to start with that. Trying to be funny is not my strong suit. But it happens when I'm nervous. It just comes out as awkward, no filter.

He laughs while uncomfortably rubbing his neck. "I would lie and say I have no idea what you're talking about, but I do."

"Great, well, I just wanted to clear that up." I strum my fingers on my thigh, letting the silence take over.

"You, uh… going to the pep rally and bonfire Friday night?"

It takes me a second to answer. One, does he really care? Two, did I actually hear that correctly? "I'm not really sure, but maybe."

"Cool. Then maybe I'll see you there." He gives me a wave goodbye and heads back down the bleachers, returning to the other half of the field. Tommy Stevenson was interested in knowing if I was going to the bonfire. Well, that's a first. I smile a bit as I watch him kicking the soccer ball around. He's cute. No, he's super hot. But every girl knows that.

I let my attention travel back to Zach, who's staring at me with a stone-cold look, and my insides turn to ice.

What's that about?

★★★

CHARGER

Zach

Fuck me. Did she really have to sit like that? Head back, tits out, not to mention the way her skin fucking glowed in the sun. Stop, Zach. She's your best friend's sister. She's *your* best friend. But I can't help it. She's the most beautiful thing I have ever seen. Sexy, smart, sassy. Damn it, I need to stop because if I don't, one day I'm going to show her everything she's been missing. I am such a pervert. Like she deserves that. *Jesus.*

I quickly turn back, facing the inside of the field before the guys notice my hard-on and before I need to go jerkoff in the locker room. My disgusting self always visualizes Jules when I'm jacking off. Sure, I'm with Sam, but she's not Jules. She's not the girl who haunts my dreams.

"Dude, why you always gotta be checking out my sister like that?" Garrett shoves the football into my chest.

"Why? Because ever since she turned fifteen, she grew tits and an ass. Now run the field before Coach blows the whistle on us."

He shakes his head, runs long, and catches my field throw. I don't know why but I turn back to Jules, and I see red. Tommy Stevenson. Tommy fucking Stevenson. This kid is a douchebag to say the least. Why the fuck is he talking to her? It's taking every part of myself to not jog up there and beat his face in. I know guys like him—word gets around—and Jules is clueless. He's the biggest manwhore in school. First Josh, now Tommy. Come on, Jules, stop attracting grade-A assholes. Trying to protect her has always been this need of mine. It sizzles deep within me and ignites on impact.

C.M. Danks

He so much as touches Jules, and I'll fucking lose it.

⭐⭐⭐

Jules

"So, why the hell were you talking to Tommy Stevenson?"

My brother whips his head in Zach's direction. "What?" He looks in the rearview mirror, meeting my eyes. "You were talking to Tommy. Why?"

I mentally prepare myself for the twenty-one questions.

"I wasn't, not really. He accidentally hit me with a soccer ball and then apologized for it."

"He hit you?" Zach flies around in his seat, now facing me from the passenger side.

"Jesus, guys, cool it with the testosterone. Yes, he hit me with a *soccer ball*." I make sure to emphasize each word. "It was an accident and he apologized. That was it. It's not that big of a deal, so can we please move on?"

"I don't want you anywhere near him," my brother demands.

"Oh, okay, um. Well, since you're not Dad, I can talk to whoever I want. Or not talk to, or whatever." I throw my hands in the air.

"I mean it, Jules. You stay the hell away from him."

"You two are acting crazy. Seriously, I wasn't even doing anything wrong." I throw my body back into the seat, crossing my arms over my chest. Who do they think they are, telling me what to do like that? Sometimes they both can be way too overprotective.

"We're not acting crazy. We're just looking out for you. So, when we tell you that he's bad news, he's bad fucking news." Zach's voice erupts throughout the car.

"Why is it okay for you two to fuck whatever female walks by, but when someone apologizes for hitting me with an accidental airborne ball, it's the end of the world?"

"I'm not discussing my sexual partners with my sister."

"Trust me, I don't want you to. I'm just trying to prove a point."

"And what point is that?" Garrett meets my eyes in the mirror again.

"Nothing, just forget it."

"No, Jules, tell me please. I want to know what the fuck that's supposed to mean? Because my sister will not be screwing Tommy Stevenson, or anyone for that matter." A deep noise, almost a growl, comes from Zach and his jaw clenches.

"Well, I'm *so* glad we cleared that up. My brother telling me what to do!"

"Stop being so dramatic, Jules." I flip Garrett off in the mirror and he shakes his head at me.

When we pull up to the house, I storm out of the car and head directly for my bedroom, slamming the door behind me. I turn on my Pandora and "Blank Space" by Taylor Swift plays. Sinking into my bed, I grab my sketchbook, making doodles of... I don't even know what. I'm just annoyed and need to do something. This is what I do when I need to escape from reality. Yeah, I want to own my own business one day, but I also love art and this, this is my escape.

C.M. Danks

A text from Zach pops up on my phone. I want to ignore it, but I'm not that strong when it comes to him.

Zach: Sorry, we didn't mean to come off as assholes. Just trying to look out for you.
Me: I don't need anyone looking out for me.
Zach: Yeah, well, that's not gonna happen.
Me: What's not going to happen?

I keep doodling, sketching, or whatever when Zach doesn't answer right away. I don't need anyone telling me what to do, certainly not Zach.

My phone vibrates again.

Zach: I will always look out for you, Jules. Don't ever think for a second that I won't.

I stare at his texted words while my stomach gets a wishy-washy feeling. What exactly am I supposed to say to that?

"Hey." Garrett pops his head inside my door and walks in. "You still love me, even if I'm the older, annoying and overprotective brother?"

"You're older by like four minutes. Get over yourself."

"It still makes me older, drama queen."

"No, you're not, ass face. It doesn't count," I tease.

"So, are you going to the bonfire with us Friday night, Miss Anti-social?"

"Ten minutes ago, you didn't want me talking to anyone. And now, you're making fun of me because I don't talk to anyone."

CHARGER

"No, I just don't want you talking to people like Tommy Stevenson."

I gently kick his hip with my foot. "I don't know. I'll probably just stay home and be little Miss *Anti-social*."

"Jules," he warns.

"Garrett," I counter, glaring into his dark brown eyes, which are nearly identical to the eyes I have.

"Fine, do whatever you want, just don't waste your senior year." He gets up and walks out, shutting the door behind him. I am not wasting my senior year. Just because I don't really want to participate in school functions, it doesn't mean I'm wasting my time.

I pick up my phone and see that Zach sent me another text.

Zach: *How did the brotherly talk go?*

There's a reason why he knows that.

Marching to my window, I unlock it, lift it up, and a blast of still summer air hits my face. Across the yard, Zach already has his window open, and a cell phone to his ear calling me.

"You know, spying on someone is rude," I say, resting my elbow on my window sill.

"Maybe you should try closing your blinds once in a while and stop giving your neighbors a view of your bedroom."

I glare at him from across the way. I probably should, although the only neighbor my bedroom window is facing is Zach. So, concealing anything from anyone would be from him only. And I'm sure he's seen me in my bra and underwear more times than he should have. The mere thought of it gets me excited, not embarrassed.

A woman yells in the background and Zach's body visibly tenses, even from here.

"Was that your mom?"

"Yeah, she's probably just mad because I hid the liquor bottles from her."

"Why didn't you just drain them and tell her she drank them all?" Unfortunately, his mom wouldn't remember (or know the difference) anyway.

"Because I can't let such valuable things go to waste, Specs." He grins, but I roll my eyes, hoping he can see it from here.

"Right, it's for all those wild parties you throw," I say sarcastically.

"Hey, you don't need a party to drink."

I tousle my hair between my fingers. "I never really drink, except for some champagne mom and dad let me try on New Year's once."

"Ah, those virgin lips of yours." The way he says it makes my body freeze. It feels almost like he is teasing me seductively. Is he flirting with me?

"Well, you'll have to let me try some of yours then," I retort, trying to salvage the conversation, but absolutely failing at it. This just became embarrassing really fast. Clearly, I don't know how to flirt.

Crap.

Abort. Abort this conversation immediately, even though the so-called flirting has my heart pounding out of my chest. I've never flirted with a guy before. God, I'm so lame.

"Uh, yeah, Jules, I'll let you have some of mine anytime you want." His mouth turns up into a one-sided grin.

CHARGER

Oh my God! Dig a hole and bury me in it. I let out an awkward, fake laugh. "Okay, well, I better go because I have homework to do."

That and some shoveling.

"See ya, Jules." He lets out a small laugh.

I couldn't hang up fast enough, slamming my window shut and closing my blinds. I press my cold, clammy hand on my warm cheek. That was not a conversation I expected to have with my best friend. The best friend I was crushing on so hard. Zach, who's been taking up all my thoughts lately while causing my heart to beat uncontrollably. I've never felt this way about a boy, ever. I'm only seventeen, but most girls my age have already experienced so much with boys. Not me, I'm over here sketching in my notebook, dreaming about what it would be like to run my fingers through Zach's hair, or trail them down his abs.

I bury my face in my hands. "God, this really sucks."

C.M. Danks

CHAPTER THREE

Jules

"So, what time should we all meet up tonight and who's driving?" Lisa tosses a fry into her mouth.

"I'll drive, because Romeo over here is taking Sam." Garrett hooks a thumb toward Zach, who's sitting at our cafeteria table with Sam on his lap. She lets out a giggle after sucking his face off. I'm glad to see they came up for air, because I was worried that she might be suffocating him to death. I am well aware I've been giving them weird looks, but I can't help myself. It does something to me—the sight of her long Barbie hair that's curled down her shoulders twirling between Zach's fingers. Maybe if he pulls hard enough, he'll yank the clip-on extensions out. Do I wish that was me sitting on his lap, his fingers twirling my hair? Yes, yes, I do.

Ugh.

"God, get a room already." Those words slip out faster than I can catch them.

Lisa stops midair with a fry dangling in front of her mouth. My brother is laughing, Samantha is shooting

CHARGER

daggers at me, and Zach is grinning—a twinkle in his eyes from the slight jealousy that overcame me.

"I'm sorry. Is this bothering you?" Sam snaps her attitude at me.

"No, not really bothering me as much as making me want to throw up the lunch I just ate." I honestly hate her and, knowing that Zach deserves better, I can't help the fact that she gets under my skin.

"You're such a bitch."

"Isn't that the pot calling the kettle black, Samantha?" Everyone sitting at the table stays silent with eyes darting back and forth between us.

Sam jumps up from her seat (or should I say Zach) and plants her hands on the table. "You're just jealous because I'm prettier and more popular than you. Or is it because you secretly want my boyfriend?"

Zach was about to say something but I jump up from my chair, causing it to almost fall backwards. "Think what you'd like, but there's no way in hell that I would ever be jealous of you. I may not paint my face with all that makeup and I may not be dating one of the hottest guys in school. But at least my hair is real and my bra's not stuffed!"

You could hear a pin drop in the cafeteria.

"Burn," Lisa mumbles under her breath.

Everyone in the lunch room has their eyes locked on me. My brother has a confused as fuck look on his face because, normally, I'm not so vocal at school.

"Screw you!" Sam storms off, and I half expect Zach to go after her but he doesn't. He stays put, zeroing in on me and my outburst. I could have sworn I saw the corner of his mouth turn up, his stare burning into me. He's loving this.

"Girl, I think Sam just pissed herself." Lisa laughs.

C.M. Danks

"Yeah, where the hell did that come from?" I wish I had an answer for my brother, but I don't.

"I'm going to the library. See you guys later." I couldn't get out of there fast enough. The silence ends rather quickly. Students start laughing, going about their business again like it never happened. I tilt my lunch tray inside the trash can and stomp through the doors.

"Hey, Jules, wait!" Zach is now in step with me and I try not to look at him. But my willpower is just not that strong when it comes to him. "What was that about?"

"I don't know. Guess she just pissed me off is all."

"I've always known you to be feisty, Specs, just not that feisty."

"Yeah, well, don't get used to it."

He grabs my arm, stopping me. He flashes a sexy smile and tugs me a little closer. His body heat turns my stomach into a fluttery mess of hell. Something passes between us, and I get trapped in his gaze.

"So, you think I'm the hottest guy in school, huh?"

I snort. "Don't flatter yourself, hotshot." Tugging myself free, I leave him in the dust. When really, I want to run back and throw myself into his arms.

★★★

"How can it be eighty degrees one day and forty-five the next? I am so not dressed for this." Lisa hugs her middle, trying to get warmth back into her body, and I'm doing the same. Even with the massive flames from the bonfire in front of us, it's still freezing out here. I have on my turtleneck sweater, jeans, boots, my brown leather jacket, and gloves. I seriously hate the cold.

We stand there while Coach Russel walks up to the podium to speak. He talks a little, then shouts a little, then talks some more, with some fist pumps thrown in the air on occasion.

"All right, everyone, let's give it up for our football team!"

The marching band starts playing and one by one, the football players run onto the field. The cheerleaders are lined up, doing their little cheering duties as they run by. Sam is shouting Zach's name, blowing him a kiss when he runs past. I wouldn't mind strangling her with her ball of streamers.

Death by pompons. It has a nice ring to it.

"I can see you planning out Sam's murder from here. What gives?" Lisa has reached the point where she is now frozen solid and her teeth are minutes from chattering. But there's no denying she can read me like a fortune cookie.

"Nothing gives. I just don't like her."

"You don't like her because she's *her*, or you don't like her because she's dating Zach?"

"The first part." I watch as the guys line up for their introductions. I purposely seek out Zach among them. "It's not like that. We've been friends for years. And besides, Zach just deserves better."

"He deserves someone like you, right?" She smirks, blowing her warm breath into her hands.

"No, that's not what I said." I pause to think about it. What would it be like, to be with him as more than just a friend? "Zach would never go for someone like me anyway."

C.M. Danks

"Whatever you say." Bobbing in place, Lisa grabs my hand. "All right, I don't feel like watching anymore. Let's go buy some hot chocolate before my face freezes and falls off."

After standing in the long line and ordering our life-saving hot chocolate, we wait as Garrett and Zach approach us. I'm confused when Garrett slips behind Lisa and rubs his hands up and down her arms, trying to help her get warm.

"Why the fuck didn't you wear something warmer?" Garret leans into Lisa as he scolds her.

Lisa stares at me wide-eyed. "I... uh, didn't realize how cold it was going to be." She nervously looks at the ground, and I mentally remind myself to ask my brother what that was about later. Zach stands next to my brother with his hoodie under his jersey, also wearing his dark, torn jeans. How can someone make a hoodie look so good? Even with it on, you can still see how broad his shoulders are.

"Aw, how come you ladies didn't buy us any hot chocolate?"

"Oh, I'm sorry. We didn't realize you were physically incapable of buying your own?" I give him an evil smile over my cup mid-sip, and Zach makes a dramatic scene like someone shot him in the chest. My brother laughs as he wraps a tender arm around Lisa's shoulders. She mouths, *"Oh my God,"* to me and her cheeks become flushed. I know my brother and I know he wouldn't go after one of my friends, so I'm not sure what he's doing right now. Unless, he all of a sudden had a change of heart and got his head out of his ass. He knows that Lisa has been crushing on him since sophomore year, maybe he finally took notice.

"Zach, you looked amazingly sexy out there tonight." Sam slips her way into our circle, and his arms. She paws her hands down his chest and looks over to me, but something causes her jaw to almost hit the ground. Zach's eyes radiate anger.

"Uh, hey, Jules." I turn around at the sound of Tommy's voice. He's tall, but still shorter than my brother and Zach. Though, anyone could get lost in those hazel eyes.

"Oh, hey, Tommy."

"What's up, guys?" He confidently greets everyone; Lisa smiles with shock but the guys don't say anything. Sam is still standing there speechless, like she can't believe someone like Tommy is talking to me right now.

Eat that, slut.

Zach looks like a bull ready to charge through the red flag at any moment. My brother also shares the same look but not as scary. You could cut the tension with a knife.

"How's it going?" I nervously tuck some hair behind my ear and glasses.

"I have a confession." He leans a little closer, and Zach's eyebrows burrow in. "I kind of wanted to ask you for your phone number ever since the soccer ball incident. Which, I am super sorry about still."

My phone number, is he serious? Okay, how cheesy is it that I'm excited about him getting my phone number? But let's be honest… I have never given my number to anyone before. He smirks, but a deep murderous noise sounds from across the group.

"Here." He hands me his phone and after a long thirty seconds of staring at it, I type my number into his contacts. "I'll text you later." I finally close my mouth as he walks away.

C.M. Danks

"Holy shit!" Lisa steps out of my brother's hold and right up to me. "Tommy just asked for your number. That boy is hot as fuck!" Garrett clears his throat in annoyance.

"Just be careful, Jules," Garrett tells me. "But you already know that."

Zach doesn't say anything as he shrugs Sam away from him. "Come on, I'm taking you home." He grabs onto her wrist and gently pulls her along. She looks like she wants to argue, but doesn't fight it.

★★★

Slipping into my covers, I turn on my book light. My head is bouncing all over the place because I still can't believe that Tommy asked for my number. Honestly, I don't think he will text me, but it feels pretty damn good that he asked for it.

I can't concentrate on reading so I turn on my Pandora and let it shuffle through my alternative playlist. A number pops up in my notifications—one that I don't have in my contacts.

Unknown: *Hey, it's Tommy.*

Holy Shit.

I jump up with my back against the headboard of my bed, tightly gripping my phone in excitement. He actually texted me. Now, to think of what to say.

Me: *Hi. What's up?*

CHARGER

My heart beats out of my chest as I save his number in my contacts.

Tommy: *Not much, just got home. I feel like your brother and Zach don't like me very much...*

He's not wrong about that one.

Me: *They're fine. Just a little too overprotective.*
Tommy: *I have sisters. I get it.*
Tommy: *Don't be a stranger, Jules. Let's hang out soon, good night.*

I smile to myself, setting my phone down on my end table.
Shutting my light off, I throw the covers back over me. Another text message comes over and I think it's from Tommy again, so I giddily check it.

Zach: *So, you gonna text him back if he texts you?*

Little does he know, it already happened.

Me: *I'm sorry, when did that become your business?*
Zach: *You, Julianna Taccarelli, are my business.*

What the hell does that mean? The possessiveness in those words... Words I wouldn't have guessed would be coming from Zach, *my* best friend, my *brother's* best friend. Not knowing what to say to that text, I ignore it and try to catch my breath as I bite my hang nail. I shut my phone off completely and close my eyes. It takes me longer than usual

C.M. Danks

to fall asleep, and I have Tommy to blame for that. Or maybe it's not Tommy's fault… maybe it's Zach's.

CHAPTER FOUR

Jules

I lazily walk to my cedar chest, which sits in front of my bed, yanking my robe from it. The smell of the big Saturday morning breakfast that my mother goes all out with every week fills the house.

In the hallway, I run into my dad, who's in front of the mirror trying to decide which tie to wear to his big meeting this morning.

"Go with the blue one. The red one means you're trying too hard," I suggest.

"Huh, good idea." He tosses the red one in the bathroom and wraps the approved tie around his neck. "Thanks, kiddo. When did you become so business savvy?"

I shrug. "It's in my blood."

He smiles, walking with me downstairs. It sucks that my dad has to go in on the weekends sometimes, but it's all part of the job. When you own your own dealership, it's not just a nine-to-five gig only on weekdays.

I stop dead in my tracks. My dad makes it into the kitchen and grabs a plate, shoveling some scrambled eggs onto it. I gnaw on my bottom lip when I see Zach sitting at the table next to my brother, laughing and watching

C.M. Danks

YouTube. I never used to care what I looked like. But that was before I started crushing on him. So, now, I am fully aware of my fuzzy slippers, robe, night shorts and hair being piled on the top of my head. I haven't even showered yet. I contemplate running back to my room, but the rumble in my stomach has already made up my mind. Zach has seen me like this a dozen times, if not more. *Get over it.*

I grab myself a plate, offering a "good morning" to my mom, who's wearing her usual authentic smile.

"Sis, why do you look so wrecked?"

Setting my plate down, I glare at my brother before going to the fridge and pulling out the orange juice. "I'm sorry I'm not a freak like you two, who seem to be abnormally chipper in the wee hours of the morning."

"Actually, in our defense…" Zach finishes chewing his eggs then continues, "It's only because we had to be up early for practice. We don't actually enjoy it."

"Well, whatever the reason, I like my beauty sleep."

"Yeah, you might need more of it." I punch my brother in the arm right before my phone vibrates in my pocket.

Tommy: *Morning, cutie.*

I practically choke on my food. The smile radiates off my face as I take a sip of OJ.

"Who's that?" Zach gives me a scowl before my brother looks over.

"It's Lisa," I lie.

"No, it's not," Zach counters.

"Yes, it is."

"Oh, yeah? Then let us see."

CHARGER

"Let you see my phone and read my text messages? No, I think I'll pass, but thanks."

"Jules..."

"Zach..."

"Okay, you two, how about we not fight at the breakfast table," my mom interjects, setting another plate of pancakes down in front of us.

"Let it go, man. She'll figure it out on her own." Garrett tries to reason with him.

"Really? That's how you're gonna let this play out, by letting her figure this out on her own?"

My dad sets down his paper, staring at my brother. "What's going on?"

"Nothing!" I quickly argue.

"Jules is talking to some guy at school who's a royal asshole."

I give Zach a "fuck you" scowl. "No, I'm not."

"Language," he says to Zach before looking back at me. "Jules, I would expect you to have enough sense to avoid talking to some jerk, if that's what he really is. However, you are old enough to make your own decisions." He clears his throat. "No one says anything about that Sam girl you're dating, Zach."

Burn. Go Dad, go Dad.

"Thanks, Daddy." I smirk at Zach. He shakes his head while shoveling a bit of pancake into his mouth.

My phone goes off again, probably because I haven't responded yet.

Tommy: *Want to go to the movies with me tonight?*

Me: *Sorry, battle at the breakfast table lol. Yes, the movies sound like fun!*

C.M. Danks

Tommy: *A breakfast battle does not sound like fun, but I'm glad you said yes. We can see the new superhero movie.*

My first date ever.

"Why are you smiling like a weirdo?" Garrett asks.

"Lisa must have said something that made you super freakin' happy." There was no denying the sarcasm from Zach. Whatever, I may as well tell them because they will obviously find out sooner or later.

"Actually, I have a date tonight. If that's okay?" I look to my mom and dad for approval. Zach drops his fork, slamming back into his chair.

My mom beams. "Oh, Jules, I'm so excited for you! Your first date!"

"Yes, thanks, Mom, for reminding everyone here that it is, in fact, my first date." I get up from the table, heading straight to my room in an effort to avoid the questions. It's okay for Garrett to go on as many dates as he wants, but when I finally get one, it's absolute insanity.

"Oh, and Jules." I pause with a cringe. "I wanna meet this boy who will be taking out my daughter tonight." My dad clears his throat.

Zach gloats with my brother. And here I was, so close to escaping.

★★★

I feel like I'm going to throw up. Could this be any more embarrassing?

"Do you two really need to be here when he picks me up?" Zach and my brother are waiting patiently in the living room for Tommy to get here. If I had known they were going

CHARGER

to be here, I would have told Tommy to run for his life and forget me. To never look back. I'm not that great anyway.

When the doorbell rings, my stomach turns. I stop the guys, running to answer it myself. "Hey, Tommy." I give him an awkward smile, hoping he doesn't run.

His eyes widen beyond my shoulder. I glance over. Zach is standing directly behind me with his arms crossed over his chest. He looks intimidating as he towers over us with his lean but muscular arms.

My dad swoops in, gently moving Zach out of the way. "All right, son, I'll take over from here." My dad's hands are on my shoulder. I could die. I love my dad for his protectiveness, but this is so embarrassing. Tommy hasn't said anything since he got here, but he looks terrified. My dad shakes his hand and starts his speech. "This young lady is very special. You treat her with the respect she deserves, and I want you back here with her by ten. Got it?"

"Y-Yes, sir. I will."

"Okay, Frank, that's enough." My mom pushes him away, pulling me into a side hug. "Okay, you two, I can't hold them off forever. Go, have fun."

"Thanks, Mom." I scurry out the door with Tommy. "I'm so sorry about all that."

He opens the passenger door to his expensive sports car. "I'll admit it is a little intimidating. Your brother, Zach, and your dad. But I'm pretty tough and I can handle anything." He smirks. Thank God for that.

Tommy had me home by nine forty-five. I don't think he wanted to risk being a minute late. When I walk inside, my mom is snuggled into my dad watching a movie. Even after all these years, they are still madly in love with each other. We all should be so lucky to have a loving marriage like that.

C.M. Danks

I greet them, telling them how much fun I had, skipping any detail whatsoever. I did have fun. It even makes me blush, thinking about how he held my hand in the theater. Yes, I know, holding hands. *Real exciting.* But for someone who is shy, and has never had a boyfriend before, holding hands is a pretty big thing.

As soon as my bedroom door shuts, I fling my purse onto my bed, and my phone vibrates.

Zach: *I'm at my window.*

The thumping in my chest beats faster. If he's going to give me any shit for tonight, I swear… I will probably fully enjoy it. I let out a huff when Zach is already leaning on the ledge of his window calling my phone.

"What, no goodbye kiss?" he says when I answer.

"Spying on me?"

"Yup."

"How nice of you. Also, are you crazy? Like he would try to kiss me in front of my house. He was probably scared to death that you guys were waiting in the shadows with shotguns."

"Good. He should be."

I shake my head. "Why are you being like this?"

"I'll always be like this when it comes to you." He straightens from his window sill, standing to his full height. "Did he touch you, Jules?"

"He held my hand if that's what you consider *touching*." He doesn't say anything, just stares. "Zach, I'm hanging up now." I go to close my window, still holding his call to my ear.

"Jules…"

CHARGER

I sigh. "Yeah?"

He pauses, and we both share a silent moment. What does he want to say? "Never mind, good night." He slams his window shut, drawing back his curtain.

"Good night, Zach." My heart does a little jump before hanging up. God, how I wish it was Zach holding my hand at the theater tonight.

C.M. Danks

CHAPTER FIVE

Jules

"So, your brother invited me to Josh's party tonight." Lisa makes a face, like she's waiting for me to scold her.

"Lisa, I don't care if you hang out with Garrett, honestly."

"Really? You sure… because if it's weird?"

"I swear. It's fine."

"Oh, thank God! Because I really and I mean *really* like your brother." Her face lights up.

"I know you do. You don't hide it very well." I shut my locker and we walk to class together. "Tommy invited me to the same party,"

"Holy shit, yeah? Perfect, now I'll have someone to cling onto all night." She laughs.

"I don't know if I'm going to go."

"Please! Please, you have to go! I need backup. I've never been alone with Garrett before. What if we run out of things to talk about?"

I bite my bottom lip out of habit. "Fine, but you have to promise not to leave me."

"I swear!" She holds out her pinky, smiling.

CHARGER

"What are we swearing to?" Zach comes up from behind me; his arm burns a hole in my skin as he wraps his forearm across my chest.

The wind's knocked out of my lungs, and despite Zach's warmth, a shiver runs down my back.

"We were just talking about the party tonight and how Jules got an invite from Tommy." She wiggles her eyebrows.

Zach's body goes stiff behind me as he squeezes his arm a little tighter to my chest. I swallow then find myself relaxing a little, sinking back into him. He moves forward into me. Even though we're already touching front to back, it's like we're craving more. Both of us.

"Well, cool, at least we'll all be there together then." Garrett shrugs.

"Yeah, awesome." Zach's bitterness is undeniable and his breath, tickling my neck, sends more chills through me.

★★★

I didn't dress too fancy, but I made sure to put on my nice skinny jeans with a black flowy top. It shows just enough chest to make me feel a little more attractive—not that I want too much attention on me. But I even put on more makeup than usual, secretly hoping that Zach will notice. I'm dressing for him. Not for anyone else.

The music blares from outside of Josh's home. Showing up to the house of someone who made an effort to make fun of my slip last year seems dumb. Yet, here I am, at his house. At his party.

C.M. Danks

Cars are lined up along the street and his driveway. The fact that his father is the mayor and his mother a doctor explains the mansion. Also, it's why no one would dare call the cops, even with his parents being out of town.

We walk up to his million-dollar mansion after having to park on the street. A Drake song is playing from the overhead speakers and girls are dancing in the front room when we walk in. Sam must have been waiting for Zach, because she comes running to him, stuffed bra and all. He lets out an annoyed groan and you bet I notice.

Interesting.

"I'm gonna go find the beer." My brother leaves us, and Lisa is right there following him. So much for not ditching me. I peek around, feeling completely lost. I don't know anyone here and coming to this party may have been a mistake.

Tommy motions a wave to me. "Hey, glad you came." He pulls me against his side as he tightens an arm around my waist.

"Do you want a drink?"

"No, she doesn't."

I'm surprised by Zach's quick response. I don't need him answering for me, even if he is right. "You speak for her too, dude?" Sam slams her hand to Zach's chest before he can move. Zach's furious eyes burn into Tommy's.

"Um, it's okay, Tommy. He's right. I don't drink." Embarrassment burns my cheeks. Sam snorts from beside Zach.

"Okay, suit yourself."

Hannah, a senior cheerleader, makes her way over to us. "Good, more people. Come on, we were just about to play truth or dare upstairs." She smiles at Sam.

CHARGER

"Oh, no, that's okay," I say quickly, in hopes of getting out of it.

"Come on, Jules, it'll be fun." Tommy's musty breath grazes my ear. Before I know it, he's leading me upstairs with Zach close behind.

We all enter a spare room, making a circle along the floor. Zach sits across from me, next to Sam, and Tommy sits next to me. There's Hannah with a few other seniors I don't really know. Josh was here, but practically ran his ass out of the room when he saw Zach.

"Oh, the rules before we start are that you have to have a drink." Hannah hands me a red solo cup. I pull my head back when the strong scent of liquor hits my nose. I know Zach wants me to decline (by the scowl on his face) but instead, I accept. Oh well, live in the moment, right? Hannah smiles then starts the game. "Okay, I'm sure everyone knows the rules. I'm assuming even you, Julianna?"

"Yeah, I got it."

"Good, let's start with… Tommy."

I take a small drink of whatever is in my cup, coughing as soon as the burning sensation hits my throat. "Fuck, that's strong." The face I make afterward proves it.

One of the guys in the circle laughs. "Didn't know Julianna had such a dirty mouth." He smirks as I wipe my lips of the leftover liquor. "I bet that's not all that's dirty."

"Knock it off, Fisher." Zach throws an elbow into the guy's ribcage.

"Tommy," Hannah starts. "Truth or dare?"

"I'm going to go with truth." He slides his arm around my waist, holding on tighter than before. Zach's jaw clicks and he sends knives through his stare. I must admit Zach showing this type of reaction makes me a little satisfied.

C.M. Danks

"Okay, where was the craziest place you ever had sex?"

"Come on, Hannah." He threatens her with annoyance.

"It's a simple question, Tommy." She glances at me then over at Sam.

"Fine, the craziest place was in the boys' locker room at school. There, happy?"

I cringe. This *is* Tommy Stevenson who's sitting next to me and holding onto my waist. He probably slept with the whole senior class of girls. Josh being the runner up in that category. What am I doing hanging out with him? He has to know that I don't have much experience in that department. Am I hanging out with him because he's the first boy to give me some attention? Do I like him? Or is it to try to make Zach jealous? Maybe it's all the above.

"Since it's going in order, I guess you're next, Jules." She flashes me one of her bitchy smirks. God, why do all the girls suck in high school? I take another drink and everyone (except Zach) laughs at the disgusted face I make. It really is gross.

"Okay, I pick truth."

"Oh, I'm sorry. We must have forgotten to tell you—our rules are different. If someone picks truth, the next person *has* to pick dare."

"You're such a fucking liar, Hannah."

She cocks her head at Zach. "Am not. It's how we play, unless Julianna over here is too scared to choose dare."

Everyone waits for me to answer, she and Sam both smiling, all eyes on me. "Okay, DARE," I challenge.

"Okay, then, I dare you to kiss Zach." My stomach drops and Sam whips her head to Hannah. The boys in the circle are "ooo-ing" into their fists.

CHARGER

"What the hell, Hannah? That's not part of what we talked about."

Hannah shrugs her shoulders at Sam, playing the innocent card. "It's what I picked, so she can either do it, or run scared."

I glance over at Tommy, who looks uncomfortable. The other guys in the circle are laughing, and then I meet Zach's eyes. He doesn't look that upset, or even phased by the dare, not at all. If I didn't know any better, I would say he is intrigued. Does he actually want to kiss me?

The room starts to get hazy and, for some reason, any nerves I felt disappear. Not being one to drink, I was a light weight for sure. So, standing up and getting ready to kiss Zach may be part of that liquid courage.

My heart stills as I connect eyes with Zach. "All right, let's do this then."

Zach looks stunned, Sam is about to have a hernia. Her eyebrows are burrowed inward with her mouth open in shock. "Jules, you don't have to…"

"Get up, Zach, now," I order.

He hesitates, but then scurries over to me like an eager puppy. Sam's still pouting. This time her arms are folded at her chest while everyone is watching in fascination.

Nothing is between us except about a foot of space. He's so close that I can feel his body heat, and he smells so fucking good.

He leans in to whisper to me. "You don't have to do this, Jules. We have nothing to prove."

So, what if I've never been kissed before, and so, what if my first time is going to be at some dumb party in front of people I don't really like? This is Zach. If my first kiss is going to be with anyone, I want it to be with him. So, what if the thought of his lips touching mine gets my heart racing out of control? The more and more he gets into my head, the more and more I want him. And the more and more I want to kiss him. To feel him touch me. To *really* touch me. To feel his hands on me. His lips.

I can hear "Wrecking Ball" by Miley Cyrus playing in the background. Nothing else. All other voices, noises, are drowned out by my beating heart.

He's standing so close to me. He's so tall. I don't remember him being this tall. He's searching my eyes, looking for something in there that is going to deny his touch, deny his kiss. But I don't give it. My eyes slowly rake over his body, his chest, his arms. That's when he slowly raises his hands, skimming them up my arms using only his fingertips.

I shiver from his touch, but I don't look away. He's staring at my mouth before he swipes his tongue along his lower lips. Then he looks back at me, into my soul, his eyes igniting with fire, like lava.

Fuck it.

I fist his shirt in my hand and I pull him down to me; his lips crash onto mine, the chorus of Miley's song playing at that exact moment. At first, he's unsure, hesitant, but then I swear I hear him moan and he pulls me closer to him, using my waist. My breasts are pushed against his chest and he tightens his arm around me, while his other hand caresses my face.

This feels so good. Too good. I should stop but I don't. Everyone is watching us kiss right now, but I don't care. If this is what kissing Zach feels like, then I never want to stop. His tongue enters my mouth and he teases it with mine. I mimic him, hoping I'm doing it right.

CHARGER

He pulls me tighter, as if I can get any closer. I'm already pressed up to him as far as I can go. My hands rest on his chest as I let him consume my mouth. He's guiding me, showing me, and I love the way he tastes. My heart is beating so fast, along with an aching throb between my thighs. *Oh God*. I pull away. The kiss leaves me breathless. Leaves us both breathless.

My eyes meet his. His chest rises and falls, his nostrils flaring, with eyes that are completely burning into me. We stare at each other like this until an angry Sam snaps. Then Hannah says something, but I tune them both out. The only thing I hear, see, feel is Zach in front of me.

"What the fuck? That was no best friend kiss. Hot damn." Hannah laughs.

Everyone in the room has the same blank look on their face—mouth open and jaw to the floor. Tommy is giving me a scowl while Sam flies up from the circle.

"Screw this. I'm out."

I look at Zach, waiting for him to go after her, but he doesn't. He hasn't taken his eyes off me since we broke apart. I don't know what just happened but I feel like it may have changed my and Zach's relationship. I just went from being excited and turned on, to a hot mess of emotions. With one last look, I turn on my heels and run out of the room. Yes, I am afraid. Could it be the alcohol and the fact that I am a little intoxicated? Maybe…

"Jules!" Zach calls out for me, but I don't stop. I keep running. My brother watches me fly by and I hear him call my name too. Then Lisa joins in.

I make it outside but keep going. I can't remember where we parked—it's not like I'll be driving anyway without the keys. I just run. I don't know where to, but I'm not stopping.

C.M. Danks

The same hand, which minutes ago was cradling my face, takes hold of my arm and I'm being spun around. "Where are you going?" I frantically whip back and forth, like a fish out of water, because I can't be around him right now. I don't want him to see me cry. Tears are starting to fall and all I want to do is get away. To hide away.

"Please, Zach, just let me go!" My brother and Lisa stand there, watching me freak out.

"Zach, what the hell is going on, man? Did something happen?" My brother has no idea that Zach and I just made out.

"Jules, stop! Stop moving. Why did you run away?"

"Because!" I scream. "Everything is going to change now. It's all going to be ruined!" At this point, I'm sobbing. There's no stopping the floodgates. I don't want to lose my best friend. He only kissed me back because of the dare, and now everything is going to be weird. My feelings for him might be real but that doesn't mean he has the same feelings for me. I can't lose him. The pain in my chest causes more tears to spill out. "I just want to go home, Zach. Please let me go." The last part comes out as a whisper and exhaustion overtakes me. The flopping and thrashing around stops.

Garrett walks up to us. "Zach, let her go. I'll take her home."

"No, fuck that. *I'm* taking her home." He looks at my brother. "I got this. She'll be fine." Garrett nods his head because there is no one else he would trust me with more than Zach.

"Jules... you okay?" Tommy joins in on the fun. But his stern facial expression burrows into me.

"Yeah, everything is fine. I got her, so you can back the hell off." Zach gives him a menacing look, right before he scoops me up like I weigh absolutely nothing and carries me to his car. I think. Honestly, I can't see anything because my eyes are blurry from crying. I huddle into his chest, even though all I really want right now is to be alone. But his warmth feels so good. His arms feel so safe.

"I got you, Jules. You're okay." He sets me down, but keeps his arm tight around my waist while he gets his keys out of his pocket. He stops to look at me. I've calmed down a little since the scene in the street. "Why did you run like that?" His eyes connect with mine, still not letting me go. My body is being swallowed by Zach's stare and my insides are melting.

"I-I ran because… because we shouldn't have done that. I don't want things to change between us. I don't want things to be weird and awkward. You're not just Garrett's best friend. You're mine too, and I-I can't lose you!" He rubs his hands repeatedly over my arms as I begin to cry again. The thought of ever being away from Zach makes me frantic.

"Jules, look at me." When I don't, he takes my face in his hands. "Look. At. Me." Obeying this time, I glance up as he continues, "You will never lose me. Don't you get that? I'm not going anywhere. I promise, and things don't have to change. We'll still go on, every day, being best friends. It's not going to be different because of some stupid fucking dare." His eyes dart back and forth between mine. "If that's what you want, we will continue like nothing happened."

If that's what I want? His face tenses at his own words.

To say the kiss didn't mean anything would be a lie. But I can't lose him. I don't want to lose him. I'm almost sure that he doesn't want me like that, so why would I ruin what we have in our friendship? I nod my head and look down at the ground. He sighs then opens the passenger door, helping me inside. What I really wanted to tell him was: no, it's not what I want. It's not what I want at all. I watch intensely as he walks around the hood of the car, and I squeeze my hands together, burying my nails into my palms.

We don't talk all the way home. I'm emotionally exhausted and I'm also coming down from my buzz. He parks in the street and I notice a man's truck (not his father's) in his driveway. The tension in the car quickly shifts. I can tell by Zach's facial expression that whoever it is, it's not someone he wants to see. He grips the steering wheel tighter.

"Zach…"

"I'll talk to you tomorrow, Jules, good night." He cuts me off, but his eyes don't leave the truck and I don't ask about it because I'm too tired. Too defeated. So, I let it go.

I drag myself to my bedroom as quietly as I can, without waking up my parents. I strip off my clothes, down to the nitty-gritty, and bury myself in my covers, snuggling them tight to my chest.

My mind wanders to the kiss. I touch my fingers to my lips, as if trying to remember the feel of Zach's on mine, and the ache in my chest starts. He tasted so good. Felt so right. And that just makes me like him even more.

I throw the covers over my head, as if I could hide from my fear. Then I let the heaviness of sleep consume me because I'm so mentally done with tonight it's not even funny.

CHARGER

CHAPTER SIX

Jules

The lunch table is quiet. Lisa looks up at me occasionally then shoots a glance toward Zach, who is sitting without Sam on his lap today. Garrett pierces his eyes into mine. I'm just waiting for it... for the question looming in the air.

"Someone wanna tell me what exactly happened on Friday night?"

Zach's eyes study mine. "If your sister didn't tell you, then maybe she doesn't want you to know. Ever think of that?"

"Zach..." I calmly press.

"What the fuck, dude?" Garrett tosses his fork down. "You've been a prick all weekend and I have a feeling it has something to do with whatever happened at the party. Am I wrong?" He looks at me. "Jules, am I wrong?"

"No! You're not wrong, okay? But it's done now and I'm not telling you what happened because it's my business, not yours, Garrett. I love you but back off with this."

Pushing my chair from the table, I rush out of the cafeteria and into an empty hall. I'm actually shocked no one spread it around school, but I have a feeling *that* has something to do with Sam.

C.M. Danks

Within seconds, footsteps sound behind me and I'm pushed against the wall. Two lean, muscular arms are caging me in. "I know that I gave you a choice. I gave you a choice to ignore what happened with us on Friday night because you were scared. You didn't want things to change between us, but guess what, pretty girl? Things did change. You liked that kiss as much as I fucking did and there's no way in hell we can go back to how things were. Not because I don't want to be your friend anymore but because I want to be more than that, and I think you want that too." He leans into me and I inhale. "I bet you can't stop thinking about my mouth on yours. Wanna know how I know? Because that's all I can think about."

"You're wrong." The soft words leave my mouth. But he's not wrong. He's anything but wrong.

"Am I?" He smirks and his lips brush my ear. "How wet are you for me, pretty girl?" Heat rises inside me.

Who is this? Because this isn't the Zach I know... Or maybe I just never got to witness this side of him before because we were never on that kind of level. No wonder all the girls get completely attached to him. He screams alpha.

"I have to get to class." My heart hammers in my chest.

He buries his eyes in mine before he pushes off the wall. "I will make you come to me, Jules, in more ways than one. You best believe that."

The breath is knocked out of me mentally. Why do I feel like I'm going to be completely powerless, completely weak, against this new Zach?

★★★

CHARGER

I tap my pencil nervously, waiting for this class to end. Of course, I have History with Zach, and of course, he sits next to me. It's only been like twenty minutes since the embarrassing hallway episode. Embarrassing not because of what happened, but because of the way my body reacted when he was close to me.

My phone lights up from my lap; trying to be discrete, I check it from the cover of my desk.

Zach: *You flipped the switch, pretty girl.*
Me: *I don't even know what that means and stop calling me pretty girl.*

Zach flashes a gorgeous grin my way.

Zach: *It means that you will give in to me sooner or later.*

I don't text back. In fact, I ignore him completely. Tommy is in this same class and he's shooting death stares at Zach. I feel my phone vibrate again.

Tommy: *Can we hang out this weekend?*

I feel Zach's eyes burning a hole into the side of my face. He knows Tommy's texting me right now, and he's not liking it at all. But, little does he know, I don't care and maybe I want to make him a little jealous.

Me: *If you want, we can watch a movie over at my house or something. My parents are going to be away this weekend and my brother is barely home.*

C.M. Danks

Looking up, I check to see if our History teacher is paying any attention to the texting war between us three, but he's oblivious, and... wait a minute.

Wait. Did I just tell Tommy that no one is going to be home at my house this weekend? If that didn't sound like an open invitation, I don't know what else could. I definitely didn't mean it like it sounded.

"Shit." This was an utterance that was meant to be a thought inside my head and not out loud. The whole class turns around to me and Mr. Gilbert stops his chalkboard writing.

"Miss Taccarelli, do you mind not swearing in my classroom?" A mixture of giggles and soft laughter erupts from the students and Tommy is grinning. I'm a complete idiot for sending him that text. Zach throws me a concerned look then eyes up Tommy. I'm in trouble.

★★★

"You guys ready?" Lisa hooks her arm around mine as we head out of our high school. The boys don't have practice today and Lisa eventually got us all to agree on going to the corn maze after school. Considering it gets dark earlier now, it actually sounded fun. The guys were *whatever* about it, but despite what happened between Zach and me, I feel like the group will always be together. Until graduation that is. Zach tried asking me what the hell my outburst was about in History today, but I didn't tell him and I have no intentions of telling him. For all I know, Zach may decide to show up this weekend while Tommy is there.

"Shotgun!" Lisa claims the front seat, which means I get to cozy up with Zach in the back.

CHARGER

On our way to the maze, Lisa turns on "Wonderwall" by Oasis. Even though I know Garrett doesn't like the song, he doesn't protest—looks like Lisa may have my brother wrapped around her finger.

Zach is sitting next to me in all his glory. He seems larger seated back here. I study his profile while he's busy looking at his phone—probably texting Sam. Jealousy rips through me.

A strand of his dirty blond hair falls in front of his eye. I love his tousled hair and I want to run my fingers through it. His lips are full and his jaw is a chiseled dream. Taking him all in sends butterflies to my stomach.

He gives me a sideward glance with a twitch of his mouth, after he realizes that I am staring at him like a weirdo. The embarrassment makes my cheeks burn.

"What's up, Jules?" He jerks his head to the side, tossing the loose strand of hair back. His full attention is on me, but I quickly turn my head to look out the window—as if I could play this off now. I got caught red-handed, drooling over Zach in the back seat of a car.

Lisa and Garrett are having their own separate conversation up front, and I'm back here losing oxygen. Man, does it feel hot in here or is it just me?

Zach reaches over the seat, which isn't far, and places his hand on my legging-clad thigh. My body immediately reacts. His touch is warm and gentle, almost like he's teasing me.

I swallow nervously.

He gently squeezes, slowly working his way up. It's like he's setting my skin ablaze as he moves. I know where he's going and I should stop him, but my body won't allow it. The ache, the throb, will not let me stop him.

C.M. Danks

I close my eyes, preparing for his touch. His hand is teasing me as he brushes the pad of his thumb right between my aroused area.

"Oh, thank God. They have a coffee stand and cupcakes. How cute is this?" Lisa squeals.

We pull into the parking lot and Zach snatches his hand off my thigh, like he is zapped by something. Without even realizing we arrived, Lisa brings me back to earth. I quickly get out of the car, tugging my sweater around me for comfort, before my insides explode. Zach just tried feeling me up in the back seat of a car and I highly enjoyed it. I breathe slowly, trying to calm myself down.

"Come on, chick, we're going to get coffee. You two buy our tickets, will ya?" Lisa drags me to the coffee booth with Zach's eyes catching mine. They're hungry, heated, and wanting more.

Our boots trudge through the grass and dirt as we line up. Two boys in front of us smile down at us. They're tall, thin, and look interested.

"You two here for the maze?" They both have brown-colored hair and a preppy look.

"Yeah, should be fun." I smile shyly. But really, all I want to do is roll my eyes.

"It is. We did this last year. You could get lost if you're not careful, and it's kind of scary at night if you're by yourselves." The brown-haired guy closest to us grins.

"Yup, so if you ladies need someone to hold your hands, we will gladly assist." The other wiggles his eyebrows. I raise mine.

Seriously?

Lisa snorts out a laugh.

CHARGER

"I think they'll be fine." Zach slides his arm around my waist, sending goosebumps through me. I get a warm feeling when he tugs me closer to him, Garrett doing the same with Lisa. Both of our boys are giving the newcomers challenging looks and they don't waste any time spinning right back around.

I shake my head.

"You guys are seriously the worst." Lisa agrees with me while she smiles giddily.

"I'm just claiming what's mine," Zach whispers to me. I want to push him away, to tell him I'm not his, but then my brother and Lisa will ask questions. Also, when he says I'm his, I don't dislike the way it sounds. So instead, as a defense, I make the rash decision to squeeze the nipple that's closest to me. "Fuck," he mumbles. *Hold up.* I look at him and he's grinning while rubbing his newly injured nipple. I felt a piercing that was never there before, at least not this summer.

"Is your nipple pierced?" I ask quietly.

"Yup. I'll even let you play with it when you finally give up and give yourself to me."

Damn, that's hot. A sensation shoots through me, all the way down between my inner thighs.

I remove myself from his hold, even though it feels so warm, and give the lady at the coffee booth my order.

By the time we drink our coffees and eat, it's almost completely dark out. The maze is already getting a line and they're only letting a few groups in at a time. The line director goes over the rules and hands us our emergency alarms. He explains that if we want to, at any time, we can hit a button and a worker will direct us out. Guess the maze is bigger than we thought.

C.M. Danks

"This is gonna be sick." My brother grabs hold of Lisa's hand. Now, I feel like we're on a double date. Zach tries to hold my hand, but I smack it away and he laughs. He's messing with me and he's loving every minute of it.

We sink further into the maze. It's now completely dark; the only light we can see is the slight illumination of the moon. "I feel like we're in a horror movie and Leatherface is going to jump out at us any minute." Lisa burrows in closer to Garrett, but Zach is nowhere to be found.

"Where's Zach?" Lisa and my brother stop mid-step. The crunching from their boots goes silent.

"I swear, if he's trying to scare us, I'll kill him," Lisa bites out.

"Yeah, this isn't funny, Zach!" I yell. We seem to be the only group in this area and I can't see anything. I hear something to my far right, so I move a little to see if it's him. "I swear to God I'm going to punch you." I move further into the field, letting the corn stalks hit my face. After I don't see him, I turn back around and walk to where I think my brother and Lisa are. But I'm not sure if I came from this way, or the other. "Garrett?" My heart thumps faster as I wait for an answer. I keep walking, hoping this way is right. I know nothing is going to murder me out here but being in the pitch black, alone, is not my thing.

"Lisa?"

Nothing.

"Damn it." Moving deeper inside the corn stalks, I confirm I'm completely lost. My feet are plastered to the ground and I'm two seconds away from hitting my button. My adrenaline picks up and I'm terrified. I mean, I sleep with a night-light for God's sake. I fumble for my button with shaky hands, and that's when someone comes up from

CHARGER

behind me. They wrap a strong arm around my waist, while the other covers my mouth. I scream out of instinct, but my voice is muffled under his hand.

"Shh, pretty girl. It's only me."

My body relaxes a little when I hear Zach's voice. But now I'm just pissed. "You jerk." I try to turn so I can smack him, but he holds me still. His arms are wrapped around me so tightly they keep mine from moving. My back is pressed firmly against his chest. Being in his embrace, I'm not scared anymore. At least not from the maze or the darkness.

"Are you going to let me go?" I ask in a whisper.

"Nah, I don't think so." He brushes my long hair to the side, exposing my neck. His soft lips touch my skin and it takes every bit of restraint not to moan. "Your skin feels so good, like silk."

My insides are screaming. He runs his hand down my arm to my waist, then stops when he reaches the top of my leggings. "Jules… you've never been touched before, have you?" I suck in air, but it doesn't seem to be enough. Everything is spinning.

"Maybe," I lie, and he knows it.

"I don't think so. And just so you know, no one will *ever* touch you but me. Now, let me finish what I started." He slides his hand down the waistband of my leggings and reaches the hot, wet area between my thighs. My body erupts with fire and my stomach is in pain. Pain for the burning, aching desire that has been lit inside me.

My eyes roll back as they close. I tilt my head until it's resting on his chest. His hot breath radiates off my temple. My breathing picks up the closer he gets. "I think you like me touching you, don't you?" He slowly slides two fingers inside me and I'm brought to life. I let out a quiet moan as he goes in deeper. "You, moaning like that, is the hottest fucking thing."

"Oh my God, Zach." My fingers grip the hoodie he's wearing.

"You want more, Jules?" Without even having to think of the answer, I nod my head. *Yes.*

"Stop denying this, us. It's obvious you want to be more than just friends." He pulls away, leaving me unsatisfied. The warmth that was once at my back is gone. I don't say anything, nor do I turn around. How insanely cruel… I want, *I need,* more.

"Fuck, finally. We've been looking for you two." I turn around at the sound of my brother's voice, before shooting daggers at Zach.

I've created a monster.

CHAPTER SEVEN

Jules

Sketching has always been my escape from the world. Like reading, I can get lost in the picture. I can zone out from everything. But ever since the corn maze, I'm having trouble focusing on anything but that night—along with the stupid kiss from the party. The stupid, incredible, make my body come apart kiss.

Foy Vance is playing in my room and I'm sitting on my window seat replicating the night sky. Taking in every detail of the moon, the stars.

I happen to glance over to Zach's house and the same beat-up truck from before is sitting in the driveway. I add more shading around the moon, blending it in with my finger, before my attention shifts.

Shouting erupts from Zach's house. He stalks out of his front door, followed by an older man. An angry older man. I study what's taking place in front of me, leaning forward a bit, like that's gonna help me see any better. The older man grabs Zach by the shoulder, spinning him around before clocking him with his fist.

"Oh my God!" I jump forward, wanting to do something, but what can I do? Should I wake my parents? If they didn't already wake up from all the yelling... Should I tell Garrett? Then I see Zach straightening up from his blow to the face, and he strikes the man back. Zach's tall—taller than his opponent. The man flies back, holding his nose. Zach's mom comes barreling outside next, screaming and crying. She crouches down to see if the man is okay. Is she serious? Her son was just punched in the face by him, and she wants to make sure *he's* okay? I'm now sitting with my legs tucked underneath me, watching everything unfold. I feel so helpless, so bad for Zach right now. I see him reach in his pocket and take out his phone. Maybe he's calling the police.

I hear my phone vibrate on the end table next to my bed. Zach's name is on the screen. *He's calling me?*

I grab it, answer, and look at him from my window.

"Zach!? Are you okay?"

"You saw that?" His head turns to where I have my palm pressed against my window.

"Yeah, I did. You need to call the police." He paces back and forth, fumbling with his hair.

"Can you let me up?" He starts walking toward my larger bedroom window, not the one facing his house.

"Zach, I think you need to call the cops." The man is still holding his nose in Zach's driveway. It looks like he broke it. Good.

"Please, Jules."

"Fine, okay." I hang up, unlatching the lock.

He climbs (like Tarzan) up my siding and into my unlocked window. I step back as he throws his leg in first with a struggle.

He hasn't been in my room, just me and him, since we were younger. I start checking boxes off in my head as I run through a list of any potentially embarrassing items lying

CHARGER

around. He smirks devilishly while holding my bra up by its strap, using only his finger. Heat immediately hits my face and I quickly snatch it away. "Give me that." I throw it in my drawer and slam it closed. When I look back at Zach, he isn't smiling anymore and a bruise is already starting to form around his eye.

Running to my bedroom door, I look to see if anyone is in the hallway before I lock it. I know my brother can sleep like a rock but I'm not sure about my parents.

After locking it, I go into my bathroom and run a washcloth under the cold water. The defeat is written all over his face. "Here." I sit next to him and hold the washcloth to his battered eye. He winces from the pain, but then draws me in with his eyes.

"Thanks." He holds my hand with his, sending waves of electricity through me.

Every time.

"Zach, who was that?"

"No one." He lets go of my hand. "Don't worry about it, okay?"

"Don't worry about it? A grown-ass man just sucker punched you while your mother watched and you're telling me not to worry about it?"

"I can handle myself."

I search his eyes, sorrow filling them. "Clearly, but you shouldn't have to. You're eighteen years old." He stands up and paces to the other side of my room, running his fingers along the books on my shelf—pretending to be interested in them.

"He's my mom's drug dealer."

My heart sinks. Like, just hit an iceberg, sinks. "Your mom does drugs? I thought she was an alcoholic?"

C.M. Danks

"She does both." He stills, then turns around to me again. "He's been showing up more than he used to. Staying the night at our house. Apparently, he's been more than just her dope supplier."

"What about your dad?"

"My dad?" He laughs. "My dad hasn't come back from his *little* business trip in two months." I gasp. I can't believe I didn't notice that. Why didn't I notice that? We live next door to each other. No wonder he's always spending so much time at our house.

"Yeah, that was my reaction. Only, I knew it was coming. He got tired of my mom's shit. But whatever—it's not like he and I had any sort of relationship."

"Zach, I'm so sorry." I was sorry. But what else could I say? It makes my heart hurt for him.

"Don't, don't you dare feel sorry for me, Jules. Not you. I don't need anyone's sympathy." I study my lap while picking at an invisible hangnail.

"Does Garrett know?"

"No, he doesn't. And I can't tell anyone because they'll make me go to the cops and if I do that, my mother will go to jail."

"But you told *me*." He scans my eyes, my face, then grazes over my breasts. I forgot that I'm wearing a tank top and night shorts. My hair is pulled up in a bun and my glasses are on. It's not my finest moment. But he doesn't seem to mind.

"I did tell you. Not sure why…" He lets out a huff. "Maybe because you're the first person I think of anymore." My stomach does a dance of excitement. He thinks about me all the time?

I quickly change the subject as he grabs my sketchpad.

CHARGER

"So, why did you guys get into a fight?"

"Because he's a prick and I told him to leave. He didn't like that, and things went to shit really fast."

I get up from my bed. "Zach, you can always stay with us. You know my parents would let you stay here."

He flips through each page of my sketchbook, ignoring my statement. "What are you always drawing in here?"

I jerk the book out of his grasp just as fast as I had with my bra. "Just stuff." I sit back down and he does the same. Our thighs touch, causing electricity to tingle through me.

"Stuff, huh, and what kind of stuff?"

I sigh. "Promise you won't laugh?"

He loses his playful smile and I open my sketchbook. I show him drawings of flowers, buildings, people. I turn the page and there he is, front and center, in his football uniform. It was their first game. The way he was happy and smiling, it made my heart full.

After realizing just how embarrassing that is, I close it. "I-I, uh, liked how you were smiling," I say softly while nervously playing with my hair.

Zach's staring at me. But without judgement. He has a spark in his eyes, giving me the impression that he really loves that I drew him. Maybe it was more special than I thought.

"Will you draw me something sometime?"

"Um, sure. What do you want me to draw you?"

"A motorcycle." He smiles proudly. "Like what the paint would look like."

Is he serious?

"You want me to design you a motorcycle, why?"

"Because, one day, I will own my own bike. And I want to always be reminded of the girl next door when I go to ride it." He reaches for my lip. The pad of his thumb parts my mouth as he runs his hand down, stopping as he nears my breasts.

"Zach..."

The sound of a very loud exhaust pipe goes off next door. We both listen as it fades away in the distance.

"Guess he decided to bounce. I should probably go." He gets up first, and I watch as he's about to climb out of my window, but then stops. Coming back inside, he steps in front of me. "Stop hanging out with Tommy, Jules." That caught me off guard.

"Why do you want me to stop hanging out with him?" I stand as he takes another step closer to me. A part of me hopes it's because he likes me. Like, really likes me. Not just him being a horny teenager.

"You know why, and trust me, he doesn't like you." He dramatically closes his eyes. *If that wasn't a blow.* "Fuck, I didn't mean it to come out the way it sounded. I meant..."

"Oh, no, I get it. You meant it's not possible for a guy to like me, right? I mean, know I don't compare to your cheerleader girlfriend, but I didn't think I was *that* repulsive."

He grabs my arm and pulls me to him. "That's not what I meant. I'm simply saying that he is an asshole, Jules. He's not interested in dating you. He just wants to fuck you."

I push him away from me until the back of his knees hit my window seat. "Why does it always have to be about having sex? Why is it so crazy for someone to just genuinely like someone?" I suddenly realize that I'm louder than I should be. That's all I need, for my parents to wake up and see Zach in my bedroom.

"Because we're boys and we're teenagers."

CHARGER

I just felt a sharp pain in my chest. So maybe that is how Zach feels. He just wants to fuck me, then forget about me. "Right, got it. You can leave now."

"Jules…"

"Bye, Zach. And don't forget to ice your damn eye."

He's staring at me, but gives up and leaves.

I lock my window and grab my sketchbook. Turning to a new page, I start drawing Zach's motorcycle. Why? Because I think I'm in love with my best friend.

C.M. Danks

Chapter Eight

Jules

It doesn't feel the same kissing Tommy like it felt when I kissed Zach. I wait for the sparks, for the butterflies when he touches me, moving his tongue inside my mouth. But there isn't anything. No spark, no fire, no desire deep inside. Nothing but a sloppy, wet kiss. There's nothing sexy about that.

I pull away from him, biting my swollen lip.

"Did you want something to drink?" I ask him, getting up from the couch. I start walking to the kitchen. He looks a little annoyed at me for abruptly ending our make out session.

"Um, I'll take a water I guess."

I stop with my hand on the fridge door handle. I touch my lips at the memory of Zach's kiss. It felt so different. It felt... *amazing*. Sure, making out with Tommy was nice. But I don't want it to feel *nice*.

I'm back in the living room and Tommy is texting on his phone. I plop down next to him again and grab for the remote. "Want to watch that movie now?" I ask him as he

CHARGER

slips his phone back into his pocket. He reaches for my hand and pulls me forward to him.

"I would rather be doing this instead." He tries lip-locking again, but I dodge it.

This would be the perfect opportunity. I should tell him that I'm not into him like that. Maybe I just need more space between Zach's kiss and his. To give myself time to forget what his lips felt like. Or how his arms felt around me, his hands touching my skin. I take a swig of my water, attempting to cool myself off.

Tommy tries again and this time his mouth crashes hard on mine. I give in to him just a little, until his hand starts moving under my shirt. I push at his chest. "Uh, maybe we should slow down."

He smiles then goes in for another kiss, this time cupping my breast.

Oh, hell no.

I push harder against him and I jump up from the couch. "What the hell are you doing? I said slow down, not speed up." I violently tug at my shirt, trying to pull it down even though it's already covering me. Suddenly I feel more exposed than normal.

"Are you fucking serious right now?" He gets up and stands there, like I'm the one who did something wrong. I don't think so, buddy.

"Pretty sure I am serious, yes."

"Right. I forgot… you'll only fuck Zach, not anyone else."

"I think you better leave, Tommy." I stand there waiting for him to go.

"Fine, whatever." He grabs his jacket off the back of the couch. He turns around right before walking out the door.

C.M. Danks

"You're a fuckin' tease, Jules. But just so you know, it's not like I really liked you anyway. I just wanted an easy fuck."

I walk up to him. "You thought just because I kissed Zach during some stupid truth or dare game, that I was screwing him?" He shrugs. "You *are* a douchebag."

"Whatever," he mutters, then stomps down my front steps.

"Oh, and Tommy!" I shout. "You suck at kissing!" With that, I slam the door. I have a quick high of Wonder Woman power before I break down. Tears roll over my cheeks and I run, faceplanting onto the couch.

I hug the pillow under me and stare at the floor. So, it was true… he didn't like me. I take out my cell and text the only person I want to talk to right now. The only person I was thinking about all night anyway.

Me: *You were right.*

I go to my music and scroll through my songs. Taylor Swift is my girl right now because her songs always know how to make me feel better.

Stuffing my phone into my pocket, I walk upstairs to change out of my jeans and into my sweatpants, before grabbing a hoodie. Just as I make it back downstairs, someone knocks. If it's Tommy trying to redeem himself, I might just kick him in his balls.

I swing open the door in exhaustion and there's Zach, standing on the top step looking like he's ready to kill someone. He's breathing heavily and his school hoodie has never looked smaller on his puffed-out chest.

CHARGER

"Zach, what are you…?" He comes stomping in and it forces me to take a step backwards. He doesn't move, just looks around.

"Where the fuck's he at?"

He was here because of my text? "He left like twenty minutes ago. It's fine. I kicked him out. How did you know I was talking about Tommy?"

"Your text wasn't encrypted, Jules. I figured it out." He moves in closer, wiping my cheek with his thumb. I have to tilt my head back and look up to see him. "Did he hurt you?"

"No, he didn't." We stare, each taking the other in, and then he relaxes. "I'm sorry."

I raise my hand. "Before you give me an *I told you so* speech, save it. I know. I suck. I'm stupid."

"I wasn't going to give you any type of speech. And you sure as fuck aren't stupid." I look down at my feet; for some reason, I have a high interest in them right now. I feel like hiding, crawling away like I do when something hurts me. "He called me a tease and said because I kissed you, he thought I would…"

He grabs my wrist, without hurting me. "He thought what?"

"He thought I would have sex with him because he thought I was having sex with you."

I hear Zach breathe in. "He's so dead."

I take my free hand and hold onto his. His attention shoots there, his eyes widening with surprise. "Will you just stay with me, at least until Garrett comes home. I don't feel like being alone right now."

It takes a second before he calms down. With a sigh, he gives up. "Yeah, pretty girl."

C.M. Danks

I get butterflies every time he calls me that. Even though I told him to stop, I didn't want him to. I walk him over to the couch, a tear escaping my eye. I'm not sad because Tommy wasn't who I thought he was. I'm crying because he thought I was easy.

I turn on the movie Tommy and I were supposed to watch as Zach holds out his arm. I'm assuming that is an invitation and I gladly accept it.

I snuggle into his embrace and he squeezes me close. It's funny because my best friend was always saving me, and tonight was the first night that I fully accepted it without overanalyzing anything.

I couldn't remember where I was, until I felt Zach's warm body underneath me. We must have fallen asleep because he's sprawled out on the couch, me on top of him.

"What are you guys doing?" My brother stands behind the couch, scaring the shit out of me. We both get up slowly.

"Nothing. We fell asleep watching a movie." I straighten my hoodie as Garrett bounces glances between us.

Zach gets up from the couch and stretches with a yawn, exposing some of his lean, V-shaped torso. Of course, my eyes travel there, and of course, I'm embarrassed when he notices. "All right, I'm out." He looks at me. "You good?"

"Yeah, I'm good. Thanks." He winks before leaving.

Garrett is staring at me like he's waiting for me to say something. "How was your date with Lisa?"

"It wasn't a date." Garrett plops down where Zach was. "Just two friends hanging out."

I smack his arm. "I swear if you hurt her Garrett... She likes you, and if you don't feel the same way, then you need to tell her."

CHARGER

"I didn't say I didn't *like* her." He rubs his arm, flashing me a smirk. Okay, so he does like her.

"Good." I give him the same smirk back.

"What's going on with you and Zach?"

"Nothing's going on with us. Why would you ask that?"

"I don't know. You guys have been weird lately. Kind of secretive too, whatever that's about." He's not wrong—we have been a little secretive lately. Before I can give an answer, he slaps his thigh. "Whatever, I'm going to bed." He starts walking upstairs. "Oh, forgot to tell you. Mom's planning a big birthday dinner for us next week, so don't plan anything. I think she wanted it to be a surprise, but I found out because I'm just that good. Don't you forget it." He points his two fingers from his eyes to me.

"Yeah, I get it, bro. You're watching me." I smile and shoo him away.

★★★

"What the hell happened on Saturday night?" Lisa's leaning against the locker next to mine.

"I threw Tommy out. He thought he was getting more out of me than I was willing to give."

"Well, did you happen to punch him in the eye too? Because I saw him this morning with a pretty nice shiner. Not saying he obviously didn't deserve it."

Someone punched Tommy? I close my locker door with force.

"No," I reply, giving Lisa a confused look. I seek Zach out in the crowd. "I'll be right back."

C.M. Danks

I strut toward him and of course Sam is there. Guess she decided to forgive him for the dare. Ignoring her, I grab Zach's arm, spinning him around.

"Hey, what's—"

"Why did you punch Tommy? He wasn't worth it, Zach. You could get expelled, or kicked off the football team!"

He raises an eyebrow. "Do you think I care about the stupid football team? And Coach Russel wouldn't let me get expelled anyway."

"That's not the point. I don't need anyone fighting my battles for me."

The annoyed tap of Sam's toe is tempting me to rip off her shoe and hit her with it. Zach grabs hold of my shoulders and lowers his head to me. "I wish, and I can't tell you this enough, how I wish it was me who punched that asshole." His warm hands leave my shoulders. "But it wasn't me."

I cock my head back as if I was smacked. "If it wasn't you, then who was it?"

"Your brother."

"You told Garrett?" He shakes his head. "Nope, the fucker bragged about what happened on Facebook, or rather, what didn't happen. Garrett saw it and obviously was pissed, so he punched him this morning."

Pulling out my phone, I text Garrett.

Me: *You know I didn't sleep with him, right?*

He responds almost instantly.

Garrett: *I don't know. I mean you're so fucking secretive lately.*

CHARGER

Me: Seriously, Garrett! You know I didn't. Stop being dumb and I hope you didn't get in trouble for the sucker punch.
Garrett: Fine, I believe you. And, no, Coach just benched me for next practice.

"Is that Garrett?" Zach looks down at my phone while I nod my head yes.

"I gotta get to class." Zach trails behind me, ignoring Sam, who throws her hands in the air. "You better not follow me or your girlfriend is gonna freak. She might even throw one of her tissue balls from her bra at you."

Zach laughs and pulls me around the corner to an empty hall. He rests his forearm on the wall above me and grabs my waist. "I broke up with her."

My heart skips like a happy grade-schooler. "Oh yeah, why did you do that? I thought you guys were *super cute* together?" I am every bit sarcastic. He shrugs and brushes a strand of hair away from my lip. "She just wasn't for me, pretty girl." I swallow nervously.

"You're turning eighteen soon." He leans in and whispers, "Which means you'll be legal, Jules." His mouth hovers over mine and I can feel the goosebumps on my skin.

"Happy birthday to me then, huh," I whisper back, having no freaking clue where that came from. Zach brings out something in me that I've never experienced. Like this new, more confident girl.

He leans back from me with a surprised as fuck look on his face. But he likes it. I can tell because of how he grins from ear to ear, how his eyes come alive. The bell rings, and I quickly duck out from the wall under his arm. Without turning around, I head straight to class. But I can feel his stare burning into my back.

C.M. Danks

Chapter Nine

Jules

"*Happy birthday to you...*" The comforting, soft sound of my mother's voice singing happy birthday to me stirs me awake. It carries on until she gets through the whole birthday song. I'm eighteen. Welcome to adulthood, Jules.

My taste buds awaken at the scent of bacon and eggs. She sets the tray of breakfast goodness down in front of me. "Mom, you didn't have to do all this," I tell her as I toss a strawberry into my mouth, the sweet taste hitting my tongue.

"You only turn eighteen once."

"Did you do the same for Garrett?"

"Are you kidding me?" My mom laughs. "Your brother would kill me if I woke him up this early on a Sunday. Birthday or not."

I laugh along with her. "That's probably true. He'd be all like... *Why can't you just let me sleep? It's not that big of a deal.* Then he would get upset later for not making it a big deal." I roll my eyes.

CHARGER

She sighs, looking at me all motherly. "Mom, it's way too early for you to start crying. I'm only eighteen—it doesn't mean I'm getting married and having babies."

"Damn right you're not." She playfully swats my hand. "But time flies by and before you know it, you *will* be married with children of your own. And then you get to watch them grow up to become amazing adults, just like today." Okay, so my mom has a way with words, for sure.

"Okay, well, now I might cry so let's calm it down." I sniffle, grabbing my glasses from the end table.

"Oh, here." She hands me a small box with an envelope. At first, I assume it's from her and Dad. But my mother wouldn't have used a brown paper bag as gift wrap. "Zach dropped it off early this morning and said to give it to you." An automatic smile forms, one that I couldn't stop if I tried.

"Well, I'm gonna go put some coffee on before your father has a stroke." She kisses my forehead before leaving my room.

After I complete my morning routine, I sit on my bed in front of Zach's present. It makes me sad that we haven't talked all that much this week. He said he was having trouble at home… with his mom. Luckily that guy never came back.

I start with the card. On the front, there's a picture of a shooting star that says Happy Birthday. Not expecting the long, hand-written message inside, I start reading it.

To my pretty girl,
Sorry I have to miss your and Garrett's birthday today. Mom has an AA meeting and I'm driving her ass. If not, I know damn well she won't go. Guess it's a start. Anyway, I'm sorry I haven't seen you much this week. I think about you every day and I can't

C.M. Danks

help but remember the sweetness of how you taste or the touch of your skin. Yeah, I'm going to tell you how I feel whether or not you feel the same. Even though, I know you do too. It's only a matter of time before you admit it. I know we've been best friends for a long time, but the feelings I have for you are real, Jules. I hope you have a great birthday because you deserve the fucking sky and all the stars in it.
Yours truly,
The hottest boy in school.

All I can do is stare at the card in my hand, rereading it a few times. Okay, my naïve self needs to stop thinking he's only a horny teenager and get over myself. So, Zach does feel the same way I do. I'm nervous, excited, and terrified. All at the same time.

With my hands shaking, I fumble to open his present. Inside, there's a necklace with a silver star charm hanging from the chain. It's absolutely beautiful and so thoughtful. It also makes me feel bad knowing that he probably spent most of his summer earnings on this. He spent a lot of his time working at his uncle's bike shop.

When I hold it out in front of me, my heart does a flip flop. The same way it always does for him. On the back, it's engraved with my initials. Zach's the first boy, (who wasn't a family member) to ever buy me a present.

My brother, half asleep, drags himself into my room. He runs a hand through his disheveled hair. "Happy birthday, loser." Pulling my desk chair out, he falls down onto it.

"Right back at you."

"Present from Mom and Dad?" He nods at the jewelry I'm holding.

"Um, actually it's from Zach."

"Oh?" His eyebrows scrunch together.

"So, what plans do you have today besides the big birthday dinner?" I say, quickly changing the subject.

"I don't know. Might take Lisa to mini golf before it closes for the winter."

"Sounds like fun."

There's a moment of silence. And I know he wants to ask me about Zach.

"So, you two have something going on or what?" His wheels are turning, as he looks from the necklace back to me. I don't know what to tell him. Does it really matter?

"To be honest, I don't really know, maybe." I pause to make sure he doesn't have a meltdown. "Are you mad about it?"

The brief hesitation in his voice scares me. I would be crushed.

"Nah, my best friend and my sister, why not?" He shrugs and I let out a sigh of relief. "Just know if he hurts you, best bud or not, I will end him."

I shake my head. "Always so dramatic, bro."

"Just sayin'." He gets up from the chair and yawns. "Well, I guess I'll go shower."

"Good idea. You don't want Lisa to smell you," I joke playfully, and he flips me off.

After my brother leaves, I jump up from my bed, butterflies taking over my stomach. Standing in front of my vanity, I latch the necklace around my neck and run my fingers over its beauty. What makes it even more special? It's from Zach. The boy next door. My best friend. The boy I have definitely fallen in love with.

C.M. Danks

★★★

All day Mom and Dad fuss over our birthday. First, it was the breakfast; then, it was the huge dinner feast. We opened our birthday gifts. I got some clothes, a new purse and makeup. I don't really wear too much makeup, but it was from my mom so I was still excited. My dad bought Garrett tickets to go see the Cleveland Browns play. I'm glad I wasn't invited. I hate sports. Unless a certain boy with dirty blond hair and gorgeous eyes is playing. Then football becomes my new favorite thing to watch. My heart flutters at the mere thought of Zach in his football uniform, running down the field, all powerful.

I walk over to my window and unlock it. A part of me hopes Zach will climb inside. When I take a peek across the yard, I don't see him or any lights on in his bedroom. In fact, I haven't even heard from him today and neither has my brother. Hoping everything went well with his mom, I lie down, putting in my earbuds.

I grab a book while listening to Blink 182's "I Miss You." Yes, the song has everything to do with missing Zach right now.

My thoughts drift, so concentrating on the book right now is not happening. I set it down and reach for Zach's card on my nightstand. I reread it like a dozen times.

I know we've been best friends for a long time, but the feelings I have for you are real, Jules. His words replay over and over in my head. I close my eyes, letting them swirl inside my thoughts. When the heaviness of sleep starts to take me, I let it.

CHARGER

I can feel my nipples harden from his touch. Using his tongue, he flicks them each in turn then gently sucks. I arch my back and moan from the pleasure, gripping onto the sheets. He works his way farther down my stomach, brushing his lips as he goes. "You like that don't you, pretty girl?"

Jerking awake, I shoot up from my bed, almost knocking heads with the person sitting in front of me. He covers my mouth as I'm about to scream. "Shit, Jules, didn't mean to scare you, but you looked like you were enjoying that dream of yours." Zach smirks and I try to control my breathing. Did I really just have a dirty dream about him? What is he doing to me?

He's wearing grey sweatpants and a plain black t-shirt, which makes his arms look fucking fantastic. The rippled abs under his shirt are screaming to be touched. And why are grey sweatpants so sexy?

"What are you doing here?" Still jumpy from the dream, I swipe loose hair out of my face.

"Your window was unlocked, so I climbed in. I wanted to see you on your birthday." He catches my stare and reaches for my cheek. "Well, technically, it's not still your birthday but I did want to see you." Checking my cell, I realize that it's 2 a.m. He looks down at the card, which had fallen off my chest and onto the bed. "I take it you liked the card and the gift." His eyes flick up to my chest, where the necklace is resting. Reaching up, I hold it in a closed fist.

"Zach, it's gorgeous. But you didn't have to buy me anything."

"I wanted to." His smile turns serious. "And I... uh, meant every word I said." I bite my bottom lip. He watches me as I try to think of what to say in return. "I hate when you do that."

"Do what?" I whisper.

"When you bite your lip. It's hot as fuck."

My stomach turns to knots, and I pull the covers to my chest. Zach reaches over, slowly tugging them back down. "Don't hide from me, Jules." He leans forward and pushes me back onto my bed with his body. With him braced on top of me, his hands on either side, I feel the heat between us. He admires me. Studies me. I swallow back the nerves, but my hands want to touch him so badly. Before I know it, my fingers are running through his soft, thick hair as he closes his eyes.

"I feel the same..." I tell him.

At my words, his eyes fly open, the intensity going from ten to one hundred within seconds. He crashes his mouth down to mine and kisses me like he never wants to stop. My insides ignite, melting little by little. His tongue finds mine and dances with it. With every flick and twirl, an achy desire hits between my legs.

He pulls away to start kissing my neck. His teeth graze my skin ever so softly, just enough that he won't leave a mark. I squirm underneath him like the horny virgin that I am and clench my thighs together.

"Do you want to be touched?"

I swallow and nod my head. *Yes*. He gives me a possessive smirk, kissing my bare chest before working his way to my breasts. He pulls down on my tank top, leaving one side exposed.

"Jesus..." I watch his arm muscles flex as he continues to brace himself up. "Let's see how wet you are for me." He grips the top of my shorts and yanks them down, leaving me in nothing but my soaked panties. He scoots lower, toward my feet, and sinks his teeth into my lace underwear, dragging them down until I am completely exposed. I feel shy because this is the first time he is seeing me practically naked. The first time any boy is seeing me in this vulnerable state. But I ache too much for him. My body is screaming for him. The waiting is torture.

"Please, Zach…"

He licks my clit and fireworks erupt.

"Oh my God."

"You taste like fucking ice cream."

I close my eyes while he continues to run his tongue in my sensitive spots, creating small, slow circles. It's getting stronger; the sensation is shooting throughout my whole body now. I grab onto his hair while he's buried between my thighs, then I clench onto his shoulders. And it hits me all at once, an overwhelming feeling like no other, and I try to hold back my scream as much as possible. He looks up at me as I'm catching my breath.

"Zach, that was…" He moves to me, eyes heated, burning like fire. "I didn't know that it could feel like that."

"Pretty girl, just wait, because I have so much more to do to you." I pull my panties up along with my shorts and he crawls in next to me.

"Crap, I never locked my door." *Guess it's a little late for that, but still…* I spring out of bed and quickly lock it. Before I can turn around, Zach slips up behind me. He turns me to face him, closing his arms around my back and lifting me off the floor. My legs wrap around him. He walks backwards until he hits my bed and sits down with me on his lap. I straddle him, locking my arms around his neck.

C.M. Danks

We stare into each other's eyes and I can feel his hard erection underneath me.

"Zach..."

"Yeah?"

"Can I make you feel good too?"

He swallows nervously. "It's your birthday, Specs. It's not about me today."

"But I want to."

He groans, tilting his head backwards, as I start kissing his neck. I yank his t-shirt up, pulling it off him. I take him in before running my hands down his hard chest, not stopping until I reach his rippled, cut muscles. I trace each rigid line with my fingers.

"Fuck," he growls.

I get up from my straddled position and push him back onto my bed. I pull his sweatpants down with his thickness on full display. I've never done this before... I remind myself just how inexperienced I am. Will he compare me to Sam, or others?

"Jules, you don't have to do this."

I allow the burst of confidence to run through me, letting it take advantage. Before he can stop me, I pull down his boxers, swiping my tongue over him. Honestly, I have no clue what I am doing, but from the sounds Zach's making, I must be doing something right. I open my mouth and take him all in, motioning in and out. He grabs a fist full of my hair. "Fuck, that feels so fucking good." I keep going until I can feel him pulsing at the back of my throat. "I'm gonna come, Jules." I refuse to let go, wanting to taste him. He grips me tighter, and that's when he releases. Gagging just a little, I sit up and look at him. He swipes the tears off my face and presses his forehead to mine. "You are fucking amazing, you know that?" I smile and his lips warm my forehead. "C'mon, I want to hold you. I waited a long time for this and I want you close to me."

We climb into my bed and he pulls me to him, wrapping his arm around me. I lay my head on his chest. This is perfect. So perfect.

"I thought maybe you would want to have sex tonight."

He tilts my chin up so he can see me. "Trust me, I did want to have sex with you. But I don't want to rush this. We have plenty of time for that."

Playing with his piercing, I find the courage to ask him. "How did today go… with your mom?"

"It went okay—she stayed for the whole thing this time. I'm hoping she gets her shit together."

"Me too," I tell him honestly.

"Go to sleep, Jules, and happy birthday."

And a happy birthday it was. I feel myself dozing off, because something about being in Zach's arms is the most comfortable place to be.

CHAPTER TEN

Jules

The bell rings, leaving the hallway deserted. I round the corner and a pair of strong hands wrap around my waist, backing me up to a locker.

"Hey." Zach's soft, husky voice gives me goosebumps.

He jerks me forward, causing me to crash right into him. It's indiscernible, how his body feels pressed to mine.

He hovers just above my mouth before he locks his with mine, sending fireworks through my whole body. I'm lost in this moment, because kissing him is something I never want to stop doing. Last night was amazing and today, *this*, well, it definitely feels like a dream.

I break apart from him even though I don't want to—each leaving the other breathless. "We're gonna get caught." I smack his chest playfully. But he catches my hand and holds it to him.

"You're worth it. I can kiss you all day."

"I can kiss you all day too."

He gives me another peck before letting go. "C'mon you're gonna make me late, Jules." I cock my head to the side, and he snickers, though I know it was only a joke.

CHARGER

We walk toward class but I stop, not caring whether I'm late or not at this point. "Hey, Zach." He turns around to face me. "What are we? I mean, like are we dating?" I feel so silly asking him.

He walks toward me with a smile. "Hell yeah, we're dating. I want everyone to know that you're mine, Jules. No one else is allowed to come near you."

My insides jump for joy—the possessiveness of his words makes the ache shoot down to my core. I'm his and he's mine. It's real. He winks, kisses my cheek, and takes off for homeroom.

At lunch, I feel everyone staring. In my opinion, they're shocked shitless that Zach is with me. Sam is eyeing me up like the bitch that she is.

"Stop caring about what everyone is thinking," Zach scolds me.

I grab a fry off my plate. "I don't. I mean, it's just..."

"It's written all over your gorgeous face. So, stop it. You're the hottest fucking girl I've ever seen and if anyone has a problem with us dating, then they can come see me."

"Can you guys not be fucking weird with me here, please." I look at my brother, who is awkwardly trying to ignore us at the lunch table.

"What your brother *means* is people like Sam don't deserve your reaction. She's clearly just jealous." Lisa smiles, throwing Sam the stink eye.

I would have been fine with keeping our little rendezvous a secret until after graduation. But when Zach pulled me into him and kissed me like a queen in the lunch room, everyone clearly figured it out. So here we are—me, trying to avoid the awkward stares and whispers, and Zach, acting like it's totally fine.

C.M. Danks

"No, what I mean is I'm okay with you two being whatever it is you two are." Garrett waves his fork. "But it doesn't mean I want to see or hear about it."

"Get used to it, man, because I've waited way too long for this." Zach is actually blushing.

"Really, you have?"

"Oh yeah, pretty girl." He leans over and kisses my cheek.

"Aw, that's way too cute." Lisa places her hand to her chest.

"Whatever." Garrett smirks.

After lunch, I make my way to the library. I take out my notebook to start rewriting my History notes. Since I have a free period, the library is kind of my sanctuary away from everything. As soon as I put my earbuds in, someone taps me on the shoulder.

"So, you and Zach are official?"

Cringing at his voice, I slam my notebook closed. "I'm sorry but one, that's none of your business and two, why are you even talking to me, Tommy?"

He shrugs, "Just thought I deserved an explanation." *He* deserves an explanation? My body erupts with laughter.

"And what makes you think that?"

"You led me on."

I place my arms on the table and look at him like he has completely lost his mind. "You must be delusional." I'll admit, maybe a part of me did use him to make Zach jealous, or maybe I just liked the attention he was giving me. But that doesn't excuse the way he treated me at my house.

He leans forward. "And you're a bitch."

He doesn't wait for a response before walking away. Had he not been a major asswipe, then maybe it could have

CHARGER

been more. Who am I kidding? The only boy I want to be with is Zach. I hate that I feel like I'm being punished for being with him. But it doesn't matter. The way I feel about him trumps everything.

"Hey." Zach leans in from behind me, tickling my face with his breath. "You okay? You look pissed."

"It's nothing." I smile, turning toward him. "So, how were you able to get out of class?"

"Eh, I have my ways." Zach pulls my face forward, kissing me like we're the only ones in the room. "I can't wait until I get to have all of you."

Licking my lips, tasting him and wanting more, I respond, "Oh yeah, and what makes you so sure I would even give it all to you?"

His smile deepens on one side. "Oh, you will. You can't resist me and my charm." He's right. When the time comes, I know I won't be able to resist him.

"You're *so* funny."

"I know. You love it though." Zach pecks my cheek, which is super cute. "So, are you coming to our game this Friday?"

"Of course, I'll be there cheering you on with my short skirt and pompons."

Zach's body turns to stone, straightening in the chair. "Wait, you joined the cheer squad?" He knows better, so I flash him a look that says so. "That's just cruel, Specs."

I laugh, shrugging my shoulders. "I know but it was also funny. I'm sorry, because I know how badly you wanted to see me in that outfit."

"Are you kidding me? I'm happy you were joking. I didn't want any other guys drooling over you." Zach gets up, throwing his book bag over his shoulder. A piece of his tousled hair falls in front of his eye. "But it would be hot as fuck if you wore my jersey to the game." With his hands on the table, he leans down, placing a kiss to my forehead and leaving me with nothing but butterflies.

★★★

"This better be one of the last games of the season, not that I don't want to see them win, but I'm just not made for this weather." I really want to agree with Lisa, but I also don't want to be *that* whiny girlfriend. Though, Zach should be happy, since I decided to go all out for him. I'm wearing his jersey like he asked me to, threw my hair into stupid pig tails and had Lisa paint his jersey numbers on my face. It's definitely something Sam would have done. Speaking of, it hasn't gone unnoticed, the way she keeps glaring at me between pompon shuffles.

Zach is on the sidelines in his tight football pants and jersey. He looks over to me sitting in the stands, puckers his lips, and gives me an imaginary kiss.

So cute.

After the game, which they won, the football players gather in a huddle on the field. Zach glances my way a couple of times, then someone walks up to him and hands him a microphone.

"What's he doing?" Lisa asks me, but I have no clue what's going on.

"I Will Follow You into the Dark" by Death Cab for Cutie starts playing on the overhead speakers. Zach knows I love this song.

CHARGER

While the music strums in the distance, Zach holds the mic up to his mouth. "So, I know this isn't really your thing, but I wanted to ask you." My heart is beating so fast. One of his teammates holds up a big white poster board that reads: Julianna Lynn Taccarelli, will you go to prom with me?

Oh my God.

Stunned, I can't move, can't speak.

"Holy shit, that's adorable!" Lisa squeals.

I'm trying to let it sink in. But all eyes are on me and Zach, as the crowd begins to chant, "Say yes!" All the cheerleaders are jumping up and down in excitement, all except Sam.

"C'mon, Jules, can't leave me hanging."

Lisa nudges me with her elbow. "Girl, go down there." My mom says the same thing as she taps my shoulder from behind. She's smiling, telling me to go and giving me that reassurance I need. Finally, breaking into the biggest smile possible, I get up and start climbing down the bleacher steps. With each vibration, each echo of the bleacher stairs, I am one step closer to him. My excitement is in overdrive.

Everyone is yelling, making wooing noises. Maybe they don't all hate me after all. But right now, my only focus is Zach. I see no one but him. He hands the mic over to his friend, then stalks toward me like he would plow anyone down to get to me. My shoes touch pavement. That's when I pick up speed. It's like being pulled by a magnet. I'm naturally drawn to him.

I fling my body into his when we finally reach one another. I lock my wrists around his neck as he lifts me up, both of his arms encompassing my back. My feet dangle midair as he twirls me in a circle. I throw my head back, laughing. Then he grips my ass cheeks and I wrap my legs around his waist. His musky, sweaty scent fills my nose as I bury my face into his neck.

"Is that a yes, pretty girl?" he whispers into my ear.

I smile but he can't see me. "Yes, I'll go to prom with you, Zachary William Scott."

Everyone claps and cheers. I unbury my face enough to kiss him. I never thought I would be so excited to go to prom until now. My brother looks over with a smile.

"I feel like you just proposed or something." I laugh, but he doesn't.

"Jules, I *will* be the one to marry you someday—best believe that." My mouth parts open and my eyes dart between each of his. Shock doesn't come close to describing this moment right now. I should be terrified. Only, his words don't scare me, they make me smile even wider. He crashes his lips to mine again before he carries me off the field.

CHARGER

CHAPTER ELEVEN

Jules

Winter flew by. Christmas was spent like it always is every year—my parents going all out with lights, movies, presents. It's just like when we were little, which is pretty cool, I'll admit. Zach spent Christmas with us this year because his mom was away with her new boyfriend. She is trying to get her act together, and I can tell Zach is excited about it. No teenager should witness their parent going through that kind of stuff.

New Year's was eventful. One of the senior football players had a party (parent-supervised) and that was the night my brother finally made his relationship with Lisa official.

Took him long enough.

What I have with Zach has been pretty amazing. We spend almost every weekend together and, on some weekdays, he sneaks into my room at night. We fall asleep together, making sure he's gone before my parents wake up. We haven't had sex yet because Zach keeps telling me he wants to wait and make it special for me.

So, here I am, a month before graduation on prom night, staring at myself wearing my mermaid-cut dress. After Zach

C.M. Danks

asked me, I think my mom was more excited than I was. That weekend, she took me shopping for my dress. It's form-fitting all the way down, silver with some sequins, and the back is cut out. It's a little out of my comfort zone, but as I turn around in the mirror and look at myself, I actually think I look hot. Thank God I haven't gained any weight—no way in hell would I have been able to fit in this dress.

I give my loose, wavy curls one more spray and swipe another application of lip gloss on. The necklace that Zach gave me on my birthday is hanging down on my chest and when I move a certain way, it sparkles. Like the star is shining.

I love it. I love it so much.

My mom yells from downstairs, letting me know Zach is here.

My heartbeat thuds a little faster. I'm more nervous than I thought. I think it's because tonight might be *the* night. Don't people usually have sex on prom night? Also, what if Zach doesn't find me attractive in my dress? What if Sam looks prettier?

Okay, Jules. Stop it. He and Sam haven't even spoken to each other since they broke up. Get a grip.

Inhaling deeply then exhaling, I try to calm my nerves. "All right, let's do this."

As I head downstairs in my four-inch heels, hoping I don't fall and humiliate myself, everyone else is huddled at the door, including Lisa. My dad is telling Zach to stop moving so he can knot his tie for him, and my mom is telling Lisa how beautiful she looks. I wouldn't doubt it, Lisa is a natural redhead, so she has the cute freckles and perfect porcelain skin.

CHARGER

No one notices I am at the top of the stairs except Zach. He seems to have a radar for when I'm in the room, much like I do for him. His mouth parts, his eyes widen, and he scans my body slowly, from head to toe.

"Oh, honey, you look gorgeous." My mom is oozing with excitement when she sees me. My dad finishes with Zach's tie, then smiles at me. Lisa is just as excited as my mom. Garrett just tells me I look nice. Zach hasn't said anything but he also hasn't stopped gawking at me since I made my grand entrance. I'm like fucking Cinderella. I chuckle to myself, bringing my shoulders back, and I finish my stride to the bottom. My dad pushes Zach forward, knocking him off his own cloud nine.

"Y-You look, um... You look amazing, like beautiful, like holy shit—"

"Language," my dad says from behind him. I smile; the constant scolding is hilarious.

"Thanks," I tell Zach. He himself looks incredibly sexy tonight. I don't think I have ever seen him in a suit before. Damn, he looks good.

"Oh, here, I have this." He takes my wrist and tugs the flower corsage on. The white and blush roses are perfect. I bring them to my nose, inhaling the sweet scent.

"They're so pretty."

"All right, everyone, line up by the door so I can get a picture." My mom shoos all of us over and Zach wraps me in his arms while Garrett leisurely slides up on the other side of me.

"You clean up good, sis."

"Not so bad yourself, *bro*." We all smile for my mom's picture and then Zach drives us to the school.

C.M. Danks

★★★

The gym is packed with students. The lights are turned down low, music is blaring, and people are lined up at the picture booth. Zach's got his arm tightly around my waist, as if he doesn't want anyone else to snatch me up.

"Have I told you how sexy and beautiful you look in that dress?"

"You have. *Many times.*" Blushing, I give his bicep a squeeze. "You look pretty freakin' hot yourself." He leans down, brushing his scrunched nose to mine.

"Okay, let's go dance."

"You dance?" I give him a curious look. It's not something I would have guessed Zach did, not even by a long shot.

"Guess you'll just have to see." He drags me to the floor with Lisa and Garrett following closely behind. The DJ is playing "Can't Hold Us" by Macklemore. The gym floor comes alive with students dancing and fist pumping. Zach twirls me around, then pulls me against his chest. We start to move to the music in rhythm together. He does a little shimmy move and I laugh hysterically.

A certain part of the song comes on and we all throw our hands up, clapping. The energy in the gym is a whole different level of crazy. It's thunder and lightning.

Dancing. Being carefree, without any worries. All of us together. I never want us to be apart.

The students in the background look like they are in slow motion, because all I see is Zach. I love seeing him this happy, not having to take care of his mother, just him tonight, having fun. Garrett's twirling Lisa in his arms. She and I giggle. She dances over and booty claps me; our hips bounce off each other's. Zach quick steps to me and grabs my hand, jerking me to him. We both laugh, throwing our arms up in the air to the song again.

When the song is over, "Everything" by Lifehouse comes on. I stop to catch my breath, as Zach holds out his hand. "Dance with me, pretty girl?" I smile, placing my hand in his. I snuggle in close, consuming the warmth from his arms as we start to slow dance.

"This song makes me think of *Smallville* with Clark and Lana. They're at their senior prom dancing to this song." I'm giddy just thinking about it. "I watched every season in like two weeks."

"I know. That's why I had the DJ play it."

"Seriously, you did that?"

"Of course, anything to see you smile."

And I do smile. He makes me smile every day. Leaning forward, I rest my cheek on his chest. He tightens his hold around me, setting his chin on the top of my head. We stay like that as we sway back and forth to the music. "I never want to let you go, Jules. Never."

"Then don't," I answer, my cheek still lying on his chest, his heartbeat no longer steady.

Being in Zach's arms, dancing to my favorite slow song, is like nothing I have ever felt before. My best friend, the boy next door, the boy who I'll always love. Because I think he just stole my heart forever. Maybe it sounds stupid because I am so young, but I can't deny what I feel for him.

After the song is over, our principal comes up on stage and says a few words. It's time for him to announce the winner for this year's prom king and queen.

C.M. Danks

A queasy feeling hits me. There's no denying who will win.

Great.

"Okay, so today's winner for prom queen is..." Principal Kramer announces Samantha as the winner, and he claps while holding the mic. The gymnasium vibrates with cheers and whistles. A student wraps the banner around her before crowning her with the plastic tiara. Nausea with an unwelcome feeling of jealousy sits in the pit of my stomach. If Zach wins, he'll have to dance with her.

"And the winner for prom king is..." Once again, our principal opens the envelope like it's a freakin' award show. *Please don't say Zach... Please don't say Zach.* "Zachary Scott." Claps immediately sound, followed by more whistles.

"Fuck." I hear Zach say next to me. "Jules—"

"Go. I know..." My half smile is so fake. "Congratulations." I pat his shoulder, letting him know it's fine, even though it's clearly not fine. Secretly, I'm dying inside.

He kisses me deeply before walking on stage to accept his equally cheap-ass crown. Another slow song starts playing and everyone makes a circle. Sam has this evil smile on her face as she wraps her arms around Zach's neck.

"Hey, Zach is crazy for you. Don't let this bother you." Lisa hooks her arm into mine.

I don't want it to bother me, but how could it not? Sam is rubbing her fake-ass boobs all over *my* boyfriend. She runs her fingers through his hair then kisses his cheek. No, she did not just do that. The music stops. *Thank God.* A sense of relief washes over me. That is, until Sam plants a kiss right on Zach's mouth. I want to puke. My body panics, my senses shooting into overdrive. I am about to lose my shit.

CHARGER

Jealousy is a vicious devil, one that's overtaking me right now. Zach isn't pushing her away. Why isn't he pushing her away?

"I can't watch." I break through the hoard of students encompassing Zach and Sam, just as Garrett calls out my name. "Don't follow me!" I yell back to him.

Without turning around, I push open the gym doors to an empty hallway. I lean against the lockers, trying to collect myself. My chest physically hurts; it feels like I'm suffocating. I'm trying my hardest not to cry. But the pain in my chest is screaming.

"Hey, you okay?" Tommy stands there, waiting for me to answer. He must have followed me.

"I'm fine." I hug my midsection and clench my fists to try to hold back the tears that want to pour out. He steps closer and touches my arm. I'm too numb from the pain right now to even care that he's touching me.

A small group of students barge through the gymnasium doors. "Hey, you guys want a ride to the after party?" One of the girls yells over to us.

I don't want to ride in the same car as Tommy, but I don't want to stay here either. Pushing off the wall, I follow them out of the school. I hope I don't regret this, especially with the way Tommy is grinning at me.

★★★

Zach

"What the fuck are you doing!?" I push Sam off me.

C.M. Danks

"Oh, what, like you don't miss this?"

"No, I fucking don't. I'm with Jules. It's over between us, Sam. It's been over."

Fuck. Jules. I whip my head around to the group. I don't see her. *Fuck.*

I leave Sam to self-wallow. "Where's she at?"

"She just wanted some space. She's in the hallway." Lisa looks pissed. But I don't give a fuck. My main concern is Jules right now.

"You're lucky you pushed her off, or I would have punched you myself." Garrett stands there, arms crossed.

Yeah, I don't have time for the brother speech. I take off toward the doors, tossing my stupid-ass crown on the floor. "Jules!" Turning in every direction, I don't see her.

In the far corner are two stoner kids. "Hey, did either of you see anyone here recently?"

"Uh, there was a girl and some dude. And a group of others. They left though."

Some dude. Who the fuck? "Did she have dark hair?" The thumping inside my chest pounds harder with each second that passes.

The one kid lets out a puff of smoke. "Yeah, she was hot. They said something about a party." My veins start to boil with rage.

"Did you find her?" Garrett and Lisa stare at me with concerned faces. Everything is muffled. The pulsing in my ears is intense.

"We're leaving. Drive us to the party now. Your sister left with some dude and I have a feeling I know who it is."

Tommy. I might strangle him with my bare hands. He even so much as lays a finger on Jules, and I'll destroy him.

CHARGER

★★★

Jules

It's only been like half an hour. But Zach has already blown up my phone, along with Lisa and Garrett. I text my brother back, letting him know that I'm fine. I don't want him calling our parents, or sending a search and rescue team.

I'm sitting on the couch in the back room with Tommy. Yes, with Tommy. Not by choice. Well, I guess by choice. But there's not many other places to go here, and at least we're not by ourselves.

"Do you want another drink?"

"No, I'm good."

He sets his cup down on the coffee table, scooting closer to me. He puts his arm around my shoulders. I can smell the alcohol on his breath. Just because I've been sitting here with him, doesn't mean we're cool. I've watched him do shots for the past ten minutes with his buddies. God, I *am* such a tease. I used him. I used him to get away.

I shouldn't have agreed to come with him. Yeah, I wanted to get away from Zach, but this was definitely a bad idea. What a mess. Just as I'm about to text Zach, Tommy whispers in my ear.

"This dress on you." He eyes me like an animal. "Is fucking insane." I scoot away from him, shrugging out of his hold. "You're serious right now?" His voice is angry.

"Yeah, I'm dead serious. What makes you think you can touch me?"

Tommy shoots up from the couch within seconds.

C.M. Danks

"You're such a teasing little bitch."

I jump up to meet him face to face. "Just because I came with you to this party, doesn't mean I want to fuck you, Tommy. Get over yourself already. We've been through this before." I fucked up, *majorly*. Now I need to get out of here.

Brushing past him, I try to head for the other room, but I don't make it. He grabs my arm, jerking me back. The sudden motion actually causes me pain, sending the ache straight to my neck.

"Ow, Tommy, that hurts. Let me go!"

"We aren't done here."

"Oh, I think you're fucking done." Zach comes flying around me, punching Tommy right in the face. He falls to the ground, holding his bloody nose. I can't hide my shock. It all happened so fast.

Zach crouches down in front of him, while Tommy holds his face, crying out in agony. "I'm going to say this once and only once. You stay the fuck away from her, Stevenson. Come near her again and you're dead." Zach stands, pulling me out of the room with him. We truck past my brother and Lisa. "I'm taking your fucking sister home, so you're going to have to find another ride later."

"Roger that." Garrett salutes and I give him the silent communication of, *"Thanks a lot."*

"Are you gonna let go of me anytime soon?" He drags me by my heels, literally. Zach doesn't say anything until we make it to his car.

"Get the fuck in."

"No, I won't get in the car with you." My hands are planted on my hips.

"I'm not kidding, Jules. Get in the car." His teeth are grinding.

CHARGER

After about thirty seconds, I give up, realizing I won't win. "Fine."

Once we're both inside, he bangs on the steering wheel, open-handedly. "What the fuck, Jules. I'm all about two seconds away from going back in there and strangling Tommy."

"*What the fuck*? Really? You have the nerve to ask me that when you were making out with Sam all of about five minutes ago."

"Maybe if you stuck around long enough, you would have seen me push her away."

"Yeah, it really looked like you were pushing her away."

Zach huffs out a breath. "She doesn't mean anything and you know that. I'm fucking crazy about you, Jules. I have been, since we were fucking fifteen. Maybe even longer... I don't know. There's no one I want to be with more than you. Can't you see that?"

I stare out the passenger's side window. Somehow, I believe him. "You didn't want to kiss her?"

"No, I didn't and I *don't*. Her kiss took me by surprise. I didn't expect it, so it took me a second before I pulled her off me."

We're both silent for a moment, before I break it. "You punched Tommy." There's amusement in my voice.

"Damn right I did, and I would do it again too. Nobody touches you like that, and I would have killed him if he did something to you. Do you hear me, Jules? I would have fucking murdered him."

I believe him. He would do anything for me. To protect me, or avenge any wrong doing that's bestowed upon me. That's for certain.

C.M. Danks

Zach pulls into his driveway, gets out and opens my door. We walk across the way until we reach my house. I stop at the door to unlock it. "Um, my parents are probably asleep. So… if you wanted to come inside, you can."

"I was already planning on it."

"Right." I swallow nervously as I step inside.

We quietly tread upstairs to my room and I make sure to lock my bedroom door this time. Behind me, Zach wraps his arms around my stomach and whispers in my ear. A warm feeling takes over my entire body.

"I would never hurt you intentionally. You do know that, right?"

"Yes." I nod my head slightly.

He kisses my neck and I close my eyes, moving my head just enough to give him more. Working his way down to my shoulders, he brushes my hair to the other side.

"Zach…" He answers with a small moan. "Will you, you know, have sex with me tonight?" That was stupid… *asking*. And I can feel the heat on my face.

He stops kissing me, gently turning me in his arms. "Is that what you want?"

"I wouldn't want my first to be with anyone else but you."

He takes my face in his hands and lightly brushes my lips with his own. "And I sure as hell don't want anyone else to be your first, or your last."

Zach unzips my dress slowly. My skin tingles as he runs the tips of his fingers down my back, sending shivers through me. "You cold?"

"No, your touch just feels amazing."

He pulls my dress off my shoulders, letting it fall to the floor. I stand there, in nothing but my strapless bra and lace

CHARGER

thong panties, knowing he's taking me all in. "You're perfect."

"Hardly, not even close." I hug myself in a vulnerable state.

"I told you before... don't hide yourself from me." He grabs me and lifts me onto the bed. He takes his suit jacket off, followed by his tie. Then he starts undoing the buttons to his dress shirt. Before I know it, I'm left with a perfect view of him. He goes for his dress pants next, along with his boxers, throwing them on the floor next to his shirt. Zach is so hot it's actually painful.

I trace his abs with my fingertips, bringing them down slowly so I can take his length in my hand. As I begin to stroke him gently, his eyes close and he leans his head back.

"Fuck, Jules." He stops me. "I'm gonna come right here if you keep that up." He lowers his body over mine and unhooks my bra, tossing it somewhere. Then he removes my underwear as he lifts my butt off the bed. "You're ready for me already."

It's not a question. He knows I am. "Zach, I don't want or need the foreplay. I just want you." He smiles before he goes to the floor to grab his wallet, taking out a condom. I watch as he unwraps it, then works it over himself. He returns, kissing my neck.

"This is gonna hurt at first, but I promise it'll get better, okay?"

"Yes, I just don't want to wait anymore."

He gently, slowly slides inside my wet opening. "Fuck, you're tight." I grip the bed sheet as he goes in deeper. I feel like I'm being ripped open. "You okay? Need me to stop?"

"No, I'm okay. Just keep going."

C.M. Danks

He pushes the rest of his way in and I wince from the pain. He stops, waiting for the approval to keep going. When I give it to him, he starts thrusting into me, slow and gentle. And the pain is gone. All that's left is this intense pleasure of Zach. Him being inside me feels so damn good. We share this moment, keeping our eyes connected with each other.

"Oh my God... this is incredible." I manage to get the words out. Zach lowers his head to my shoulder, while he moans. I grab onto his hair, scraping my nails down his back. The way he rubs my clit is going to make me explode. "Zach, I think I might—"

"I know. Me too."

We both release at the same time. Pure magic. My vision blurs from the intensity.

I just had sex with Zach. I try to wrap my brain around that one as he sinks into me. His heavy breaths touch my skin.

"Fuck, that was everything, Jules."

"Yeah, it was." I rub his back with circular motions. We stay like this for a couple of minutes before he pushes himself off the bed. I just let Zach take a part of me. A part of me I will never get back. But there are zero regrets and it was amazing.

"I better take this thing off." He kisses my shoulder then heads for my bathroom.

I rest my arm on my forehead, staring at my ceiling. It might sound cliché, considering we just had sex, but if I wasn't already thinking that I might be in love with Zach, this confirms it. Not that I would tell him as much. I can't. He might take off running.

CHARGER

I put my panties back on, followed by my Blink 182 t-shirt, and snuggle inside my covers. Zach sinks in beside me. "Jules, don't freak out over what I'm about to tell you, okay?"

I sit up and rest my elbows on my bed. "What's wrong? Was it not good?"

"Hell, it was better than good. It's not that. It's just that, well, the condom broke."

"What?" My heart jumps. Well, shit. "Zach..."

"It's okay. They have things for these kinds of emergencies."

"Things? What kind of things?"

"They have a morning after pill, so tomorrow morning, you can talk to your mom and she can take you somewhere to get one." He cups my cheek. "Actually, I can take you. Or... if something were to happen, Jules, I mean, it wouldn't totally suck. I would be there for you."

Did he just say that? I shake my head, trying to knock myself back into reality. "Uh, Zach. We're eighteen years old. I don't fucking think so. And oh, great! I have to tell my mom we had sex, and I need a pill to make it all go away because the stupid condom decided not to hold up its end of the deal." I crash back down on the bed in frustration. "Crap."

"Look, I'll take you. It'll be okay." He rubs my arm in comfort. "Let's just lie down."

He wraps his arm around me and pulls me to his chest. We don't say anything. How could he be so calm about this? Well, fuck. I mean, what are the chances of something happening? Probably slim.

After what feels like hours of lying there in silence, we both finally fall asleep.

C.M. Danks

CHAPTER TWELVE

Jules

I jolt awake. The once warm spot next to me where Zach was lying is empty. He must have snuck out before morning, which is a good thing. My parents would kill me if they found out. But something doesn't feel right. I don't know what it is, but something's off. I grab my phone from my nightstand and check my messages. The first one I read is from Zach—he sent it this morning.

Zach: I hate leaving before you wake up, but didn't want your folks to murder me. Sleep tight, pretty girl.

I read the next one, which is from Garrett last night.

Garrett: Hey, sis, getting a ride from one of the guys. Thanks for asking btw lol. Anyway, be safe tonight and don't do anything stupid. Meaning, tell Zach to wrap up his fucking shit. Whatever, love you and p.s. Tommy's nose is broke as fuck. Lol. Ttyl.

CHARGER

I was so dumb last night. Jealous rage got the best of me and I acted like a complete idiot. I should have just stayed at the dance.

Making my way to Garrett's room, I open his door slowly, in case he's still sleeping. The bed sheets haven't been touched. He didn't come home last night?

Weird.

The doorbell rings and multiple voices are being carried up from downstairs. The gut-wrenching, ear-piercing scream emanating from my mother stops time. The thumping in my chest is all I can feel; the thumping in my ears is all I can hear.

My mother's screams are loud enough to send the neighborhood into panic mode. Finally, ungluing my feet from the ground, I run… only to stop dead at the top of the stairs. Two cops are standing in the doorway, with sympathetic looks on their faces.

Something happened to Garrett.

I've had this feeling, this feeling ever since I woke up, of being unable to sense my brother's presence anymore. Call it a weird twin thing, but it is definitely real. Part of me doesn't want to continue down these steps, afraid of what I already know to be true.

Mid-descent, I watch in horror as my mom sobs on the floor, my dad holding her as he rocks her back and forth. Tears fall from his face.

"Mom… D-dad." It's like I'm being strangled.

My dad looks up with the most devastating face I've ever seen. That's when I know. In that moment, without the words being said, I know Garrett is gone. I collapse on the bottom step, as the tears drown my soul. I let the sobs from the agonizing pain overtake me. The stab, the twist of the knife inside my chest hurts so badly I can barely breathe.

The nightmare, the one you never think could possibly happen, has become my reality. This very moment just changed our lives forever.

★★★

Two months later

I stand outside Zach's house, box in hand with a letter taped to the outside, staring at the door in front of me. I fiddle with the letter, deciding if I should even be here. Prom night was the last time I saw Zach. The last time I got to look into those baby blues. That was it. The silence on the phone, as I told him Garrett was killed, was deafening. Nothing. He didn't say anything. Just hung up. He just fucking hung up. I haven't talked to him since.

Our world changed that morning. Life as we knew it would never be the same. One of the boys driving that night had been drunk. He swerved into the other lane, hitting a car head-on. He was killed along with his girlfriend and my brother. Lisa was the only survivor, leaving her in bad shape for a long time. She was physically, *mentally*, broken. We all were. We still are.

It kills me to see my parents grieving every day. A part of them died alongside Garrett. My mother doesn't smile anymore. Her normal, bubbly self is gone and might even be lost forever.

As for me? The pain in my chest has yet to go away. I don't think it ever will. And there hasn't been a day I don't

CHARGER

mourn for him. I sob, knowing I will never see him again. I will never get to joke with him or tell him what a jerkface I think he is. I am crushed, shattered, wrecked... from losing my brother. From *just as suddenly* losing Zach. Two months without a word, without seeing him. I've sent him texts. Yet he avoids me. To lose two people you love, all at once, it fucking sucks—to say the least.

Zach didn't show up for graduation, nor did he attend the funeral. I needed him. Selfishly, I needed him.

So, I stand here, feeling ridiculous holding this box for him.

After the long contemplation, my knuckles tap on his front door. It takes a few minutes before his mom answers. "Oh, hi, Jules. How are you doing, honey?" She gives me the same look everyone else has given me over the past couple of months. The look that says, "I'm so sorry but I don't know what else to say." She does seem better though. Being sober has done her good, and I'm glad she got her act together. Though, you'd think her son up and leaving would break her more.

"Hi, Mrs. Scott, is Zach here?"

"No, dear, he's not." She sighs with a sad smile.

Disappointment hits me, not that I was expecting him to be here. "Well, if he does come back, will you give him this please?" I extend my gift to her.

"Of course, hon." She takes it and hugs it to her midsection. I smile and turn to walk back to my house. "Hey, Jules," she beckons from the doorway. I turn back around to her once more. "He calls every so often. He's doing okay for himself. Well, I think he is anyway. Give him time. He'll call you."

C.M. Danks

I nod solemnly, but I can't deny the slight wave of relief that follows. Am I glad he's okay? Sure, but the fact that he hasn't tried contacting me breaks what little heart I have left. I needed him and he wasn't there. I still need him—something I don't think I will ever forgive him for. His mom's words repeat in my mind. *Give him time. He'll call you.*

Yeah, too bad he never actually did.

★★★

One Month Later

Zach

The demons grow bigger inside me every day. I'm unable to shake this misery. All I can do is take this little pill to make me forget. Maybe if I was less of a coward and more of a man, I would have been able to face her. But instead, I ran. I ran from her and I ran from the pain. I ran from the girl I was in love with. From the girl I am *still* in love with. Only to inflict more pain. But how could I face her now? Just look at me... I am a complete mess and she would never forgive me. Just one more hit. One more instance of letting myself fall unconscious, of forgetting about the ache inside my chest. Once I am able, I will come back to you. I will come back to you, my pretty girl. Just wait for me, please. I will come back for you. I promise you that.

Too bad I never actually did. I left that promise to her broken, as broken as the rest of me.

CHARGER

Chapter Thirteen

Six Years Later

Charger

"Surprise!"

Fuck. I skid to a stop just as a balloon floats by my head. A goddamn balloon. Streamers? Balloons? This isn't happening. Not for my birthday. Fuck my birthday.

Chain approaches me with a slap to the shoulder. "Say anything about the fucking streamers or any of the other decorations, and I'll cut your balls off. Oh, and happy birthday, kid."

Ha, kid. Guess turning twenty-five means I'm still a kid. Well shit, I don't feel like one. Not after the shit I've seen or been through over the years. That little boy with the Batman underwear is long gone.

From the sound of Chain's warning, I can assume that his Ol' Lady had everything and anything to do with this shindig. I don't do birthdays. And I sure as fuck don't do surprises. I haven't celebrated a birthday in a long-ass time and I would like to keep it that way. But Mags, being the sweet woman that she is, just had to throw me a birthday party. Her heart is in the right place, but this shit just isn't me.

Maggie, aka Mags, is also Chain's Ol' Lady. Which means by default, hands off or you get them sent through a meat grinder along with whatever other body part he feels is necessary. That's what it means to have an Ol' Lady. It means to claim her. To protect her as yours. That's real shit right there, and more than any piece of paper could offer.

I catch her from the corner of my eye as she walks over to me, with a smile that could light up a dark room. The small hint of age around her eyes lets us know she's been through hell and back in this club. She's the "momma" of the club, so to speak. But I don't think it's a title she regrets, not even a little. Chain was the one to start this biker club from the ground up. Maggie was with him from the start. Side by side.

"Happy birthday! I hope I didn't go too overboard. I mean, maybe I could have eased up on the decorations a little." She stares at the balloons in question.

"You, overboard? Never, woman." Chain winks.

"Nah, I appreciate it, Mags. Everything is great, even the balloons and streamers."

"Oh, good." Relief fills her eyes. "We just couldn't let your twenty-fifth birthday go unnoticed, now, could we?" *Oh, you definitely could have.* "Well, I'd better go check on the cake and make sure no one has stuck their grubby fingers in it." She kisses us both on the cheek, then heads straight for the kitchen on a mission.

"Well, kid, go mingle, drink, get some pussy. I don't know? Do whatever it is you want. It's your birthday so live it up." Before I can say anything, he yells over my shoulder. "Hey, you!" He points at a prospect. "Don't fucking touch that balloon. Damn kid," he rambles under his breath as he walks away. Yeah, he would do anything for Mags—that's for damn sure.

The place is packed with the usual club hang-arounds, some members, and those prospects waiting (hoping) to get patched-in. Lucky for me, I earned my way in just fine, got patched-in last year. I owe a lot to this club and I would gladly put my life on the line for any one of them. Most days I do. Not because it's part of the job description. There's more to it than that... Chain, along with the others, saved my life. These guys are my brothers, maybe not by blood but definitely by bond. It helps fill the void that's been missing for the last six years.

"Hey, man." Tank strolls over to me, holding two beers. He hands one off to me. Dude's a big fucker, half the reason for his name. The other reason? He served his time in the army, drove those armored machines around like a boss.

He takes a swig before we sit down at the bar. "How's it feel to be at the mid-point to thirty? Think it sucks now? You just wait till you're my age."

"Your age? You realize that you're only six years older than me, right?"

"Yeah, yeah, but it feels like I'm a hell of a lot older. My fucking knees crack like a seventy-year-old. But..." He takes back another swig of beer. "At least my dick is still in pristine condition."

"You're fucked up, man." I shake my head. But laughter follows.

"I know. The ladies dig it though. Makes me a freak in the sheets." He leans back and stretches his massive arms above his head. "Speaking of ladies, I noticed you haven't touched Stiletto lately. She's been hittin' up Throttle and

C.M. Danks

Bullet for an easy lay." He laughs, which sounds like thunder. "Those guys would fuck anything with a pussy, doesn't matter who it is. But something tells me you don't give a shit."

"Nope. I *don't* give a shit." Leaning forward onto the bar, I signal for Tequila to get me another beer. "She can fuck whoever she wants. She isn't my Ol' Lady. Never will be." Stiletto doesn't mean anything to me. But the feeling is mutual. She's there when I need a good lay, but that's it.

Tank whistles. "All right, all right. Fair enough."

Tequila comes back with another beer, setting a shot glass down next to it. "Here you go, handsome. It's your birthday after all." She leans forward, letting her tits spill out of her shirt. Would I be lying if I said she wasn't hot as hell? Yeah, but for some reason lately, only one girl keeps showing up in my mind. The same one I haven't spoken to in years. She's been consuming me, today especially. Every birthday has been hell since I was like twelve.

I slam the shot back, feeling the burn from the alcohol. "Thanks, Tequila."

She smiles with her pouty lips, swaying her hips as she works her way to Hush, who's at the other end of the bar. "Now, *that* is one hot piece of ass." When I don't say anything, Tank leans forward, finishing off his beer. "Where's your head been at, brother?"

"Ah, fuck. I don't know, man, just been off lately. Birthdays and shit always have this effect on me."

"This have anything to do with that girl that you won't talk about?"

That girl.

CHARGER

I get up off my stool, slapping a twenty down for Tequila. "I gotta get outta here. Clear my head and shit. I'll see you later. And tell Mags I appreciate everything."

I make a beeline for the door, but Tank is already on my heels. "Yo, brother, wait up. I know this chill bar about five miles out. We can go there. Haven't been there yet, but the girls like it."

Whatever, I just need to go somewhere. Somewhere the focus isn't on me. It's too much right now. "Lead the way." I gesture with my hand toward the door then follow behind.

Our rides are parked along the strip of pavement. When I reach my bike, I swing my leg over my pride and joy then start her up. Nothing beats the open road and a Harley, especially this one.

After a little while of riding, we pull up to the small honky-tonk looking bar and park our bikes. The bar is set by itself on the outskirts of a highway—a bad location in my opinion. Not a safe one. Trees and woods tower from above. I straighten my cut as we both walk up to the door—the leather cut-off is a symbol of the club. It indicates where our loyalties lie, where we belong. Each member has one, showcasing our club patch and road name.

"I thought you said this place was chill. There's a shit-ton of people here."

Tank reaches up, scratching behind his head. "Yeah, well, last time I drove by, this place wasn't as busy. But we're here now, so fuck it. Let's go in."

The sign above the door reads: Fallen Star. A feeling immediately kicks me in my gut.

Fallen Star.

Tank looks back at me. "What's up?"

"Nothing. It's fine. Let's go."

C.M. Danks

When we step inside, I expect some country pop shit to be playing, but it's not. "Don't Stop Believin'" by Journey is rocking out in the background. We get some stares as we walk in, but I ignore them. It's not uncommon. People see us and automatically think we're trouble, judging us for being in a biker club. Because of what we wear, our tattoos. People will always judge.

We approach the bar, sitting our asses down on the tiny stools. You would think whoever owned this place would be generous enough to have seats that were semi comfortable.

There's a guy to the left of us nursing his beer; he hasn't stopped his glaring since we walked in. He doesn't want to find out what happens if he keeps that up. I didn't get the name *Charger* for no reason.

Tank strums his tattooed fingers along the wood-grained counter top. We wait for the hot-ass bartender to turn around and serve us. Her ass in those jeans is a fucking sin. And the way her jet-black hair is pulled into a high pony reminds me of *her*. This place is actually worse than being back at the clubhouse.

As I'm just about to tell Tank that we need to split, the pretty little bartender turns around and heads are way. She gets stopped by the jack-hole who was staring me down, and for some reason, my protective instincts go into overdrive. But she gives him a killer smile.

That smile. Wait, it can't be... No, there's no way it's her.

She walks her perfect, familiar, petite body over to us. Tank says something to me about her, but I can't hear him. I'm lost in a trance, lost to the woman in front of me.

"What can I get you gentlemen...?" Her words trail off as she notices me. Her whole body stills, and so does mine.

CHARGER

No, this isn't happening. I know it can't be her. There is no fucking way on God's green earth that Julianna, that *my* Jules, is standing here right now. In front of me. Beads of sweat start trickling down my forehead as my heart is pounding out of control. Those eyes, I would remember those gorgeous big brown eyes anywhere.

Fuck Me.

C.M. Danks

CHAPTER FOURTEEN

Jules

"Get the fuck out and stay out!"

Joe throws out yet another intoxicated man from my bar. "You know, Joe, if you kick out every man who attempts to grab my ass, I think my bar is going to go out of business."

He smirks, returning to his stool. "Jules, I've been sitting at your bar almost every day for the past year. You're like a daughter to me, so don't expect me to sit here and let some drunken idiot mistreat you."

It's true. Joe has been like another father to me ever since day one, when I opened the Fallen Star. He's been sitting in the same spot at the bar, drinking the same beer for a year. "Well, as much as I appreciate it, maybe just back off a little. Besides, you know I can handle myself."

"Oh, I know, honey, but that doesn't mean you should have to." He takes back his Miller in one big gulp.

"You're a very sweet man." I place my hand on top of his, giving him a *thank you* smile.

There's a clunk at the end of the bar, where Lucy exhaustedly plumps down her tray. "Hey, Luc, what do you need?"

CHARGER

She slumps into the bar stool with a huff. "I need three shots of Crown Royal for table three. Actually, make that four—the last one is for me."

I laugh. "You're killin' it tonight, just so you know." Lining up the glasses in a row, I pour the whisky down each one. "I didn't expect it to get so busy on a Monday."

"Busy is an understatement. My feet are screaming. I didn't even wear heels tonight." She does a double take at the door. I glance up, noticing the two men who just walked in.

The very tall, broad-shouldered men make their way over to sit at two stools on the other end. Their black leather vests form to their bodies, and each one has an embroidered name on the back that I can't quite make out.

"Think they're part of that motorcycle gang?" Lucy suggests.

"I sure hope not."

I stalk toward them, stopping when Joe grabs my wrist. "They give you any trouble let me know." I offer his hand a reassuring squeeze before he lets go.

When I eventually make it over to them both, I can't help but swallow nervously. Yeah, it's intimidating. But I hold my head up.

"What can I get you gentlemen…?" My stomach drops.

My body tightens as I look directly into the eyes I could never forget, no matter how hard I tried. No matter how much I wanted to wipe my memory clean of him, he has never and *will never* truly leave my thoughts, my head, my mind, my body. The days and nights I spent wishing I could forget everything about him, I couldn't.

He will always have all of me.

But I never thought this day would come. Zachary Scott, the boy I loved.

My best friend.

My protector.

My everything.

Even being only eighteen, there was no doubt in my mind that I was completely in love with him. So, it's not hard to believe that the boy who had my whole heart would be the same one to rip it out.

I can't form any words, let alone a sentence. He must recognize me too because he hasn't said anything either. Nor has he taken his eyes off me.

The handsome boy I used to know six years ago has definitely grown up. His shoulders are wider and his arms are twice as large. Not to mention, the tattoos painted on each of them. He's still lean, but his muscles are more visible. And who could forget about those piercing blue eyes that are just as penetrating now. Maybe just not as alive as I once remember.

A wave of sadness hits me because my heart is being ripped out all over again. Seeing him reminds me of the three of us... of being back in high school. I never stopped missing Garrett and I never stopped longing for Zach. His presence is like a knife to the chest. *Damn it.*

I swallow hard, to hold back any tears that want to start forming. I'll be damned if I let him see me cry. He disappeared without any explanation, without any reason. So, you know what, *fuck him.*

"Uh, do you two know each other?" The guy sitting next to Zach is just as good-looking. Large, with long hair and some daily scruff. The confusion on his face shoots between each of us.

CHARGER

I smile, more like smirk, to the best of my ability. Zach literally hasn't been able to look away from me. I take in his leather vest, which is draped over his tight-fitting t-shirt. He's in a motorcycle club now? Chills run up my spine.

"No, we don't know each other. And I'm sorry, but I have the right to refuse service to anyone, and I'm refusing to serve you both. Have a good night, gentlemen." As I turn to take care of another customer, I can hear his buddy throw a few F-bombs as he gets up to leave. *Don't do it. Don't do it.* My eyes wander over to Zach, connecting with his as he watches me. I hurry, drawing my attention back to the man in front of me.

After taking his order, my hands shake as I try to pop off the top of the beer bottle. I set it down, not able to hold back sneaking another glance.

Disappointment rushes through me when I realize he's gone. How could I be so angry at him, but at the same time, disappointed that he left?

Again.

"Hey, you okay?"

I sigh, turning toward Lucy. "I'm fine. Just a run-in with my past. Someone I didn't expect to see."

"That wasn't *him*, was it?"

I think she's referring to Zach for a second before realizing I never told her about him. I haven't told anyone. It's like I thought if I never talked about it, the hurt would go away. I hoped the pain would disappear if I didn't mention his name, but it hasn't. Lucy is referring to a different past...

"No, it wasn't him."

"Well, that's good at least." She sets her tray down on the countertop. "Why don't you take five? I can watch the bar. My tables are caught up."

"No, I'm okay, really. Thank you, though."

"Well, I'm glad they're gone. Don't need no bikers around here, causing up a commotion," Joe grunts.

"Somehow I don't think they'll be coming back anytime soon." Yet another disappointment. Damn him for coming back and breaking my already shattered heart.

★★★

"Mommy!" Chloe runs to me, arms out, latching onto my leg with brute force. Well, as much force as a five-year-old can give.

"Hi, my little bug. Did you have fun at grandma and grandpa's?"

"Of course, she did. Grandma and grandpa's house is like the best place ever." My mom playfully teases as she tugs on Chloe's pigtails. "Isn't that right, angel?"

Chloe detaches herself from me with an overly excited head nod, jumping up and down, pigtails flopping in the air. "Yes! Mommy, I never wanna leave."

"That's nice, Mom. Really? Thanks." I smile, crossing my arms over my chest.

With a shrug, she rectifies herself. "But I know you would miss your mommy."

Chloe stops hopping in place, holding attention to her pink tennis shoes. "I *would* miss you, Mommy, a lot."

CHARGER

My dad comes to the door, holding Chloe's little ladybug backpack. "All right, Miss Thang, don't forget this." He crouches down, helping Chloe shimmy into the straps.

"Okay, you, time to get home and into bed. It is way past your bedtime."

My parents watch Chloe while I pull in shifts at the bar. Some nights are worse than others—depends on when I'm able to leave.

Even though I own the Fallen Star, I'm still fully involved. I pull my own weight. If I'm too late, Chloe will usually spend the night but tonight, I made sure I got out of there—not that I thought Zach would come back in for a nice little chat about the past.

Chloe swings her small arms around my father and he kisses her head. "Behave for your mom. We'll see you soon." She walks over to hug my mom and then I shoo her out the door.

"Thanks for watching her."

"Jules, you don't have to thank us every time for watching our own grandchild."

"I know, I know, but I feel better doing it." I hug them both, then walk Chloe down the driveway of my childhood home. Each time, it seems to get harder and harder. Memories play in my head, memories of me and Garrett, and the way we used to ride our bikes down this driveway. Then there are those of Zach and the number of times we sat in a circle just talking and laughing. It never gets any easier.

I avoid looking at his house. It's obvious neither he nor his mom live there anymore. Six months after graduation, Zach's mom moved out. I don't know where to, but another family moved in and they've been there ever since.

C.M. Danks

Everything still stings as though it just happened. They say time heals everything... I'm still waiting.

We make it to my somewhat new Malibu and I strap Chloe into her car seat, tugging the straps tightly to her. She lays her head to the side, already starting to doze off. I can't help but stand there for a second, watching her. She is the best damn thing to happen to me and I wouldn't change it for anything in the world.

Tucking a small strand of hair that fell loose behind her ear, I smile when she doesn't even flinch at my touch. She's out like a light. I gently kiss her forehead before climbing into the driver's seat and heading home, never once glancing at Zach's old house. I never do.

I'm carrying Chloe through the back parking lot of the bar. Renting the upstairs apartment, and making it our home, was a huge convenience.

Stepping inside the bar entrance, I practically jump out of my black boots. A large, dark silhouette sits at the counter, helping himself to a beer. The only light is from the one above the bar. I can make out small details only—like his leather vest. How did he get in? Is it Zach?

I flick on the lights and my stomach twists.

"Hello, Jules." He doesn't move. He continues to face forward, resting an elbow on the bar while casually drinking a beer. *My* beer. I tighten my grip on Chloe in pure protective instinct. Peeking at her, I breathe a sigh of relief. She's still sleeping.

He finally swings his massive thighs around, leaving the stool and stalking toward me like I'm his prey.

I take a step back. "I have to put her to bed. And *you* need to leave."

CHARGER

"Nah, I'll wait." He stops with a smirk. Of course, it wouldn't be that easy.

I exhale, making my way to our upstairs apartment. Once we're inside, I carry Chloe to bed, day clothes and all. I give her a kiss to the forehead after tucking her in.

Knowing she'll be fine for now, I make my trip back downstairs, smacking right into his stone chest. It takes a second to regain my balance.

"What are you doing here, Venom?" I ask him in disgust.

He smells like cedarwood. Had this been months ago, I would have found it to be a turn on. Now? Not so much. Even though he's tall, muscled, and screams bad boy biker, his eyes stare at me with darkness. Emptiness. I may have made a mistake before, in being with this man. But I sure as hell learned my lesson.

He casually walks back to the bar. "I haven't heard from you in a good while, so I thought I would swing on by," he says it with amusement, like he's taunting me.

"Yeah, well, I can't say I'm happy to see you."

"Now, it hurts me to hear you say that. I thought what we had was special." He sneers, rubbing his thick dark hair.

"If you honestly thought what we had was special, then you are clearly delusional." I throw my hands on my hips, jumping back when he makes it over to me in two easy strides. He pushes me against the wall, holding me there with his hand to my chest. He leans forward and I can smell the alcohol and cigarettes on his breath.

I turn my head to the side, to avoid his *way too* closeness, but he grabs my chin and turns me back with aggression, before planting a hard kiss to my lips. The sick feeling in the pit of my stomach forms and I hold back the bile that fills my throat.

C.M. Danks

"Don't think for one second that we're done here." His voice is low and gruff, but I try to hold my own. However, looking tough and being tough are two completely different things. I refuse to show him weakness. Besides, Venom gets off on that sick sort of thing.

He relaxes and takes a step back, that venomous smile never fading from his twisted face. I now understand why they call him Venom.

My palms are still flat against the wall, and I hold my head high.

"I'll be seeing you around, babe."

Spinning on his heel, he walks out, gets on his bike, and takes off down the road. When he's finally gone, I feel like I can breathe again. I sink against the wall with my hands on my knees. Fuck him and the Steel Valley Skulls.

CHARGER

CHAPTER FIFTEEN

Charger

Fuck this. I whip the bed sheet off me after another sleepless night. Resting my elbows on my knees, I slouch to the side of the bed. My thoughts immediately go to *her*. It's not like I've been able to think of anything or anyone else since seeing her. Shit, she was all I could think about before. Now, I can't sleep, eat, jack off, without her inside my thoughts.

Not even bothering to put a shirt on, I head downstairs in nothing but my grey sweats and Converse. It's summer in Ohio so there's no need to bundle the fuck up.

I leave the clubhouse, walking next door to Tank's gym. The only one who would be awake this early is our very own spitfire, Angel.

Pulling the doors open, I see her violently kicking, before throwing punches to the standing bag in the middle of the gym floor. Her long blonde hair swings with every movement. She's sexy, that's for sure, but it's never been like that between us. To be honest, she's a little too intimidating for me—probably could cut my balls off in seconds.

Chain wasn't happy at first, letting a chick into our club as a patched member. It's unheard of… It's also hard to get the shit we need to get done, when we have to worry about her getting hurt. But the girl has proven herself enough, proven she's got more balls than some of the dudes.

I cringe when I hear Avril Lavigne blasting from the soundbar. It's that song "Girlfriend" or some shit. She doesn't notice me as she makes one quick move. I lean back to avoid the insane round-off kick she just gave the bag.

She stops to catch her breath as soon as she realizes she almost decapitated me. "Shit, Charger, a few more inches there and you would have been smoked. What the hell are you doing sneaking up on a girl like that?" She swipes a strand of hair that's stuck to her cheek from the sweat. "And Jesus, you look like hell. When was the last time you slept?"

"It's been a couple of days." I grab the jump rope to begin warming up.

"Ah, does this have anything to do with the raven-haired hottie you saw the other night?" She gives another punch then a kick, causing the bag to swing back and forth.

"And how do you know about that?"

"A little birdie told me." She smiles as she wipes the sweat from her chest. Any other guy would get a straight fucking hard-on watching her right now. And a little birdie? Guess I'll have to remind myself to pound Tank into the ground later. "So, who is she?"

"She's no one." Even that statement doesn't settle right.

"I doubt she's no one."

"Oh yeah, you read minds now?"

"It's a girl's intuition. Besides, as you know, I like to wake up early and work out. But you've been in here at the ass crack of dawn. I've left you alone because you looked like you needed it. And while a girl could appreciate looking at someone as hot as you, I've been missing my alone time."

CHARGER

She comes over and slaps my arm. "So, whatever it is you need to do so I can have my gym time back, please fucking do it already." She winks.

"Ha, can't make any promises. But I need a sparring partner. Help a guy out?" I clap the boxing pads together.

"All right, stud, but I'm going first. Give me those gloves."

I take out my phone and connect my Bluetooth to the speakers. "What are you doing?"

"What's it look like I'm doing? If I have to hear one more Avril song, my balls are gonna shrivel up."

She laughs. "The fact that you know who she is tells me that you might secretly listen to some Avril."

"Not a chance." I tap on a Disturbed song. "Now this, this is a workout song." I hold up the boxing pads for Angel while she hits them with her closed fists. One by one, my hands vibrate from the blows.

After a couple of rounds, Angel taps out and leaves the gym.

Left to my own devices, I decide to do some high-intensity interval training. I change the song to "Talk to a friend" by the Slaves.

Using the battle rope, I slam each of the ends to the floor until I do my set, then I rush over to the pull-up bar. With each rep I do, her face flashes in my mind, sweat beading down my body, muscles flexing with intensity.

Her smile.
One.
Her lips.
Two.
Her eyes.
Three.

C.M. Danks

Am I justified in calling myself a monster? Damn right. I hurt the only girl I have ever felt anything for.

Landing palms down on the mat, I start with a few push-ups, knocking out a rep then five more. My back muscles break down with each pump. Yeah, I'm the one who ghosted her. I'm the one who left, but every day without her fucking sucks. Every day since *that* day has changed me. I'm not the same boy she used to know. I'm Charger now, and that boy back in high school is gone.

★★★

With my palms flat on the tiled shower wall, I slouch over with my head hanging low, letting the hot water pour over my sore muscles. That workout left me drained, sore, tired. Not that I had much energy to begin with. I can't shut my mind off.

A fist bangs on the bathroom door and I hear Tank on the other side. "Church starts in ten. Chain says if you're late, you gotta work the pit."

Church is what we call our club meetings.

I shake my head under the water, letting out a laugh. The pit, the underground fighting arena we have in the back of the bar. Every week there's a fight that goes down and I (in particular) like to get my hands dirty with some of those fights. It's UFC-style fighting and I hold the title for first place. My signature move: charge, drop, and tap the fucker out.

But when Tank says working the pit, he isn't referring to fighting. He means cleaning up the aftermath. Blood, sweat, broken beer bottles, and the used fucking condom

CHARGER

wrappers. Usually, it's the prospects' job but if you fuck up, you get sent there. Like a poor student with detention.

Shutting the water off, I wrap the towel around my waist and open the door that leads to my bedroom. I throw on what's probably a dirty pair of jeans and a black t-shirt.

"You look like shit."

"You're not the first one to tell me that today."

Tank and I round the corner and head downstairs. When we walk into the room, cigarette smoke hits my face. Everyone's sitting around bullshitting. Hush is the only one standing in the far back, feet crossed at his ankles and arms to his chest. Weird fucker, quiet and strange. No one knows much about him, but he's basically a psychopath with good intentions so no one questions him.

Chain looks at his invisible watch, then gives Tank and me a glare. "All right, assholes." He pauses when he looks at Angel, who's giving him a disgusted look. "And ladies." She winks in satisfaction. "Since these two decided to finally join us, let's start this shit, shall we?" Tank and I find a seat next to Angel and Throttle. "Got some good news and some bad news…" I'm looking at our Pres, but not really hearing a word he's saying. My mind wanders off. Jules's face is swirling in my visions. She looked the same. More grown up obviously, and more beautiful than I remember from high school, which I didn't think was possible. And it makes me miss her and Garrett all over again. Even though I never stopped missing them both.

Chain grunts at the head of the table and the room gets quiet. All eyes are on me including Chain's. He's resting his chin on his fist.

Fuck.

C.M. Danks

I straighten in my seat and brace myself. Throttle blows a puff of smoke at me while Chain gears up to rip me a new asshole. "I'm tickled fucking pink that you volunteered, Charger."

Throttle claps my shoulder. "Better you than us, brother," he snorts out, then laughter erupts. I sigh, knowing whatever Chain decided to volunteer me for won't be fucking fun.

"Uh, yeah, boss, whatever you need. I'm your guy." I clear my throat.

"Fucking fantastic, you and Hush will meet with the Skulls MC's finest President, Scorpion, and his equally humble Vice President, Venom." Sarcasm pours out of him. "Apparently, they wanna talk business, but I have a prior engagement tonight and so does Bullet." Bullet being our Vice President. It's unusual for the Vice of a club to be absent at a meet, but I guess Chain has his reasons.

Chain takes the glass of scotch that's sitting on the spot in front of him and swigs it, wiping his knuckles across his mouth. "Hush, you getting all this back there?" Everyone's head darts over to him, still leaning against the wall with an *if looks could kill* expression. He just jerks his head forward into a nod.

Chain shakes his head. "Crazy fucker," he mumbles to himself. He looks back at me. "I'll send the address to your phones along with the time you two gotta be there, got me?" I nod. "Fucking great. Meeting dismissed." He slams the gavel down and chairs start screeching against the floor. Chain points in my direction. "You. Stay."

After everyone disperses, he shoots me a curious look, scratches his beard and interlocks his ringed fingers inside his folded hands. "You look like shit."

CHARGER

"Fuck, is everyone gonna tell me that today?" I grunt, rubbing my palm down my face. "I got some stuff that's been going on. Mind's been shit lately. But I won't let it affect this club. You have my word."

Chain squints before answering. "It better not. That includes the meeting tonight. I don't know what those fuckers have planned, but I'm sending you and Hush because you two are my best guys for this sort of shit. Hush might be a weird fucker, but he's good, and I need you guys sniffing out their motives."

"I got it, Pres. What sort of business do you think they have?

He sighs. "Who knows with those pieces of scum? I hate that we already have to share a turf with them, but because we do, I wanna keep shit civil between us. We don't need the unnecessary drama and attention." He gets up from his seat. I follow suit. "Do yourself a favor, kid. Whatever it is that's eating you up, deal with it. Because the longer it eats away at you, the worse off you'll be, and I don't want to see you in that place again."

The memories haunt me to this day, being completely numb, inside and out. If there were any type of time machine, I'd use it in a heartbeat. "Yeah, I'll do my best."

"Good, now get the fuck out." He smirks and lights up a cigar from the tray table.

Walking out of Church, I have some type of fucking epiphany or some shit. I know what I have to do, or what I want to do anyway. Should I open up that can again? I don't know, but I don't give a fuck. I can't go another day (or night) without talking to her.

I left that bar without saying a word. Without saying a goddamn word. I really am a piece of shit. Now, all I have

C.M. Danks

to do is ask Bullet for a little favor, one that involves finding out where she lives. Because I'll be dammed if I let my pride or self-doubt get the best of me. That was one mistake I made before, not going after her. I won't do it again.

CHAPTER SIXTEEN

Jules

"Mommy, I don't like this stuff." Chloe picks the green bean off her plate with her fork, making the worst face at it.

After setting her juice down on the table, I snap my fingers at her plate. "Eat them. Vegetables are yummy and healthy for little girls. They make you grow up beautiful and strong."

"They are not yummy. They're gross." The green bean drops off her fork. I smile, holding back a laugh.

"All right, here's the deal, you eat some of those green beans and I'll let you watch extra cartoons today."

Chloe makes a face like she's thinking, then holds her thumb up. "Deal. It was good negotiating with you, Mommy." She mispronounces the word "negotiating" and I chuckle. The girl is way too smart for her age.

"Hey, Mommy." She chokes down her green bean, sticking out her tongue in disgust. "Are you gonna show me more pictures of Uncle Garrett today?"

The question hits me like a hammer to a nail. The pain works its way up again, taking its usual residence in the middle of my chest. Chloe started asking me about Garrett when she saw the prom picture sitting on my end table. I couldn't say no. He was her uncle after all. It sucks to see that picture in the same spot every day, but it's also comforting.

"And what about Daddy?" Before I could answer, a knock sounds at the door.

Saved.

"Finish your beans, little girl." Walking to the door, I look down, remembering I'm wearing a very low-cut tank top with comfy shorts. I wasn't planning on having company or going anywhere before work tonight. I decide not to change, because it's probably just Lucy.

My stomach drops after whipping the door open. Leaning against the frame with one arm, the other in his pocket, is Zach. His outstretched arm openly displays his muscled bicep. His black t-shirt is lifted a tad under his leather and I can see that he still has his lean, solid abs. I swallow, trying not to salivate too much.

He gives me a once-over, starting with my legs and only stopping when he's at my breasts. "Jesus Christ," he mumbles. But it's loud enough I can hear him.

I quickly cross my arms over my chest, in hopes of hiding my cleavage. After Chloe, my breasts may have gotten a tad larger than what they were in high school.

"How did you know I lived here?" Staring right into his blue eyes, I wait for him to answer. I blink, finding myself getting lost inside them.

"We need to talk."

"Oh," I let out a sarcastic laugh. "You're only about six years too late. Goodbye, Zach."

I go to close the door, but he holds out the palm of his hand, stopping it. "It's Charger."

"What?"

CHARGER

"My name is Charger now. I don't go by Zach anymore."

"Charger... like the car?" I say it in almost a mocking way while he glares at me.

Looking at the patch on his leather, I can see the name: *Steel Valley Chains MC*. He really is in a motorcycle club now.

"Let me in, Jules."

My attention snaps back to his near perfect face. Hearing my name from his lips again stings in places all over. What's even worse... I miss him calling me *pretty girl*. Hell, I would even settle for *Specs*, although I hardly wear my glasses anymore. Thank God for contacts.

"Pass."

But this time he's too fast. He brushes past me, right inside.

"I said leave, Charger." I tell him as I grip the door, waving my hand to shoo him out.

I shouldn't be trying to kick him out before telling him. I glance over at Chloe, who's building some kind of tower with her food.

"You're giving me five minutes. And I'm not asking."

"I see you've lost any charm you ever had."

He steps closer to me, but I take one back. Not because I'm scared, but because I don't trust myself to be close to him. I'm afraid I'll remember what his scent was like.

He pushes his way in until I'm cornered and tucks his hand under my chin, tilting my head up to meet his eyes. "Five minutes." The words leave his mouth as a soft whisper, causing my body to erupt. My lips part slightly. Why the heck am I reacting to him like this? Jesus, Jules. Calm your "horny for your old high school boyfriend" vagina. It's been six years.

C.M. Danks

"Mommy, is he your friend?" Her cheerful voice pulls me out of my fixated trance. I close my eyes because, well, *shit*. Chloe stands right next to us. His body tenses in front of me as he scrunches his eyebrows in confusion. I watch him as he turns around slowly. He's staring at Chloe as if he's a deer in headlights.

No. No. No. This was not supposed to happen this way.

Chloe sticks her hand out to Zach as he glances down at it. His mouth opens, as though he's trying to process a million things inside his mind. With his chest rising and falling in a less than normal fashion, he finally takes her hand. It's so tiny compared to his.

"I'm Chloe. What's your name, Mister?"

"I… uh…" He clears his throat. "My name's Charger."

She giggles and the floor underneath me feels like it's sinking. I have so many emotions right now. I guess I never did prepare for this moment.

"That's a funny name."

I pry my feet from the floor, moving forward, toward Chloe. "Okay, sweetie, why don't you go to your room and play. I need to talk to *Charger* alone, okay?"

"Fine." She stomps to her room. I turn on her Barbie radio, and then close the door without latching it. I spend a few seconds with my back to him, not removing my hand from the doorknob. When I finally have the courage to turn around, Zach is still staring where Chloe had been standing. He doesn't say anything.

"Zach…"

He holds up his hand then finally shoots his eyes to mine. He points at her door. "How old is she?" When I don't say anything, he repeats himself, angrier than the first time. "How. Old. Is. She. Jules?" If he mentally did the math, he would know. He would know how old she is. Not to mention the fact that she inherited every single feature from Zach. Blond hair with the same piercing blue eyes.

"I can explain." The burning that's setting in is making my eyes blur.

"Is she my daughter?" His voice cracks.

We can't have this discussion here, so I grab onto one of his solid, tattooed forearms and guide him into the small hallway. We're right above the stairs leading to the bar, but it's not open yet.

After I close the door, I lean against the frame, letting out a breath.

"Yes, she's your daughter." I feel the wetness slip down my cheeks. Anger, hurt, confusion, regret. Any emotion, you name it, and Zach has it in his eyes.

That night, the night the condom broke, I didn't think it would actually happen. That slim chance of getting pregnant... I didn't even notice until about a few months after. The morning sickness started, the obvious weight gain, the missed menstrual cycle. I just thought it was stress, until my mother sat me down and asked me what was going on. It eventually clicked. I mean, I was eighteen. Young and naive. She went with me to get a test and here we are, six years later. I would have never, ever, in a million years kept this from him. He had every right, he deserved to know. But how could I tell the father when I had no idea where he was? How could I tell someone who didn't want to be found?

"I have a daughter. I have a fucking daughter and I didn't know. How could you not tell me I had a daughter?"

"Are you kidding me?" I leave the safety of the door to stand right in front of him. Since Zach was always taller than me, I have to look up. *Did he grow even more?* "How could *I*

C.M. Danks

not tell *you*? Well, it might have been because I didn't know where the fuck you were. Or maybe because you left without a trace. No phone call, no text, nothing. Your old number was disconnected. Your own mother didn't even know where you were. I tried to find you, Zach." I stop only to take a breath. "Do you think I enjoyed keeping her from you? I didn't want her to grow up without a father, and I sure as hell didn't want you to not know about her. So, you have the nerve, the audacity, to stand here, at my house, accusing *me* of not telling *you*." I let out a laugh. "Now that's hilarious. As far as I was concerned, you died along with my brother that night." I swipe a tear off my cheek just in time for another one to replace it. His shoulders lose their stiffness and his eyes soften.

"You could have found me if you really wanted to. And when we saw each other two nights ago, you could have told me then. What would have happened if I didn't swing on by tonight, Jules, huh? You just would have kept on going about your everyday life."

He's right—that should have been my first priority. But the shock of seeing him after all these years was too strong. I needed time to process it. I didn't know what to do.

"I'm sorry. I should have told you that night, yes, not let you leave. But it was too much seeing you again. And what did you want me to do exactly, hire a private investigator all those years ago? So I could find a man who didn't want anything to do with me. To find someone who didn't want to be found." The last part came out in a screech. "Just go, Zach."

He cocks his head back, as if I hit him. "Go, you serious? I just found out that, that little girl in there is my daughter and you think I'm just gonna leave?"

CHARGER

There's a silent pause between us before his phone buzzes in his pocket. Since he didn't answer, it goes off a second time. He snatches it out of his pocket in frustration.

"Fuck," he snaps. Huffing out a breath, he looks down at the ground, balling his fist. "You want me to be honest about all those years ago? About why I left without a word, without calling, without anything?" he asks me softly. I swipe another tear off my face. "I blamed you." His words are like a sledgehammer to my chest, like the walls suddenly collapsed all around me. The feeling of losing oxygen swirls in my lungs. "I blamed you for your brother's death. The night of the party... I felt like if you hadn't overreacted to me dancing with Sam at the prom, then you wouldn't have run off to that party. I wouldn't have had to take you home. Garrett had no other choice but to get a ride with someone else. The sick fuck inside me... *blamed you*. The girl I loved, the girl who I wanted to marry. I blamed you. And because of that, I left. I ran like the coward that I was, *that I am*." He stops to breathe. "Jules, I was an asshole and for that, I'm sorry. I am so fucking sorry. But it wasn't true, not really. I was a dumb kid who didn't know any better." He steps forward, but the hurt he sees inside me stops him. I shove at his chest.

I carry the weight of my brother's death with me every day, so the fact that Zach is standing here, telling me he blamed me for Garrett's accident, makes it so much worse. The pain. The hurt. The guilt.

"Get out." My shoulders shudder from crying. "Get. Out."

"Jules..."

"Get out." My voice is soft, but defeated.

C.M. Danks

He starts to walk away, but turns back. "You can't keep me from seeing my daughter." I hear the sound of his heavy footsteps hit each stair, with the chains on each boot rattling, then the slam of the door.

I walk backwards until my body hits the door, letting myself slip to the floor. He blamed me? Did my heart just get ripped to shreds all over again? Those words cut like a knife. Missing Garrett has become a daily routine. I didn't need more backlash from it. But the sad thing is that I *want* to hate Zach. Hate him with every breath I have. Let the hatred fill my body, ignite my mind and soul. But I can't. After everything, I can't.

CHARGER

CHAPTER SEVENTEEN

Charger

I storm out of Jules's place, kicking the dirt in frustration, like I'm ten years old again.

I have a fucking daughter.

Turning my bike on, I notice that "For You" by All That Remains is playing.

The pain in her eyes gutted my insides. The urge to grab her, hold her in my arms until she stopped crying, was unbearable. I needed to be honest with why I left, but at what cost? Seeing her in pain took me back. Back to a dark place. A place I never want to go again. I was a stupid kid who didn't know shit. I was just someone who lost his best friend. I didn't know how to handle my emotions. My selfishness over losing my best friend made me forget that she also lost her brother. I would give anything to undo the pain I caused her.

Still, she can't keep me from seeing my daughter.

I knew… I knew the moment I looked into that little girl's eyes that she was mine. Explaining that feeling is impossible, but I just knew.

Slamming my fist into the handlebar of my bike (again out of frustration), I dial Hush's number. Losing out on five years of my daughter's life makes me physically fucking ill. No more wasted time. I knock the kickstand up with my boot and take off down the pavement.

When I pull into the meet-up spot, Hush is waiting for me. He's twirling a baseball bat like a fucking baton at a pep rally—cigarette in mouth, hood up, eyes dark. The dude would probably blend right in if he stood in a dark alley.

The place is secluded so we don't have to worry about any outside eyes.

Hush gives me a head nod, exhaling a puff of smoke. I can't let tonight throw me off. I have to get my head in the game.

"They here yet?"

Hush pulls down his hood. His lifeless, emotionless eyes give me the chills. "No, looks like they're late."

A roar of bikes from the distance catches our attention. Hush throws down his cigarette, pushing himself off from his ride. Venom pulls up with his President, parks, and starts heading our way.

The grass and dirt underneath their steps crunch as their boots hit the ground. Our boots mimic theirs as we approach them.

"Gentlemen." The President of the Steel Valley Skulls is a prick and I can't say I can tolerate the fucker much. Same goes for Venom—I want to wipe that stupid smirk off his face. "Too bad your President couldn't be here himself. I like to conduct my business with the one who actually runs the club."

"Yeah, well, you got *us*. So, start talking."

"I can see patience is not your strong suit." He says it with a smug fucking look. Refusing to acknowledge the comment with a response, I just stare, waiting for him to get this over with. "I'd like to negotiate a deal with your club. You see, we have a business we want to start. The profit being very beneficial. However, the more people we have in on this, the better."

Keeping his enemies close. Smart fucker. Not that we're enemies necessarily. As clubs, it's just how it is. Same turf, but we aren't pals.

"Which is…?" My voice is stern. He smirks. Venom rubs his facial hair, glaring at me. I give him a scowl in return, holding it with hatred.

"GTA, grand theft auto."

I let out a laugh. "Yeah, I know what that stands for. I don't think so. We ain't into anything illegal, so count us the fuck out." Attempting to turn around, I lead with Hush at my tail.

"We thought you might refuse." His sleezy laughter carries over my shoulder.

We stop dead in our tracks.

I sigh, rolling my eyes back. "Oh yeah?"

Scorpion grins with a shrug of his shoulders. "If you boys don't want to work with us, that's a damn shame. But if I were you, I'd watch my back. We hear that the business of pretty girls—willing or not, especially not—is very lucrative." His voice takes an ominous turn. "And it seems to me that there are a lot of pretty girls hanging around Steel Valley Chains…"

My stare goes cold with every part of my body tensing. I feel the rage inside my blood rise by every ticking second. Hush taps the end of his bat into his palms continuously.

"What did you say? Are you threatening us?"

"We may have some hot ones already lined up." He looks to Venom. "Isn't that right?"

C.M. Danks

"Oh yeah, lots of fresh ones. By the looks of them, I'd say we would really be bringing in the cash for sure." Venom follows the statement with a crude gesture, grabbing his cock. That's when Hush lunges forward. I grip him by the shoulders, walking us both backwards.

"Not now," I tell him in a low hiss.

He's angry. I can see it because so am I. His eyes are shooting daggers at Scorpion and Venom. Twenty more seconds of this and Hush is going to unleash on these guys. And I have no doubt in my mind he will rip them apart.

What the fuck kind of point are these fuckers trying to make?

Turning around, I stalk back over. Venom takes a step forward, meeting me right in my face. My eyes linger, burning into him. He's lucky I don't tear through him to get to his President. He might be taller than I am, but only by a cunt hair and that doesn't mean shit.

"Get in my face anymore and he..." I point to Hush, who's standing behind me. "Well, he might just gut you from the inside out." Hush grinds his teeth, juggling the bat. "Now, your President there is going to retract that statement because if he doesn't, our club and yours are going to have a major fucking problem. Got it?"

"No can do... Charger, is it?" Scorpion steps around Venom. "Tell your President that we'll be in touch. We do hope that you and your club will reconsider. It would be nice to have more manpower."

"Oh, you can be sure that we'll be in touch." I grind my teeth and watch them walk away. Their bikes rumble as they take off, and I turn to Hush. "Fuck. this is bad."

Hush is silent as his eyes follow them down the road.

CHARGER

"They're fucking dead if that's the game they wanna play." The anger in my voice is undeniable. "Chain's not gonna like this."

I swing my leg over, start my bike up, and dial Chain. "Think they'd be that stupid?" Hush asks, while he secures his bat in place.

"Knowing the Skulls, I wouldn't doubt it."

★★★

"What the fuck?" Heads turn when Chain comes barreling down to where Hush and I are standing in the doorway. Bullet isn't far behind. I knew he would be pissed. "My office, now!" We follow him. He slams the door then thunder erupts. "These pricks serious? Because I can assure you his plan A will not be happening. And his threat, he can go fuck himself with it."

"They got some fucking balls." Bullet crosses his arms as he stands next to Chain's desk.

"We know. I'll be honest; they definitely caught us off guard."

He starts pacing, his boots clunking with every giant step. "Fuck!" Resting his palms on his desk, he lets out a sigh. "So much for a quiet, relaxing evening."

I raise my eyebrow. "I thought you two had important shit to take care of tonight?" He doesn't miss the hint of accusation in my voice. He gives me a look. Bullet smirks, letting me know this was a test for us. But I get it—Hush and me being the two newest members besides the prospects.

"You two were tested tonight so congratulations, you both failed."

C.M. Danks

"To be fair, grand theft auto didn't exactly sound like a fun idea. We didn't really know he was gonna blindside us with an ultimatum either." I pause to study Chain. But he doesn't say anything, so I continue, "Knowing Scorpion and his club, I wouldn't say he's one to bluff."

The Steel Valley Skulls hold the record for a piss-poor reputation. Usually, they stay out of our way and we stay out of theirs. So, the fact that they reached out, wanted to partner up... well, it rubs us the wrong way—down to our cores.

"Agreed," Chain exhales. "All right, we'll figure this out, but until we do, we keep an eye on those pricks. Any funny business, any sign they're doing shit we don't like, they're gonna have problems with us. And we keep extra close eyes on the girls. If Scorpion and his club even bat an eye at one of ours, I want to know about it. If he isn't bluffing and he really is giving us an ultimatum, I don't wanna take any chances."

They will be signing their own death warrants if any one of them comes near our women, that's for sure. Or any woman for that matter. My blood boils with the thought of someone coming near Jules. Jules or our daughter.

"Okay, I'm going home to make love to my woman. You two good?"

"Make love?" Hush's low question has us turning slowly toward him.

"Yes, make love. Something you two don't know the first thing about. Think about settling down, men."

Settling down? There's no woman I have ever thought about settling down with, except Jules. I would have gladly married her straight out of graduation. That's how in love with her I was. Fuck, still am.

CHARGER

Hush releases a grunt as we both head out of Chain's office.

There're two things I can do to make this right: try to convince her I didn't mean what I said, or take out my frustration in the pit tomorrow night. Her face flashes in my mind. I hated leaving her like that and I sure as fuck don't want to see her hurt.

I decide to take the first option. Flipping through my contacts, I find her name, *pretty girl*. That's a name I haven't called her in six years. I hope it's the same number. Her number was the first one I saved into my new phone, way back when. Never did find enough courage to actually call her.

Here goes nothing...

C.M. Danks

★★★

Jules

Settling for a glass of wine sounded fabulous right now, but I decide on a creamy pint of something tastier instead. Scooping my spoon into the delicious mint chocolate chip flavored ice cream, I moan when it hits my tongue. I've been saving this, in case of emergencies. And this was definitely an emergency.

I decided to skip out on work early tonight, which is rare. But considering Lucy was ten seconds away from pulling out her hair due to my bitchy-ass moodiness, it was probably better to just come back upstairs.

I snuggle up with my Sherpa blanket, fuzzy pj's, and my favorite ice cream flavor. *Priceless*. Only the muffled sound of music fills my apartment.

I flick on Netflix, in hopes of finding something that'll stop the ache in my chest. Zach's words hit me hard. How could he blame me for everything? Like I didn't feel bad enough, he had to bury me deeper. A tear slips down my cheek. Wiping it off, I inhale with confidence. As I get ready to spoon another huge scoop of ice cream, my phone buzzes.

Unknown: *Jules, I'm sorry about everything. Please, we need to talk.*

My pulse races. I stare at the words on my screen, obviously knowing it's Zach. I hover my finger over my

CHARGER

phone's keyboard. When I finally manage to type out a response, it's long and complicated. My leg bounces up and down as I contemplate if I should send it. He deserves to see his daughter and he will, but I just can't right now.

I turn my phone over on the coffee table, ignoring it. Then I shovel in the scoop of ice cream that has practically melted off my spoon.

C.M. Danks

Chapter Eighteen

Jules

The Fallen Star is packed again tonight. The dart board is being overtaken. The old arcade game, Pac Man, has the younger crowd entertained. And when I say younger crowd, I mean *my* crowd. Groups of young men hover around, watching. I was pretty excited when I won that at an auction—gives the bar a fun vibe.

Lucy is running around here like a mad woman and I love her for it. The chick knows how to work her ass off. Owning your own place can be tough, that's for sure, so having the right people to work for you is key. And you might just gain some friends along the way. Like Joe, who's in his usual spot. Maybe he'll eventually meet the woman of his dreams, sitting here every night. It kind of hurts, seeing him lonely all the time at my bar.

"Need a refill, Joe?"

"Nah, I'm good, honey."

Two men sit down a couple of seats from Joe. Loud, laughing, drunk. The one barely made it into his seat. I'll be cutting them off soon. The other flags me down with a wave of his hand, whistling like I'm a damn dog. He's clearly

CHARGER

lacking manners. Showing off a fake smile, I approach them while he scans my body, lingering on my chest longer than welcomed.

I snap my fingers. "How about I get you two some water, yeah?" They both laugh. The one with a fascination for my breasts, and disgusting teeth, slurs out his words.

"No, dollface, we would like two more Millers and bring us two shots of Crown."

"I can do two beers and two waters, no shots. Deal?" Negotiating and compromising—the best solution, being a bar owner (and bartender for that matter). Lucy walks by juggling her tray and he slaps her ass. She shakes her head, but keeps walking, mumbling *asshole* under her breath. "And no touching my waitresses." My politeness takes a plunge. The guy holds his hands up in surrender then slouches into the seat, licking his lips at me.

Gross.

As I fill the glasses with water for the two asshats, someone walks into the bar. Not just someone, *Zach*. It happens like something out of a movie. Slow motion. His large frame, muscled everything, leather... before his blue eyes connect with mine. Why is he here?

"Shit." I dab the puddle of water, which accidently spilled over the cups, with a towel just as he plants his hands on the counter.

"You never answered my text." His eyes are glued to mine. I finish wiping up the spill, then crack open the two beers. My body feels weak, powerless. Whenever he's around, it's like everything goes out the window with a toss of a hat. There go my morals, toss. My confidence over telling him to go fuck himself, toss. What I really want to do is jump on him... have him take me. *Right here. Right now.*

C.M. Danks

"Yes, I'm aware of that. It was kind of on purpose." Juggling the glasses, I place them in front of the rude men.

"Thanks, dollface, it's always nice to get served by such a fine piece of ass."

Zach's head whips in their direction, and I swear if this were a cartoon, it would have flown off his body. He gives them each one hell of a nasty glare. His jaw ticks. But, by some miracle, he ignores the comment and sits down. A sigh of relief leaves my body.

"Zach, what are you doing?"

"What's it look like I'm doing? I would like a beer, please." He emphasizes the word *please*. I pop my lips, giving him a stern look. His forearms rest on the counter. His tattooed, muscular forearms. "I'm just here to see you, have a beer, and talk."

Joe looks at him, then to me.

"Old acquaintance," I explain, trying to reassure him I don't need a rescue. "I can't talk right now. Clearly, I'm working."

"Uh, excuse me, dollface." The rude guy laughs, swinging his empty bottle back and forth in the air. I would love to take the bottle from his grubby hand and whip it at his face. I give him an irritated look, and I'm about five minutes away from throwing him out, when Zach starts to lose his cool. He cracks his neck.

"Yes?" I grunt.

"Can we get another beer? Seems we ran out." He's sneering, showing off the fact that he's never been to a dentist.

"I'm sorry but you two have had enough. So, take your pick: water with or without lemon." His face turns cold, all playfulness gone. Staring at me with his glazed over eyes, he stumbles to a stand.

"Listen here…"

"Sit. Down." Zach's voice carries over the music, each word drawn out. He says it with such a demand, but also a calmness. His fingers flex around his beer bottle, turning his knuckles white.

"I'll sit down when this little bitch shows me some respect. Now, I said I want another beer, so get me another beer." He moves forward, trying to grab my arm, but Zach is out of his seat in seconds. The guy falls back, landing ass-first in the stool. Zach towers over the man, his hand resting on the counter. Zach's other hand grips the stool behind the drunken asshole. Only inches from the guy's face, Zach is every bit as intimidating as I remember.

Joe spins himself around, watching the scene unfold. Some others are in the distance, also watching. Me? I'm not surprised. Zach has always been one to stand up for me, even now, six years later.

"You're done. Now, get the fuck out." His stare is intense, his eyes filled with rage.

The guy's Adam's apple dips up and down as he rises hesitantly. "Yeah, man. We were just leaving." Zach straightens, watching until they are both out the door. Lucy is staring… or salivating? I can't tell which one. Maybe both. He turns his muscled body back to me, connecting us in a powerful moment. His eyes don't leave mine. No, Jules, you do not want to jump over the bar and tackle him. Let him devour you. Rip every piece of clothing off your body. You do not want to feel his hands running over every inch of your naked body.

I pull my bottom lip with my teeth and he raises a brow.

C.M. Danks

Damn, it's hot in here.

"Outside, now."

At the sound of his growl, it's like I have no control; my body just moves. I yell to one of the waitresses, asking her to cover for me. I tell Joe that it's fine and before I know it, I'm following Zach out the back door.

As soon as the screen door shuts, I'm backed up against the brick wall. His hands are softly pressed on my arms just above my elbows. With hardly any room between us, he scans my face, my body. "Does that shit happen a lot?" He grinds his teeth together.

I swallow. "Yes, I'm a bartender. Of course, it does. But I can take care of myself. I don't need you fighting my battles like we're back in high school."

His chest expands, his eyes darting between mine. Inching forward, he brushes his nose on my cheek, then he hovers just above my lips. "You're still so fucking beautiful."

Our lips almost touch and I can't help but part them slightly. Like I'm inviting him in. Does he taste the same? Does his mouth feel the same? My bottom teeth capture my lip. The heat rises in my body, soaking the area between my thighs. Because my neck is exposed from my hair being pulled up, his breath tickles my skin. I close my eyes, trying to imagine what it would feel like if he made the connection, his lips on me. Such a desirable thing. I want it, need it. But the cool night air is the only thing I feel against my skin.

Zach's warm body, which was shielding me moments ago, is gone. I catch my breath, watching as his attention focuses on the ground. I'm disappointed he backed away, but nothing can keep me from admiring how good he looks. How sexy, how powerful.

"You look good too," I tell him. He picks his head up. "I mean, you know, you look…" I pause. "Bigger." I mentally roll my eyes at myself. He smirks. "So why are you here, Zach? Is it really just to talk?"

"I wanted to see you. I told you inside… you didn't answer my texts, so that's why I'm here."

"I just didn't know what to say. You left me with a lot to process. I had quite a bit of emotions to try to deal with. I mean, blaming me for my brother's death is a pretty big fucking thing." Crossing my arms over my chest, I can feel the emotions resurfacing. I've always been one to wear them on my sleeve. Sitting nice and pretty. Front and center, with a flashing neon sign.

"Fuck, Jules, I messed up. I'm not the same kid from high school in so many ways. But I can tell you this. I blamed you so I didn't have to blame myself. That's why I did it. I was fucked up and I am so sorry." The sincerity in his voice is real. The sadness in his eyes is real. "And I want to be active in Chloe's life, Jules. Don't keep her away from me."

My heart strings are playing tug of war. "No, Zach, I would never purposely keep you from her. It's just… I need time to tell Chloe."

"You had time, Jules. Five years. You had five years." I want to argue, but I don't. He's not wrong. But, on the other hand…

"That's not entirely fair."

He sighs, stepping closer to me once again. "I know, fuck." He runs his hand through the longer part of his hair. He's kept his hairstyle the same. I love when his loose bangs fall against his face. "I'm not sure how to do this. This whole dad thing. Co-parenting thing. I just found out I have a daughter so my emotions are all over the place too. Just don't shut me out like I did to you."

All I can do is nod my head yes. We stand like that for a minute before he nods back, then trudges off through the front parking lot. I exhale the breath I have been holding for what feels like a century.

***

Charger

I start up my bike, not wanting to leave, but needing to remove myself from a situation that makes me a weak fucking man. It's taking all of me not to throw her over my shoulder and walk that perfect ass upstairs.

Gripping my fist around my handlebars, I think about that fucker who was giving Jules shit. He was lucky. Had he touched her, he would have been dead. Is this the kind of bullshit she deals with while owning this place? *Fuck.*

I catch a single small headlight in the distance, my body on high alert when I realize it's a bike. Whoever it is, they were just scoping out Jules's bar. The bike makes a quick turnaround then takes off. I don't recognize the ride. So, it couldn't have been one of our guys. Then who the fuck was it?

CHARGER

CHAPTER NINETEEN

Jules

"Chloe Star, what in the world are you doing, girl?" Watching my daughter, I honestly wish I knew what was going through her mind sometimes.

"I wanted to be as pretty as you, Mommy."

Chuckling, I bend down and pick her up into my arms. My red lipstick, which I didn't even remember owning, is now drawn all over Chloe's face. "Okay, Joker, how about we scrub this stuff off your face."

"Joker?" Her small face looks at me like she has no idea what I'm talking about.

"Never mind, you're too young." With her tiny frame still in my arms, I walk her to the bathroom. I set her on the counter, running a washcloth under the water.

"Where in the world did you find this lipstick anyway, little bug?"

"It was in a box... with *this*." Chloe holds up a necklace. A star necklace. *The* star necklace.

With the washcloth still in my hand, I freeze, studying the dangling charm. I haven't looked at that necklace in years. I wore it for almost two years after graduation, but thinking that I would probably never see Zach again, I couldn't bear to wear it any longer. It hurt too much.

"Was it from Daddy?"

With a sigh, I smile. "Yes, it was from your daddy. It was a birthday present."

"Am I ever going to meet him?" Her "light up the room" smile fades.

Just when a heart couldn't break anymore...

"How about you let me worry about that and let's focus on getting that lipstick off your face." Her cute little smile is back. "How about this... remember when I told you that Daddy had very important things to take care of?" She nods with enthusiasm. "Well, what if his important things are over?" Her smile is growing bigger by the second. My heart warms. Being able to tell Chloe that her dad is going to be around is by far the best feeling.

After about an hour of trying to stay busy, my curiosity gets the best of me. Zach has seen where I work, has seen what *my* life is about, maybe it's time I did the same. If he is going to be active in Chloe's life, I need to know what exactly his biker life is like. *Biker club* doesn't exactly scream *family fun zone*.

A knock at the door has me guessing that Lucy has arrived. I called her, asking if she would watch Chloe for a while. She gladly accepted the offer. She loves Chloe.

"Thanks for coming over last minute, Lucy."

"It's totally fine. It's either come over and play dolls with your adorable five-year-old, or sit home on my day off, binge watching Korean Dramas and wishing I had that kind of love life."

"You watch K-Dramas?"

"No..." Lucy smiles, setting her purse down.

CHARGER

"Lucy!" Chloe darts over, clinging to her leg. "Do you want to play with my dollhouse?"

"Uh, yeah, totally. How about you go set it up and I'll be there in a sec." Chloe runs back to her room, pulling out all her doll pieces. "Are you going to be okay? Going there by yourself, I mean? You don't know how those club places can get."

"I do. I dated a club member, remember?"

"Yeah, well, just be careful is all."

"I will. I need to see what the life of Zachary Scott is all about."

Having dated Venom for almost a year, I know how these biker club's work. But that's Venom's club, not Zach's. So, let's see what the difference is, shall we?

★★★

After googling the address, I realize I have driven past here numerous times. He hasn't been that far away from me after all.

I park off to the side on the dirt lot and head up to their club, which is basically a large bar. It looks pretty nice but I make sure my pepper spray is handy on my keychain, clenching it to me. Venom's club was anything but kind so I have to be prepared.

They have a gym and a bike shop on either side of the bar. The buildings are clean, the landscape is kept up, and they don't give off any "danger" vibes. This is the nicest looking biker bar I have ever seen.

I take a deep breath in, then exhale before opening the door. There's not a lot of people here but it is a Monday.

C.M. Danks

They have your average pool tables toward the back and a stage, which I'm guessing is for live music, on the left; whereas the bar is to the right. I swallow nervously, walking past a group of men—each spinning around in a slow circle. I try to seek out the person I came to see.

"Hey, sweetheart, lookin' for someone?" the girl behind the bar asks me. She's pretty. Her chocolate brown hair makes her green eyes pop.

"Um, I'm looking for Za—Charger," I quickly correct myself.

She eyes me up and down before smiling. "He's in the pit, sweetie."

"The pit?"

"The pit is the fighting arena. He fights there like all the time." She sets a glass in the soapy water in front of her. Zach fights? "It's the dingy place out back."

Well, now I definitely have to see this for myself. What kind of fighting is this? Sounds like an illegal underground thing going on. "Okay, thank you." I start walking straight for the back.

"Now, hang on, the pit is no place for someone like you. Those men will eat you up."

I flash her my keychain. "I'll be fine, nothing a little pepper spray can't handle." I'm out the door before she can say anything else.

As soon as I make it outside, I can hear the music thumping. Bikes and cars are lined up in the back lot. When I reach the door and pull it open, the smell of smoke, sweat, and beer hits my face. Letting out a cough, I continue down the narrow entryway, only to be stopped by a huge bouncer at the end.

CHARGER

He raises an eyebrow in question. "This is no place for you, doll."

"I know, but I really need to speak to someone who's supposed to be in there." With his arms crossed, his chest puffed out, he studies me. Okay, this guy isn't going to let me through for anything. I'll have to resort to the oldest trick in the book.

"Hey, who's that?" Within seconds, the bouncer looks down the hall for the imaginary person I just made up. Super corny, but it works. They really should consider a new bouncer, one that isn't so gullible.

I make my way toward the crowd of men. They're all shouting and watching whatever is happening at the center of the ring.

I hear "Blood" by Breaking Benjamin.

My eyes pan over to where the men are focused. I see him. Zach is in the ring, hopping back and forth, dodging his opponent's fist like its easy.

When did he start fighting?

I slowly make my way to the ring, weaving in and out through the crowd and getting bumped on the way there. I stop when I'm as close as I can get. I take all of Zach in. Without a shirt, his tattoos are displayed perfectly on his bare, sweaty body. He still has that sexy nipple piercing. Grown, tattoos, and a hell of a lot more muscle than when he was eighteen. The intricate designs move, as if dancing with every motion he does. I lick my lips slowly, tilting my head in admiration.

His opponent spins around fast, throwing a roundhouse kick to Zach. I jump with a gasp, thinking the guy's going to strike him, but Zach quickly dodges, then takes him down with one hard charge.

C.M. Danks

Charger.

With the quick maneuvering, Zach is now on top. He then slowly rolls his body, twisting the man's arm before pulling it back. Agonizing screams of pain sound from his opponent and his hand quickly taps the matted floor. The referee blows into the whistle, grabbing hold of Zach's arm and raising it as the crowd cries out in victory. A swirl of pride hits me in this moment. Seeing him like this sends something through me. I tighten my thighs, in order to draw in some type of friction. I want to relive the feeling of Zach. The feeling of his lips on my skin. Him touching me without regret. Maybe send my nails down his back, while his body is caging me in. *Damn.*

He removes his mouthguard, chucking it to the floor, then scans the crowd only to connect with me. When he sees me, he doesn't look away, his face turning hard and cold.

A set of strong hands grab me from behind. They are strong, yet gentle. Spinning around, I practically face-plant with a large chest, a long necklace dangling in front. I have to look up to see that it's the same man from the bar—the one Zach came in with when I first saw him. His shoulder-length hair lies perfectly along his collarbone, with his half pony man-bun drawing loose strands away from his face. I glance up—he's tall with the sort of brown eyes you can get lost in because they're so kind.

"Hey, honey, let's get you out of here. This is no place for you." His biker friend looks around before taking hold of my arm and leading me down the long hall I came from. I don't get a chance to look back at Zach before I'm out the door. I do give the bouncer an apologetic look as I pass him. He smirks.

CHARGER

The fresh air immediately feels like a warm welcome. The muggy cigarette smell mixed with sweat and beer was making me ill.

The bartender from earlier watches me as I'm led to one of the stools. "Tequila, get her a drink, will ya?"

"Yeah, of course." She grabs a glass. "Nice to see you made it out alive." She smirks. "What's your poison, love?" she asks me. I can still feel the large biker behind me.

"Um, I'll take a cosmopolitan, please." I should have said *a beer*—now I sound like a high-maintenance brat.

"Coming right up." She turns, grabbing the bottle before pouring each liquid into the glass. "Told you not to go down there. Those men are not exactly gentlemen and I wouldn't be surprised if one of them tried something with you." She places the drink on the square napkin in front of me. "I'm Tequila by the way, and this giant of a man is Tank."

He leans in next to me, with an elbow on the bar countertop, and winks. "Nice to meet ya, sweetheart."

"I'm Jules. Nice to meet you both. I didn't know Zach was a fighter." They scrunch their eyebrows together. *Shit.* "I mean, Charger."

"Where the fuck is she!?" Zach stalks through the back door, grey sweats, no shirt. *Dear God.* I get up from the bar stool, standing toe-to-toe with him. "You don't ever, and I mean ever, come to the pit alone. Do you understand?" Tank is ready to jump in, and I prepare to argue when an older woman comes over and places a calming hand on Zach's shoulder.

"What in the world? The whole state of Ohio will hear you if you keep up that shouting." The woman looks at me. "And who might this be?"

C.M. Danks

"I'm Jules." I smile shyly, awkwardly. Zach's chest looks much bigger when he's angry. She darts between Zach and me. Then she smiles a huge smile.

"I'm Maggie. I'm Chain's Ol' Lady." I don't have to ask her what that means. I already know. Having been with Venom, I've learned some of the biker lingo. Though, his club was not as kind. When Maggie gives me a hug, it's not something I expected. She smells of older perfume, like citrus and lilies. It's comforting. Her short brown pixie haircut matches her sweet face. "Charger, can you not yell at this poor girl. You're frightening her."

"It's okay. I shouldn't have been there."

She doesn't know me, but Zach could never scare me. He *has* never scared me. There's never been a man I've felt safer with. He takes a deep breath in and then out before he steps away, rubbing his hand over the back of his neck, his bicep flexing.

"Are you two friends?" Maggie asks. We both look at the ground.

"Something like that." I didn't mean for it to sound so bitter.

"Well, any friend of Charger's is a friend of ours. You're welcome here anytime."

"Thank you. That's very kind of you, but I don't know how much I'll actually be around." My eyes scan over them all. From Tank, to Maggie, to Zach, and then Tequila leaning over the bar. "I just needed to talk to Charger. See this place for myself. See what our child is going to be around." My eyes snap shut, realizing what I just said. By the shocked look on their faces, I would say no one knew. "Sorry, I meant…" Zach swiftly moves around Tank, taking hold of my arm. He leads me outside the clubhouse, guiding us around the corner. Well, if this wasn't a repeat of the other night... "Sorry, I didn't mean to spill that out in front of everyone."

He stands with little space between us. He's so close, my heart beats out of my chest. For some reason, I can't focus on anything, hear anything, see anything but his bare, smooth, muscled chest in front of me. The way his sweatpants hang low, showcasing his subtle V-shape... The tattoos inked across his arms...

I squeeze my lips tightly together to stop myself from licking the bead of sweat trickling down his rippled abs. If he keeps doing this, I will lose every ounce of willpower I have.

"Pretty girl..." I snap my focus up to his eyes, which are peering into me.

I get lost again.

A small piece of hair is stuck to his forehead, but with that too, I have to stop myself. I want to reach up, swiping it ever so slightly away. *Stop thinking about how good he looks.*

"You fight now?" The words leave my lips in a seductive way, almost as if the thought of him fighting is turning me on. Damn, it is. His eyes burn into mine with his chest practically pressed up against my smaller frame. When I lay my head back onto the stone behind us, he eyes me like he wants to lick and suck me dry. *Please, do it.* Put me out of my misery.

"Yeah, I fight now. But I don't ever want to see you down at the pit again, get me, Jules?" I hear him. I want to say, "Sure, fine," but my mouth doesn't seem to function right now. "Would you like me to go put a shirt on?" He leans forward, brushing his lips against my ear. "You seem distracted." He smells of pure man right now. I can't see beyond his body. His frame covers everything from the outside world. I'm shielded, completely protected from anything dangerous. I don't want to leave his comfort, but I know I should.

Spinning around, escaping the proximity between us, I cross my arms around myself. "No, I think I'll be okay. Thanks. Try not to flatter yourself."

"Just like old times." He smirks, and my lady parts do a dance.

"I just needed to see what exactly was involved in your life. Chloe can't be around you if it's dangerous."

"You think I would expose my daughter to these people or this place if I thought it was dangerous?" He sighs. "Look, Jules. There might be some things that are out of my control, being involved in certain things, but I can promise you that I would never put her in harm's way."

There's no denying the sincerity. "Everyone seems nice." I smile. "A lot nicer than..." I catch myself, not wanting to finish that sentence. Zach steps to me.

"A lot nicer than what?"

"Nothing, I should go. And I am so sorry for just showing up like this. Guess it was a little spontaneous." When I hug my midsection, his smile disappears.

"Jules, I can also promise you this..." He waves his hand around. "This place, my club, is completely safe. They would die for me and whoever I care about." My heart skips. Does he mean me too, along with Chloe? "I just want to make sure you understand that."

"Yeah, I get it. Although, you being involved with an underground fighting pit is a little scary."

"Trust me, it's taken care of. You'll be kept safe from it. As long as you listen to me and do what you're told."

CHARGER

Oh, hell no.

"I'm sorry, do as I'm told? Look here, buddy." I point my finger into his chest. His very hard, muscled chest. "You don't get to tell me what to do. You don't own me."

"I've always owned you, Jules."

The air grows heavy and I swallow nervously. "Whatever." I turn, heading toward my car, but I spin back around. "I'll be in touch about our daughter. Goodbye." Once again, I stomp to my car like a little pissed off high schooler. Zach grabs my arm. Why does he always have to touch me? It's radioactive. It's torture. Complete and utter torture.

"I'm just trying to keep you safe. So, when it comes to things you know nothing about, things involving my club, you *will* listen to me." He rubs the pad of his thumb down my bottom lip. "Now, tuck that sass away, Jules."

Staring at him in silence, I nod.

Before I get in and take off back home, like my life depends on it, I decide to give him something to hold onto. "She's amazing." I rub my arm because of the slight awkwardness. "She's so smart and polite, but also has this spunky side. Which I think she gets from you." I chuckle.

"Yeah?" His face lights up.

"Yeah." I smile back. "I, uh, I'd better go."

I go to open my car door, but Zach plants one of his hands on it, slamming it shut. I'm sandwiched between my door and Zach's body. The little flutter my heart does electrifies my body, sending it straight to my lady parts. The throbbing starts, then the aching. His chest comes in contact with my back, causing me to scream on the inside. Dying. A slow and torturous death. His hardness growing more and more the longer we stand like this, he presses it into me. I can only imagine what it'd be like now. What *he* would be like now. My mouth is open as I breathe deeply. He skims my arm before planting his other hand on the roof of the car. Can't we just stay like this? Let me soak him in. Let me feel him touching me, so I can hold onto this feeling. A feeling I never want to let go of now that we have been reintroduced. His breath, the warm subtleness of it, hits my neck in a quickened pattern.

"Zach, I think…"

"You're the only one who's allowed to call me that, pretty girl." *Pretty girl.* Damn, if that still doesn't affect me… "But don't call me that in front of anyone here again, got it?"

"Yes," I answer softly.

Giving into him more and more, I lean back. Yes, I lean back into him and I think I hear him growl. He feels too good. It's warm, safe, and familiar. The last time I remember ever feeling this way was with him, six years ago. There was never this kind of chemistry with Venom. It was just physical, nothing mentally connecting us like it does with Zach. My body never reacted the same way.

The roaring sound of bikes breaks whatever moment we had, and he steps away. Two men covered in tattoos approach us after they park. "Hey, brother, put a damn shirt on! What the fuck you…" He stops. "Oh, sorry, didn't know there was a lady present. I'm Throttle." He smiles. A smile that can make your panties wet. His boyish good looks and chocolate messy hair are sexy too. There has to be something in the water these men are drinking. Because this shit is just unreal.

The other guy side-glances at me before he passes by. He's just as good looking, but his eyes are dark, somewhat scary. There're tattoos covering his neck and I catch a

CHARGER

glimpse of his patch, which reads: *Hush*. Just as I'm about to introduce myself to Throttle, Zach interrupts.

"Keep it moving, man. This one isn't a hang-around."

Throttle shakes his head with laughter. "Well, hopefully you won't be a stranger. You seem to have made an impact on my brother's life." He claps Zach on the shoulder, then follows Hush up to the clubhouse.

Zach rubs the back of his neck while I scoot into the driver's seat of my car. "I'll be at your place tomorrow to see Chloe."

I tilt my head in confusion. Was he not present throughout our conversation? Did he not here the part where I wanted to give this just a little more time?

"That's a little soon, don't you think? I said give me some time for it all to sink in with Chloe."

He leans forward, holding onto the car door. "It wasn't a question. I'll see you tomorrow." With that, he shuts it, then walks up the long stretch of the lot.

My hands grip the steering wheel as I watch him in my mirror. He's so hot and cold. The Zach now and the Zach back in high school are not the same people. But still, there's little pieces of him left. The protective, gentle boy is still in there. The only difference now is he seems even more dominant. But to be honest, my body has never wanted him more.

C.M. Danks

Chapter Twenty

Charger

Yeah, I just showed up today. No call, no text. Tough shit. She'll just have to deal with it. Backing up my bike into an empty spot at the bar, I throw my kickstand down before swinging my leg over.

After that night I saw Jules, I called up Bullet—to have him do some investigating on where she was living. The first time I showed up at her place, she wanted to know how exactly I knew she was living above her bar. I ignored her question; I didn't think she would like to find out I was having her searched. I can't say that I am surprised she owns the bar though. Jules was always smart. This was always what she wanted to do one day, own her own business. I just wish it wasn't a damn bar. Mix alcohol with men who have nothing better to do, then add in a woman who looks like Jules. *Fucking animals.* I got a taste of that when I decided to swing by for a visit the other night. I would have murdered that piece of shit had he touched her. Because no matter how much time has passed, I will always feel the same way. The idea of other men touching, or shit, even looking at her for that matter fucking makes me insane. And

CHARGER

what if she's seeing someone? I just assumed she wasn't. She's gorgeous, successful. Any man would want to be with her. She deserves someone other than me.

Not bothering to see if the front was open, I make my way to the back door leading upstairs, which is unlocked. I shake my head. I'll be sure to talk to her about why the fuck a single mother living alone is not locking her damn door.

I go to knock, but the door flies open. Standing there is Jules, wearing a pair of tight black pants. Maybe yoga pants. I think that's what the fuck they call them. Her tank top hides nothing and her hair is pulled up on top of her head, which makes me fantasize about grabbing hold of it and fucking her from behind like there's no tomorrow.

Fuck. I really am scum.

"Zach?"

"I could have been anyone. Why did you just open the door like that? And you need to start locking your back door."

"I was expecting someone. I heard footsteps so I thought it was them. What are you doing here?"

I step inside. Our arms touch as I walk by, the slight contact passing electricity through me. "Who were you expecting?" I take a quick glance around. Chloe's at the kitchen table coloring with her pink headphones on. She's so concentrated on that drawing that she doesn't even realize I'm here. My heart beats a little faster, knowing that my daughter is real, that she's sitting right here. I'm nervous, excited, but still trying to wrap my head around it all.

"Zach, you should have called. I have to go downstairs to help prepare for tonight. I had a ton of call offs. My mom is on her way to watch Chloe."

C.M. Danks

"Your mom? If anyone is going to watch her, it should be me. Besides, I'm here already. So, I can watch her." I've never watched a kid in my life and this isn't just any kid. This is *my* kid. I can do this. I *want* to do this.

"I mean... have you ever babysat before?"

"No, but how hard can it be?"

Jules's eyes widen, her face turning sour.

Light footsteps sound from the stairs. I don't hesitate to see who it is.

The petite woman in the doorway is an older version of Jules. Her face aged just slightly since the last time I saw her. The normal light in her eyes I remember from years ago is gone. It doesn't take a genius to figure out why.

Without moving or saying a word, she stares at me. A blank but honest expression on her face tells me she knows exactly who I am. Anger spikes in her as she slowly stalks toward me, stopping only when she's a foot in front of me. A quick sting of pain hits the side of my face. My cheek's left burning from her slap.

"*Mom,*" Jules says only loud enough for us to hear. I hold my hand up, letting her know it's okay. It wasn't what I was expecting, but I definitely deserve that.

"How dare you. My daughter not only had to suffer the loss of her brother." Her voice shakes and a tear slides down her cheek. "But she had to endure the pain of losing you too. She needed you and you weren't there."

I keep my eyes on hers, giving her the respect needed. I can take the abuse. Hell, I want the abuse. Take me, string me up, and let me have it. I deserve nothing less. She takes another small step toward me. Should I brace for another hit? Instead, she lifts her motherly arms before wrapping them around my back. "But I'm glad you're okay and it's good to see you." Jules's body relaxes before she flashes me a smile. I return the warm gesture. It feels like home to hug her mom—something I hardly ever did with my own.

Pulling away, she looks at me with a smile. But it fades when she takes in my patch, reading my MC's name. "I just hope whatever you have going on doesn't affect my granddaughter or my daughter."

"I'm sorry about everything. About leaving, and for you guys losing Garrett." Saying his name out loud is harder than I thought. "And there's a lot that goes on in the club, Mrs. T. But I can promise you that I'll try my hardest to keep them both safe from it."

She studies my eyes, then steps away. "I hope you do." She smiles. "Since Chloe's father is here, Jules, I guess you don't need me," she says in a low voice, glancing at Chloe who is, yes, still drawing—guess she got her artistic interest from her mother. She kisses Jules on the cheek and I hear Jules thanking her. Before she leaves, she flashes me a smile, then disappears out of the apartment.

"That went better than I thought." Jules laughs with some sarcasm behind it.

"Yeah, thought it went pretty well." I smirk, rubbing my cheek. We both turn to Chloe, who is removing her headphones.

"All right, so much for giving her time. Chloe bug, can you come here please."

"Hold on, Mommy. I'm drawing a masterpiece right now."

I laugh deeply, which catches her attention. She turns in her chair to look at me. "It's Charger!" She hops down, her small feet running over to me, barely able to keep up with each other. I crouch down to her level, so does Jules. "Mommy, he's less scary than the other man."

Jules hums out a groan and my blood instantly boils. Who the hell is Chloe talking about? I give her a look, but she ignores it.

"Chloe, we have to tell you something." Jules places a gentle hand on her arm.

Holding back my curiosity for now, I return my attention to Chloe. To her million-dollar fucking smile, her eyes. Christ, she has my eyes.

"Is Charger my daddy?" She looks up at Jules. *Kid is smart as hell.*

"Yes, Charger is your father." A tear slides down Jules's cheek. She closes her eyes, waiting for Chloe's reaction. Chloe reaches up and brushes her small hand in my hair. Then, she slams her body into mine, wrapping her arms around me. Though they don't quite make it, the feeling of her hugging me is by far the best moment of my life. Yet another hug today that I don't deserve. But I return it nonetheless and engulf her in my hold, overcome by this overwhelming urge to always protect her with my life.

Jules has her hand over her mouth, tears slipping down her face. Tears of happiness, not sadness. I'm glad I can give her some type of joy, considering all the pain I've caused.

"He's going to watch you for a little bit, okay?"

Chloe pulls away, nodding her head with excitement. "Yay!"

For the first time in a long while, I feel weak. Almost dizzy, like the floor beneath me will collapse at any second. An overwhelming feeling that I can't explain hits me hard. I think being a father just sunk in.

CHARGER

"Um, well, if you need me, I'll be right downstairs. You sure you're going to be okay?"

"Yep, I got it." I swallow nervously. *I can do this.*

She kisses Chloe and takes off for the bar downstairs. Chloe stares at me, then grabs my hand. Guiding me to the sofa, she sits down with her feet dangling over the edge. "Why do you wear *that*, and why is your name Charger?" She points to my patch and what I'm guessing is my leather cut.

I clear my throat. "This name was given to me by a special family. And I wear *this*." I tug at my cut. "To show love, respect, and loyalty." I have no idea if she understands what I'm saying. She might be too damn young, but she smiles like she does.

"Oh!" She jumps down from the sofa and practically face-first onto the coffee table, and my heart skips a beat. My hands fly up ready to catch her, but she doesn't fall. She runs off to the other room. The urge to keep this child, *my* child, safe is off the charts. It's like a natural instinct, appearing out of nowhere.

When she comes back in, she holds up a necklace. "Mommy said that you gave this to her a long time ago. You should give it to her again."

I take the necklace from her tiny hand and my stomach drops, remembering the day I picked it out for her like it was yesterday. I knew it was perfect as soon as I saw it. Jules will always be like the stars in the sky. My star. The fact that she's kept it makes me love her even more. Yeah, I love her. I never fucking stopped.

"I like the way you think, kid. And I think you're right. I do need to give her this present again."

C.M. Danks

She smiles proudly as I tuck the necklace into my pocket while being mindful not to tangle it up. Her feet are kicking off the couch as she looks at me with her big, bright, blue ocean eyes. It's as if I hung the moon in her eyes, which leaves a swell in my chest.

"Why did you leave Mommy?"

There it is, the question no kid should ever ask their parent. I hate how that question sounds coming from her. It makes me feel ashamed. "It's complicated, kid. I wasn't thinking clearly, but that was a long time ago. I'm sorry for not being there for you and your mom." I'm actually getting choked up. Jesus.

"Are you going to stay?"

"Yeah, kid, I'm going to stay."

"Yay! Let's go. I want to show you my room." She flies off the couch again but this time, I hold out my arms. Ready (unlike last time) to catch her. She falls right into my embrace, and I set her down. The kid weighs about nothing.

She takes hold of my hand, trying her best to drag me with her. Jules's bedroom door is open. I catch a glimpse of the paintings and drawings along her wall. I'm glad she is still involved with art in some way.

Chloe waves her tiny hand at the small plastic chair sitting in front of the equally small plastic table. "Uh, I don't think so, kid."

She looks back and forth, her eyes darting between me and the chair. "Okay, you sit on the floor. We're having a tea party!"

She hands me the small toy cup and pours the invisible tea into it. Here I am, sitting cross-legged on a pink fluffy rug and drinking invisible tea with my daughter. But for some reason, it's exactly where I want to be.

CHAPTER TWENTY-ONE

Jules

The bar was complete chaos. Between three people calling off and the cooks being down to one person, it was a challenge. But we made it, and I was able to finally escape. Hoping that Zach did okay with Chloe was on my mind all night.

I set my keys down on the entryway table and look around at the empty living area. I walk a few more steps to Chloe's room. But I don't think anything could prepare me for this. A wave of heaviness sits on my chest, but it's anything but negative. There Chloe is, her small body sprawled across Zach's broad, much larger chest. He has his right hand resting on her back while they sleep, both spread out on the floor. So peaceful, so quiet. The warmness in my heart is unexplainable.

A chuckle escapes me when I notice Zach is wearing one of Chloe's princess necklaces. He startles awake and glances down at Chloe before moving. He sees me in the doorway, nodding his head in acknowledgment. He positions himself upright—Chloe still a bundle of dead weight on top of him—before transitioning her from his chest into his arms. He then gently places her in the bed, moving the covers over and around her. He takes a second before he leans in and kisses her forehead, princess necklace dangling and all.

My ovaries just exploded. Zach was irresistible before. But Zach as a daddy... *Dear God.*

My feet are still planted to the floor when he approaches me. After a gentle closing of her door, he yawns. "Didn't realize what time it was." When he runs a hand over the slight facial hair along his chin, his bicep flexes.

I look down at the necklace, trying to stifle another laugh. "That is the cutest thing I have ever seen. I didn't know you liked the color pink."

He takes the costume jewelry up and over his head, placing it down on the entryway table. "Ha, yeah, well, I couldn't say no."

"She has that effect on people."

"Yeah, she does." We share a moment before Zach heads toward the door. "Well, I guess I'll go then."

Don't go. "Um, did you want to stay for a drink?"

He pauses with his hand resting on the doorknob. "A drink would be nice."

"Okay, great!" *A little too enthusiastic, Jules.*

After grabbing a cold beer from the fridge, I pop it open before handing it to him. It's like I'm watching in slow motion, as his throat bobs and the liquid slides down. I run my tongue over my lips, feeling my cheeks getting warm. I step away and pour myself a small glass of wine. To fill the silence, I turn on "Surrender" by Natalie Taylor, making sure it's low enough so as to not wake Chloe.

With the soft sounds of the song in the background, Zach has his eyes set on me. "She's pretty great. Just like her mom." Sadness fills his eyes. I know he still feels guilty. Guilty because of what happened and why he left.

"Thanks, she is pretty amazing." When I go to sit on the sofa, I gesture for Zach to do the same. With a head nod, he sits down next to me, our knees touching.

"Oh, here." He pulls something out of his pocket. Taking my hand in his, he uncurls my fingers and places what looks like a necklace into my palm. My heart thumps a little harder. "Chloe said I should give it to you. Well, again." He shifts in place.

I swallow back a rush of emotions. "You wrapped it in a lunch bag. I thought it was adorable." He lets out a sexy, deep but quick laugh. "I haven't worn it in a long time."

"Well, maybe if I wasn't such an asshole, you would have kept wearing it."

My eyebrows twitch.

"I mean, you're not wrong. But the past is the past and if you're going to be here for Chloe, then we need to move on, right?" I smile. But my mind shifts to Garrett. "I miss him so much, Zach." Looking at the necklace, I then close my eyes. "I wish time could go back, so that I could stop myself from running out of that gym." I fist my hands, sagging my head in defeat.

"Hey." Zach tilts my chin up. His warm touch is welcoming. "It's not your fault. Do you understand me? Blaming you... what I said to you... it's not fucking true. I was a dumb kid, I was a coward and shit, Jules, I still am. I never tried to reach out because I knew you hated me or... at least, I thought it was too late. I didn't think there would be anything left to salvage."

Don't cry. Don't cry.

"Like I said, it's in the past. So, we move on, for Chloe's sake. We can try to get back to being friends, if that's okay?" Friends, I have to laugh inside. Or die. At least, that's what saying those words feel like. Sure, we were best friends. But I fell in love with mine. How am I supposed to just be friends with this man? The man sitting across from me, the father of my child. The same man who, all about half an hour ago, was wearing costume jewelry and playing tea party. The gorgeous, raw, powerful man who drips testosterone. Friends? Sure.

"Sure, friends." He clears his throat. "Since we agree to move on, how about I help you put that back on. If you want..." I turn in place, so my back is now facing him. My hair is already up in a bun so I don't have to move it. But heat shoots through me as soon as his touch hits my neck. Using his fingertips, he takes the tiny strand that must have fallen and slowly, extra slowly, brushes it off to the side. I quietly suck in a breath, closing my eyes. He swings his hands around, letting the necklace drop on my chest, then he clamps it from behind. His fingertips brush from my neck down my back, and my body goes stiff as a board. I turn my head slightly to get a peek from the side. He edges forward, but then stops himself. "I should go." The deep, husky whisper of his voice sends chills through me.

Before he reaches the door, I quickly ask him, "What happened after that night?" Rising from the couch, I hug myself protectively. "I mean, where did you disappear to. Zach, what happened to you?" Waiting for him to answer, I watch as he slides his hands inside the pockets of his athletic, slim, charcoal-colored jeans. His black tee stretches across his muscled back, which I can still picture in my mind even with his leather vest concealing it.

"I was in a really bad place." He turns to face me. "I did shit I'm not proud of. Got into some stuff that was hard to break free of. I'm not making excuses but... Garrett and you were my everything, so after that... After losing him, I just didn't know what to do. I felt lost. But the club took me in. Saved my life in a sense."

"You all sound like one big family." I smile.

"We are. They're the only family I have. That is, before I found out about Chloe." I nod my head, but I still feel pain for him. "And you, Jules. You are both my family." A wave of emotions hits me. I press my tongue to the roof of my mouth, in order to stop any form of tears from showing up.

His hand grips the doorknob. Just before he walks out, I take a step forward. "I have Sundays and Mondays off. I know, I own the bar, but I still like to work and do my part. Anyway, you can see her those days. Together or separate."

His eyes soften. "Together would be good. I'd like that."

"Perfect. And of course, you can call or text anytime you want to see her." My voice starts to crack.

"Thanks, Jules. I'll see you around then. Oh, and lock your damn door." With that, he walks out, closing it behind him. I can't help but laugh as I go to throw the deadbolt on. I lay my forehead on the door, clenching my necklace in my fist and holding onto it for dear life. For the first time, in so long, I cry happy tears.

★★★

Charger

Pulling up to the club after leaving Jules's place, I feel a sense of relief. Like something was lifted off my shoulders. I haven't felt this way in a long-ass time. Spending those few

C.M. Danks

hours with Chloe was incredible. Though it hurts in a way, because I wish I was a part of her life from the beginning. But I'll take it—finally having that closure with Jules.

Damn, friends. That's not something I want between us. I guess a part of me will always want more. But I have to take what I can get, considering. But damn it, if touching her didn't feel right... My body awakens like a beast when I feel her. Or whenever she's around. Christ, I'm a horny teenager all over again.

There's a loud commotion coming from inside the club, breaking me out of my trance. I jog the rest of the way up and see Tank, Chain, and one of the club hang-arounds. The girl looks upset, holding an ice pack to the right side of her face. Maggie has her arms around her shoulders in a comforting way. Chain looks pissed.

"What's going on?" I shuffle in and look at our Pres questioningly. But his look doesn't need words. I have a clue as to what happened.

I now recognize that it's Kitty who is sitting at one of the tables. "I was just walking out to my car when some fucker grabbed me. I fought him off. Thank God for my four-inch pumps. Kicked the prick right in his balls," she snickers. "No one touches me, not unless I fucking ask for it." Uneasiness settles over all of us.

"All right, dear, let's go get you something to drink and switch out the ice pack. Let the guys talk." Kitty nods slowly and walks to the back with Mags. Chain looks around before speaking up.

"It might have been one of Scorpion's guys. Kitty said she saw *Prospect* on his cut. Fucker's sending guys to snatch our girls. He's sending us a goddamn message." The vein on Chain's forehead pulsates. There's no stopping him when he gets like this, no reasoning with him, but I can't say I blame him. I'm right there with him.

"All right, so let's go pay those bastards a little visit." Tank towers over everyone as he starts to head for the door. His black combat boots dip over his jeans, with his man jewelry clunking together as his massive arms sway at his sides.

"Stop. No one is going anywhere." Chain grinds his teeth to his own words.

"Boss, c'mon, we know it's them. Let's go teach them a fucking lesson." Tank is visibly angry, his hands moving at a mile a minute.

"As much as I would love to ride down and rip havoc on their club, we can't just go in and start a war."

"Start a war? They already started one. Chain, they tried to snatch one of our girls. As either a message or maybe worse." Chain's eyes bore into Tank, sending him a warning look. "Sorry, fine. You're right." The big guy is usually all fun and games, but right now our jokester is anything but laughs.

"Everyone, breathe and relax. We come at this smart. Got it?" Tank and I nod in agreement, followed by Bullet and Throttle, then Hush. Bullet, our Vice, shakes his head. "They don't know who the fuck they're messin' with."

No, they don't. Because if they were to come after Jules or Chloe... if they were to even think about it... well, *regret* isn't a strong enough word for what they'd feel when I hunted them down.

C.M. Danks

Chapter Twenty-Two

Jules

Chloe's with my parents. So today, today is a me day. A day I take a long, hot bath, chill the hell out by listening to music, and try to come down from my high that is Zach. Everything seems okay. Our daughter now has her father in her life. Things are going well at the moment. Though, I'm trying desperately to ignore the leftover feelings I still have for Zach. I have to try to pry the vision I have of him out of me, from his gorgeous face, down to his amazing ass. If this "friends" thing is ever going to work, then I can't look at him like I want to straddle and ride him home. Good thing he's the only man to ever make my lady parts sing *hallelujah*. Sure, sex with Venom was good at the beginning, but there were no feelings there. And before Venom, this one guy who Lucy set me up with, well, what a dud he was. He made Venom look like a five-star winner.

So, needless to say, I never really dated too much or slept around. There's not much time for that when you're raising a child on your own, even with the help from my parents.

Just as I'm about to start the bath, a knock on the door has me groaning with annoyance. Zipping my hoodie up to

CHARGER

conceal the fact I have nothing underneath, I stomp to the door.

Tugging my leggings up at the waist, I swing the door open and find myself in a full jaw-drop moment. On the other side is a gorgeous badass woman, who is standing with her hip cocked to the side like I've kept her waiting for hours. Her long, wavy, blonde locks are hung over her super cute leather jacket. Correction, *cute* would be the word if I wore it. Hot is more her vibe. On the corner of the jacket, there's a patch that reads: *Angel*. Her tight skinny jeans are tucked inside her heeled boots. She looks like she just stepped off a super hero set. I find myself a tad jealous. Considering I'm standing here with no makeup on and a hoodie, I'm more like the extra in the background.

"So, you're the girl who has my boy all worked up."

Her boy?

"I'm sorry, what?"

She struts inside with her curvy hips and whips around with a hair flip. She's taller than me and it's not just because of her heels.

"Are you part of Charger's club?"

"Sorry, I'm Angel." She winks. "Yup, I'm a member of the Steel Valley Chains. And I came to steal you away for the day. We're going shopping."

I try to wrap my mind around what is happening right now. "Wait, hold on, back up. You seem nice and like super cool. But I don't know you." *Super cool?* I laugh at myself. She would have been the popular "I don't give a fuck what people think about me" girl in school. I would have been the one to watch in the back, wishing I had her confidence.

"Girl, that's why we're going shopping. To bond and shit. Also, Charger sent me." He sent her to hang out with me… Why? She struts around, taking everything in. "It's a cute place. I like it. And you're adorable. I see why Charger has his balls all wound up."

I can't help but wonder if they had a thing. It sounds like they had a thing. She's gorgeous. He's gorgeous. So I wouldn't be surprised. Jealousy hits me hard. I feel about as small as dirt, even with her compliment.

"Um, thank you."

"Okay, so go change and then we'll leave, because if Charger knows I let you leave with that on, he'll flip his shit."

Standing there still stunned, I literally don't get why this woman is in my house right now, or why I have to go shopping with her. "I'm sorry… You seem cool, but why am I going shopping with you?"

"Club party tomorrow night and you're coming."

"I have to bartend at my bar tomorrow night. I can't go to a party."

"It's already taken care of. One of our girls is taking your place." What is happening right now? "Okay, so I'll be downstairs."

Before I can argue over who the hell is taking my place tomorrow night, she's gone. Did that just happen?

I give up, shimmy into a pair of jeans, and put a damn bra on. I hustle outside, where Angel is waiting in her shiny black Camaro with the windows down.

"Holy… this is yours?"

She laughs while cranking the stereo volume up. The song "Hurricane" by I Prevail is playing. "Yeah, girl, he's my pride and joy." I want to ask how in the world she can afford something like this, but it's probably better not to ask. It would be rude. "Get in."

CHARGER

As I slide into the seat, I happen to notice that scary biker friend of Zach's is leaning against his bike behind Angel. He throws his cigarette on the ground, then swings onto his bike before starting it up.

"Why is the scary dude following us?"

She nudges her sunglasses back down from in her hair, looking in the rearview. "Who, Hush? He's not scary, just quiet." She throws the car in drive and we take off. I lay my head back, laughing. The music is blaring and this car is sick. My adrenaline is on fire with excitement.

"So why exactly is he following us?"

She glances at me. "Don't tell him I told you, but your man has a person on you at all times. Got some weird stuff going down and he just wants to make sure you're safe.

"One, he's not my guy. And two, what kind of weird stuff?"

"Nothing you need to worry about."

Hate to tell her, but I do need to worry if it's something dangerous that can hurt my daughter. We pull up in front of the boutique. It looks expensive and definitely out of my price range. "You know, I could just wear something I have."

"Girl, please. Charger is paying. Take full advantage." I really don't need him to do me any favors. She looks at the scary biker dude. "Hush, we shouldn't be too long." Angel winks at him as he pulls out another cigarette before leaning on his bike. "Unless, of course, you would like to join us?" Angel blows him a kiss, but he ignores it. "Quiet, but hot as fuck."

I giggle to that. She's not wrong.

Angel heads straight for the shoes. "Yes! Look at these. These are hot and would be perfect." She holds them out in front of her. They're black bootie pumps with buckles. They are sexy and cute. "Now we need to find you a hot little tight black dress. Charger will lose his mind."

"I'm not trying to impress him, Angel. We just started being friends again."

"Yeah, sure... Oh! Yes, this is hot as hell." She ignores my comment and flocks over to the short black dress on the mannequin. "You're trying this on." I catch it as she takes one from the rack, shoving it to me. "Your body is killer and this would look amazing on you!"

I hold it out in front of me. "Um, where's the rest of it?" She laughs. "No, seriously, I can't wear something like this."

"Yes, you can. And you're getting those shoes too."

I stare at the hanger for a couple of seconds before giving up. "Dear Lord. All right, I'll go and try it on." I laugh. I mean, the dress is sexy.

Thirty minutes and some wallet damage later, we're sitting at a small café by the boutique. Hush is seated at a table by his bike. "You know, I try to convince these guys I can handle myself, but they insist that because I'm a *woman*, I need a tail too." Angel takes a sip of her mimosa.

"You definitely look like you can handle yourself." I snort. "Thanks for this. This is fun. I don't get out much. Having a business and kid doesn't allow for much outside fun."

"No problem. I like you. You're definitely my kind of peeps." She takes another sip of mimosa. "So, Charger's got a kid, huh? Who would have thought?"

"Yeah." I let out a small laugh. I don't know why, but I really want to ask Angel if she and Zach were ever a thing. She's so beautiful and confident in herself. I can't help but

CHARGER

feel a tad envious. I'll just go for it. "So, you and Charger ever...?"

She practically chokes on her drink. "Oh, *no*. No, we haven't. I would never get involved with one of the guys. They're all like my brothers. Except maybe for Hush over there." She laughs. "Nah, not even him, sadly." Relief rushes over me in one giant wave. There's no way I could compete with her. "And you say there's nothing going on with you two? What happened between you guys? Just say if I'm overstepping."

I fiddle with my hands. "No, you're not overstepping. We have a past. He, and my brother and I, we were all best friends. After my brother passed away..." I swallow back the sadness. It never gets any easier. "He kind of disappeared."

"Sorry to hear about your brother. Sucks, that's for sure. You and Charger were obviously an item?"

"Yeah, we were. I fell in love with him. But when he left without a trace, it destroyed me and I was already pretty much shattered."

"Shit, yeah, I get it, girl. Here's to hoping you two work out your demons, because he's a good guy and you seem legit. We've all done stupid things we aren't proud of." Guilt showers her face. "Not to mention, you two have that kid together." I chuckle. "Here's to working shit out, and hot men." When Angel raises her glass, I follow suit and we clink our drinks together.

"Yes, and don't forget new friendships," I say with a smile.

"Hear, hear, sister."

We each take a sip, smiling.

C.M. Danks

★★★

After Angel drops me off, I decide to text Zach. I have to thank him for buying me an outfit, not really understanding why he did it in the first place. Although, my guess is that he feels like he owes me. But he doesn't owe me anything. I'm just happy to have him back in my life and now Chloe's.

Me: *Hey, even though I wish you didn't, I appreciate the day out with Angel. I like her.*

I set my phone down, waiting for a response. My heart starts to race like I'm in high school again and waiting for my crush to answer.

Zach: *You deserve a hell of a lot more, but it's a start.*
Me: *You don't have to buy me things, Zach. By the way, why did you invite me to this party at your club?*
Zach: *Because I want you there. I want you to see what kind of family I have here and what kind of family Chloe will have too. Plus, maybe I just want to see you. I've been away from you for too damn long.*

I smile at his last text and thank all the stars in the sky that I found him again.

Admittedly, I'm a little worried about some random person taking my shift tomorrow, but also excited to go to the party and see Zach. I feel like I can trust these people he's involved with. So, I guess I'll hold onto that feeling.

CHARGER

★★★

Charger

I watch her as I straddle my bike in her parking lot. The shadowed silhouette darkens the window shade with every movement she makes. She doesn't know that I come by every night to scope things out. After what happened back at the club, I'm not taking any chances.

She's probably working tonight. But I want to take her away from it all and wrap her in a goddamn bubble. But I'm proud as shit of her. And she's not that type of woman.

I do fight the urge to go tearing up into her place and rip her goddamn clothes off. Hell, I want to do a lot more than that. My dirty fucking mind has been consumed by thoughts of her every fucking day and night. I want to make her scream my name, over and over again. It's a thrill I can get used to. But fuck, I just got her back in my life and if *friends* is something that we're going to have to be, then so fucking be it. Sure, I'll be her best friend again. But I don't think it's going to be in the way she thinks. Because honestly, keeping my damn hands off her is going to be a big fucking challenge.

C.M. Danks

Chapter Twenty-Three

Charger

The club is full of brothers, hang-arounds, and whoever else decided to drop by. As club members, we host these parties a lot. It's a way to have fun, cook up some good-ass food, and just give back to the community. The money we receive at these parties is donated to local charities. Despite what people may think of us, we're not the bad guys, at least not all of us.

The Skulls MC, they're a different story. They're scraping the bottom of the barrel when it comes to our patience. It all started when Scorpion took over. He wasn't always their President. No, that happened recently. Not that they were saints before, but now, now they really are fucking scum. Their old President was decent enough to at least keep his distance. Back then, they didn't mess with us and we didn't mess with them. Sometimes I wonder why we all can't just get the fuck along. We share the same turf, but that doesn't mean we have to be enemies. We can make our own rules. Who gives a fuck?

"Man, oh man, did you smell that barbeque out there?" Tank leans back in his stool, stretching his oversized legs out to the side. "Can't wait to dig into... that." Following Tank's line of sight, I see why he faltered. In walks Jules. My dick twitches at the appearance of her—her long, dark locks flowing over her shoulders with strands falling between her tits. My eyes travel along her body, over her hourglass shape, then down her long, toned legs. She has the tightest, shortest little black number on. Why the fuck is she wearing something like that here? I have to readjust myself in my seat, because my jeans suddenly feel a bit tighter. Just the view of her might get me off right here.

Julianna Taccarelli is the most beautiful woman I've ever laid eyes on. There's no comparing her. No one could ever match up. I'm not the only one to notice either. Every guy in the room has their eyes fixated on her, making me want to break all their fucking necks.

Jules looks around then smiles after spotting me. It's that same sweet, sexy smile she always has. She struts over, hips swaying with each step. Hips that are wider, sexier, and more woman than before.

Tank claps me on the back. "How's that *just being friends* thing working out?" He smirks and I shake my head.

A prospect steps out in front of her, his body blocking her from me. That asshole. I see red, my ears burning and my insides fuming.

"I don't know yet. I'll get back to you on that." I finish off my beer in one big swig, slam it down, and head over to remove this ass-twat from Jules. When I make it over to him, I tower behind the dumbass, watching as he feeds her some bullshit lines. Jules's eyes slowly rise and widen at the sight of me. What? Like she's surprised I would be here? Doesn't she know by now? She's mine.

C.M. Danks

I take a fist full of his leather, pulling him back and lifting him so the tops of his shoes scrape the ground. "You got five seconds to get lost, prospect." After I release him, he scurries to the side and out of my reach, like a scared little puppy.

"Shit, sorry, Charger. I didn't know she was yours or I wouldn't have tried anything. My bad." He runs away so fast, almost falling face-first on that ugly mug of his. *My Jules.* That does have a happy ring to it. But unfortunately, I don't have a claim or hold on her, which means every asshole here thinks she's up for grabs.

I pull my glare away from him, taking her all in. Now that she's closer, she's more beautiful than I thought. How is that possible?

Even with her heels, she still only comes to my chin. The scent of dessert fills our space. She smells like a damn cupcake. Her eyes shine and her lips are plump with a gloss that makes me want to run my tongue across it, giving her a little taste.

"You look…" I swallow, trying to get the words out. "Gorgeous. But it is just a barbeque. You didn't have to wear something quite so, um, quite so revealing." My eyes scan her again. *Fucking hell.*

"Yeah, well. I'm going to blame Angel for this one. Apparently, she left out the small detail of what kind of party it was and basically picked this dress out." She fidgets with her hands. "I feel kind of stupid."

I look over to Angel. She winks at me with a little wave. She also mouths, *"You're welcome,"* like I'm supposed to appreciate Jules in something like this. I told her to take her shopping, to make sure she buys nice things, not a fucking dress like she's going to a club. Now I'll be fending off every cocksucker in here all night.

CHARGER

I inch closer, placing my hand on her waist. She's so small compared to me. So delicate, like a flower. I want to wrap her up and make sure nothing happens to her. *Ever.* "Don't feel stupid. You look beautiful. Just don't leave my side." When I brush her cheek with my thumb, her mouth parts. I force myself to step back, taking her hand and leading her to the bar where Tank is openly gawking.

"Close your fucking mouth, brother."

He grins. "Hey, Jules, don't you look breathtaking tonight." He leans in, giving her a kiss to the cheek.

"Thank you, Tank. But if I would have known... I would have just worn jeans."

"No way! You look hot." Angel slides into our circle, handing Jules a shot. "Here, this will loosen you up a bit." Jules takes it without hesitation, knocking it back in one quick motion.

"Thanks, I needed that. But I'm still pissed. Just not *as* pissed." She nudges Angel with her elbow.

"I got you, girl." Angel turns to Tank. "So, you gonna sing tonight or what, big guy?"

"You sing?" Jules asks with curiosity.

My gaze falls on Jules's lips as she wipes the remaining liquor from them. *Fuck.*

"On occasion, mostly covers. Some country, mainly rock." He grunts. "But, I'm kind of rusty, so..."

Angel slaps his chest. "Nah, you're fine. We need some entertainment to liven up the place. Now, grab your guitar and go make the ladies swoon."

"When did you get so bossy?"

"I've always been bossy. You just haven't had the pleasure of sampling a taste." She flicks her hair and Tank shakes his head. That's Angel, our spitfire.

C.M. Danks

"Jesus, woman." Tank claps his hands together. "Well, guess I'll go suit up, upon the request of Angel over here."

"You'll thank me later, when you have two girls in bed with you tonight." We all laugh. Both Angel and Tank walk away.

Tequila slides a drink over to Jules, and to me a beer. We stand at the bar. I hesitate, only for a second, before placing my hand at the small of her back. There's no denying the fact that she moves in closer to me, letting me soak in that sweet scent of hers. I know she likes it when I touch her by the way her body reacts.

"Thanks for inviting me. I don't get out much and it feels good to have some fun. Not that having Chloe isn't fun. It's just... sometimes, it's good to get out." Her cheeks turn a rose color. She's blushing and it's cute as fuck.

"It's good to have you back in my life, Jules." We share a moment, her eyes filling with lust, sadness, appreciation. Everything. Too much. I deserve none of it.

"All right, folks, come and get her. Food's out back, keg's nice and full, and for the single folk, girls are hot and ready." Jules giggles at Chain's announcement. He walks over hand in hand with Mags. She clunks the floor with her high-heeled boots and chains. She's still got it. "Sweet baby Jesus. I see why our boy Charger here has a protective barrier around you." Chain lands a kiss on Jules's cheek. Why does everyone feel the need to do that? "I'm Chain, darlin'. President of this club. And you must be *the* Jules everyone's talking about. Why are you dressed like you're going to the club, sweetheart?"

Maggie cuts in. "Don't ask a woman that kind of question. You're going to make her uncomfortable. Besides, I think she looks absolutely stunning."

CHARGER

"I mean, me too. I was just asking."

"There's kind of a story, to why I'm dressed like I'm hitting up a strip joint. But we'll just say I was tricked by a friend into wearing this thing." She smiles at them and Mags chuckles.

"Well, you look pretty as a button." Mags glances over at me and grins. "All right, old man, let's go mingle and say hello to our guests."

"Old man? Who you calling old, woman?"

"Yeah, yeah, I'm sorry. I forgot you still act like you're in your twenties." They walk away and I'm left alone with Jules once again.

"Wow, they seem perfect together." She nods at the end of the bar. "Why is he always so quiet and alone?" I look over to Hush, and I have to wonder that myself. He's sitting there, nursing his whiskey and watching the crowd. No one knows much about him. I guess that's our fault, for not asking. But I can almost guarantee he wouldn't tell us anyway.

"I know someone like that at my bar—name's Joe. He's kind of like a second father to me. He's been coming to the bar since I opened it. No family. It's sad in a way." She must be referring to the guy who looks like he wants to beat my ass every time I walk in.

"Maybe he's got this sick thing for you."

She practically chokes on her drink. "No, no way, not Joe."

"Just saying, we think with our dicks."

She cocks her head to the side. "Oh, really, that so?"

Shit.

"I mean, yeah, but..." I'm saved from having to explain that one.

C.M. Danks

Tank gets on stage, clearing his throat. The music overhead stops playing and everyone focuses their attention on him. "As some of you might know, I like to sing and play some guitar from time to time. And tonight, our own Miss Spitfire, Angel, told me I needed to get back up here and show off my manly skills." The crowd laughs. "So, here we go. Hope you all enjoy."

Tank messes with some buttons. Jules leans in and whispers, "You know, you guys are like the worst bikers ever." She laughs. I smirk.

"Oh yeah, and why do you say that?"

"Because I've never been around a biker club with folks as nice as yours—you know, the kind that throws benefit parties and has acoustic guitar playing members."

"We ain't your typical biker club, babe." *Hang on...* "And what do you mean you've never been around one as nice as ours?" I lean in closer and Jules's friendly expression drops. She swallows nervously, like she knows she just let something slip. Maybe this has something to do with whoever Chloe was talking about. Her eyes tell me she's keeping something from me.

"I just meant..."

Tank starts playing and Jules avoids the question completely. That's the second time she has me nervous over what she means. Tank is strumming to a song we all recognize immediately. "Wherever You Will Go" by The Calling. Jules squeals in her seat. "I love this song, and holy crap, Tank is good! She turns to me. "Hey, Charger... will you dance with me?" Her big, brown eyes stare up at me and I smile down at her. I try to ignore the sting of her calling me Charger instead of Zach, even though that's exactly what I had asked of her when we're around the guys.

"Sure, pretty girl. I'll dance with you." I will? I don't fucking dance. Maybe I did in high school.

She hops off her stool, but stumbles. I catch her around her waist, holding her to me. The gentle touch of her hands on my chest sends lava coursing through my veins.

"Thanks," she whispers.

She plays with my shirt with her fingertips. I gently take her hand, walking us to the middle of the club floor. I have a feeling I'll get shit from the guys for this later. My hand wraps around her waist keeping a small distance between us, but she steps in closer, slowly raking her hands up my chest until she rests them on my shoulders.

She rises on the tips of her toes to whisper into my ear. "Hold me closer, Zach."

She stares into my eyes. That's when I wrap my hands fully around her waist, gently tugging her flush against my chest. She relaxes into me, laying her head above my thumping heart. Then she wraps both arms around my neck.

"This reminds me of our prom."

My chest goes heavy and I can feel my t-shirt getting wet. Lifting her chin with my hand, I wipe her tears away.

"Don't cry, pretty girl. You don't ever deserve to cry, got it?" Her breathing picks up as her eyes burn into me. Smiling, she lays her head back down. We stay like this, swaying to our past and welcoming the future.

C.M. Danks

★★★

Jules

I never wanted to leave Zach's arms. They were warm, safe, familiar. I wanted to stay in his arms forever. But Tank stopped singing and Zach broke apart from me. He smelled so good. Why do men always have that minty cedar smell? It's such a panty-soaking scent.

A couple of hours and a few too many drinks in, I feel like I'm inside one of those funnels in a fun house. The ones that turn in rotation. I'm sitting at the bar with Angel but I can't even remember what we were talking about.

"Girl, you okay? Please don't hurl."

"I'm fine. No need to worry about me. I am totally fine." I wave my hand, almost unintentionally smacking her in the face.

"Right. You stay here and I'll be right back."

I shoo her off with a laugh, more like a hiccup. "Tequila, can I please have another drink." I drag out the word *please* longer than intended.

"Sorry, Jules. But I think it's my job to cut you off right about now."

Now I get why my customers are so annoyed when I tell them the same thing. "I totally understand." I laugh, attempting to put my elbow on the bar but missing. My stomach flops, preparing me for the shameful fall. But a strong arm catches me around the front of my waist.

"Okay, babe. I think it's time we call it a night." With Zach's arm bracing the front of me, I lose the ability to think,

CHARGER

to speak. He's so beautiful it hurts—the way his blue eyes are shining under the strands of his hair. All those tattoos on his arms are like a work of art. No one can be this beautiful. "Let's go, babe." He scoops me up by hooking one arm under my knees with the other on my back. I move my arms around his shoulders and neck, melting into him. He carries me through the crowd as I watch him intently, studying his handsome features as we trek all the way to his room. *Wait, room?* He sets me down, then closes the door behind us. "Chloe's staying at your parents, right?"

I nod wordlessly. I'm in his room. Where his bed is. I. Am. In. His. Room. "Um, Zach, is this where you live?" He stands by the door, peering at me with features shadowed by so little light—the only illumination radiating from the lamp on his bedside table.

"I never really needed a place of my own. Living above the bar kind of suits me."

"Guess we both have something in common, huh?" I laugh.

"Guess so." He rubs the back of his neck. "You can crash on the bed, unless you want me to take you home, but I'll be honest… I'm not completely sober either."

"No, no. It's fine. But where are you sleeping?" He points over to the chair in the opposite corner. "Zach, please, that doesn't look comfortable. I'll sleep there. I'm smaller anyway." He walks into the bathroom, strolling back out with a cup of water and two pills, which I assume are Aspirin. Our arms touch as he passes by before snatching a pillow off his bed and laying it on the chair.

"It'll be fine. Go ahead and get comfortable." Zach takes his leather off, placing it on the dresser. He then grabs the hem of his black t-shirt and pulls it over himself, throwing it on the floor. I swallow. His tattoos are so seductive, along with that damn nipple piercing. Even his abs are provocative, with the small rays of light shining on them. I can't pry my feet off the floor, and I sure as hell can't take my eyes off him. I'm standing here like an idiot while he unbuttons his jeans and runs the zipper down.

"Zach, wait. What are you doing?"

He pauses. "Sorry, babe, but I can't sleep in anything but my boxers. Is that going to be a problem? It's nothing you haven't seen before."

He's right, but I haven't seen this raw, powerful twenty-five-year-old in boxers. Just the eighteen-year-old boy from next door.

"N-no, no problem at all." I roll my eyes back, breathing out. He tugs off his jeans and, good God... His thighs are pure muscle and his ass looks like he squats his motorcycle. Okay, alcohol talking. Chill out, girl.

He sits down in the chair (which he makes look like dollhouse furniture), crossing his arms over his chest with one ankle over the other and his eyes closed. I set my shoes off to the side, then burrow into his bed sheets. They smell like him. I bring the fabric to my nose, inhaling and breathing him in. The scent is comforting. But something is missing. Oh yeah, *him.* I glance over, to check if his eyes are still closed. They are. I slowly, quietly, leave his bed. Stumbling a bit, I don't stop until I'm directly in front of him.

"Zach," I whisper and his eyes fly open. I'm still wearing my dress. Finding the zipper behind my back, I begin pulling it down.

"Jules, what are you doing?"

CHARGER

"I'm sorry, but I can't sleep in this." I smirk, and his throat bobs up and down. I finish unzipping my dress, and shimmy as I tug it down over my hips. Hips that are slightly wider after being pregnant. I step out of the pooled material and toss it away. Zach's eyes widen with lust. I know that look because I've seen it before. The unsteadiness of his chest, the way it rises and falls... I know he wants this. The burning desire written all over him is telling me as much.

"Jules, I-I don't think..."

"Shh." I place a finger to his lips. "Don't think, Zach. Let's just be in this moment *together*." I close the distance between us and climb onto his lap, straddling him in my lace panties and strapless bra, which might as well be nothing.

"Fuck, Jules." I can feel his thickness growing harder underneath me. He moans in pleasure when I start to rub myself on him. He lays his head back, closing his eyes. "Jesus Christ." I trace my fingers around his pierced nipple, then run them along his chest and down his steel abs. His hands close around my hips and I kiss his neck. "Fuck," he drags out breathlessly. He wants this, and so do I. At least I believe he does. But he stops me by holding onto my waist. "Jules, stop, you're drunk."

"So? It doesn't matter. I want this, Zach. I've never been more sure." I nibble at his ear, feeling his calloused hands trail down my back before stopping at the latch of my bra. "Take it off, please." He searches my eyes while fumbling with the clasp; he starts to unhook it but hesitates.

"Jules, I think we should stop."

Pain and disappointment hit me hard. I lean back to really look at him. He's serious. "You don't want me?"

He huffs out a breath. "You think I don't want you, are you kidding me? You're sitting on my *hard* dick, practically naked, fucking beautiful, and you think it's because I don't want you?"

"Then what is it? You really only want to be friends and nothing else?" He doesn't say anything. Nothing, he just looks at me. *Oh my God.* The tears start to burn in my eyes. Blinking, I try to stop them but one falls. I push off his chest and climb down, reaching for my dress and violently putting it back on. After redressing, I stomp to leave but he grabs my wrist, jerking me back to his body.

"I want you. Just not like this." He takes my face in both of his hands. "Get back in bed, Jules." I tilt my head forward, wanting to bury myself in his chest, but I give up.

"Fine." Climbing back into his sheets, I hope he'll change his mind and nestle in with me, hold me close, but he doesn't.

CHARGER

CHAPTER TWENTY-FOUR

Jules

I wake up to the smell of bacon and coffee. The sun is shining through Zach's blinds. I move just a little, but it's enough to remind me of the heavy amount of alcohol I drank last night. The massive pounding going on inside my head feels like someone hit me with a sledge hammer.

I look to the chair where Zach had slept last night, but he's not there. Slowly swinging my legs over to the side of the bed, I take the Aspirin he left out last night. There's also a t-shirt and a pair of sweatpants neatly folded beside me. Assuming his clothes are for me, I do my thing in the bathroom and get dressed.

I hear a lot of commotion downstairs. As I enter the kitchen area, people are grabbing plates and scooping up the breakfast food that surrounds the tables. Zach spots me and meets me at the door.

"Did you sleep okay?"

"Yeah, I think so. Although my head feels like it's going to explode. I should probably get going." I try to avoid Zach's eyes, and the humiliation of what went down last night. God, could I have thrown myself at him any more? I'm such an idiot.

"Eat first, then I'll take you home."

"Good morning, grab yourself a plate before it's all gone, honey." Maggie walks over to me, taking my shoulders in her hands and guiding me to the plates. "Eat, and then later Charger will take you and that daughter of yours to the street carnival."

"Street carnival?"

"Yes, we have a booth there every year. Kind of like a bake sale." Maggie smiles.

"She's got the best fucking muffins on this planet," Tank shouts from the table, his mouth full.

"Manners, young man," Mags scolds him.

"Oh, but it's so true." Angel walks over, snatching an apple from Tank's plate.

I look at Angel questioningly. "Are you even human? You drank just as much as I did. How are you so functional?"

"Oh, I'm just used to it." She shrugs.

Functional and still beautiful hungover… *Must be nice.* "You guys sure do a lot of charity events."

"Well, we want to let people know we aren't as scary as they think we are. Plus, we like doing them." Maggie smiles, swiping a piece of her brown hair back behind her ear. Her cute pixie bob makes her stellar cheek bones pop. Her skin is equally as amazing. I hope when I'm older I look that good.

"That seems fair. Really, thank you for the invite and for last night, but I need to get going. I have to pick up Chloe and…"

"Nope, I won't take no for an answer."

CHARGER

"It's true. You might as well give in." Zach shrugs and before I know it, I'm eating Maggie's homecooked bacon and eggs.

★★★

I open my door and there's Zach. His hair is tousled, his jeans are hugging his thighs, and his leather is draped over his white t-shirt, which of course always looks good on him. To be honest, I still feel embarrassed about last night. Being rejected by Zach kind of sucks. I wanted to hide out today, but seeing that it was a fair, Chloe would be excited to go, and this gave Zach more time to spend with her.

"Hey." His voice is deep.

"Hey." I grab my hair, tossing it in a pony as he walks inside. Zach watches me as if tying my hair up is the most seductive thing. But the way he looks at me makes my nipples perk up.

"About last night…"

"Let's just forget it, please." I stop him, basically to save myself from more humiliation. There's no hole for me to crawl inside, so let's not.

Chloe comes running out from her bedroom. "Charger!" Zach crouches down to Chloe's height, catching her in his arms.

"What's up, kid? You ready to go eat cotton candy until your teeth fall out?" They both laugh together. "I was just kidding. Your mom wouldn't be too happy with me."

She pats his arm. "Can I call you Daddy instead?"

He looks at me, then back to Chloe with a smile. "Sure, kid. I would love that."

"Yay!"

C.M. Danks

He taps her on the nose, then glances up at me.

"Ready?" I nod my head yes and we all head downstairs.

I catch a glimpse of Zach's bike parked off to the side. This is actually the first time I'm seeing it in the daylight. I have to do a double take, stopping dead in my tracks. I recognize something. While Zach carries Chloe ahead of us, I walk closer to get a better look. The detail is so familiar. And now I know why. It's my drawing.

"I had your drawing hand-painted on as soon as I was able to afford it. The guy who painted it was actually worried about messing it up, since yours was so good."

I'm stunned, and that's just touching the surface of how I am feeling.

Gently running the tips of my fingers on its surface, I take in the exceptional detail. The lion looks so real. I'd hate to brag but it looks just like my sketch. Its eyes are fierce, watching, protecting.

"I can't believe you did this."

"I told you I would."

"Yeah, but, how did you... when did you?"

Chloe sings from the back seat of my car and Zach shrugs.

"I came back eventually. My mother, before she skipped town and relapsed, gave me the box with your sketch in it."

I smile, biting my lip. "You want to know why I chose a lion?" I move closer to him. "Because lions protect. You were always my protector, Zach."

He tugs me into him and instantly, I melt. His strong arms circle around me all while I breathe him in. "I will always protect you, Jules. You and Chloe both, got it?"

"Mommy! Daddy!"

He pulls me away slightly. "Will I ever get used to that?"

CHARGER

"No," I whisper to him with a smile. "Come on, *Dad*." He takes my palm and we walk hand in hand to the car.

★★★

Everyone is already here when we arrive. Mags is with Angel at the booth. Tank and Throttle are hanging out on the side, with a small circle of women ogling them up. I can't say I blame them. The guys all look like they stepped off the *hot and sexy* train.

Chloe tugs at my jeans. "Mommy, I want to ride the Ferris wheel."

"Okay, honey. One sec." All three of us walk over to the booth. Tank is the first to introduce himself.

"What's up, squirt?" He kneels down and Chloe gives a big tug to his hair.

"You have long hair like mine. Can I braid it?" Everyone laughs.

Tank pretends like he's thinking. "Sure thing, squirt. But no pink hair ties. Not my color, deal?" She nods her head violently and giggles. We introduce Chloe to everyone around the booth. Each member spends a couple of minutes with her, telling her how pretty she is and how they like her outfit. It's comforting, knowing how different it is with them versus the Skulls. The club never hurt Chloe, neither did Venom, but the vibe was different. Maggie has that motherly touch, even if she is dripping in leather and chains. I look over at Zach, who's watching me. He knows when I lose myself in thought. He knows me better than anyone. I know it's going to come up eventually. I just want to avoid the subject of Venom for as long as I can. Or even better, maybe he won't find out.

"Hey, pretty girl. You good?" Zach rubs my arm with a smile.

"Yeah, of course."

"Can we go on the Ferris wheel now?" Chloe begs. Zach scoops her up in a cradle.

"I bet you'd rather go on the scrambler. Now that..." He taps her nose. "Sounds like more fun."

Chloe gives him a questionable look. "Daddy, are you scared of the Ferris wheel?"

I try to hold in a laugh. "Yeah, Zach, are you scared?"

"Me, scared? Fu... I mean, heck no, I'm not scared."

The guy takes our tickets and we climb into the bucket seat of the Ferris wheel. Zach stiffens immediately, grabbing onto the sides. Chloe and I share a look, then smile.

"So, you're scared of heights? How come I never knew this?" His biceps bulge with each grasp. The ride starts and Zach takes a deep breath in.

"Guess we never went on a Ferris wheel together. For good reason, I might add. We weren't meant to be in the air. That's the reason for gravity." He chokes out the words as he swallows.

I laugh, and Chloe giggles before taunting Zach, "Ooo, look how high up we are!"

"Yeah, kid, I'd rather not."

Chloe climbs over and sits down next to him, rocking the car along the way. "Just breathe, Daddy. In and out." She pats his shoulder.

"Big bad biker is afraid of heights," I joke but Chloe scolds me.

"Mommy, that's not nice."

CHARGER

Zach smirks and so do I. "You are so right. That was not nice at all." I place a hand on my chest playfully and smile.

After the second go around, he relaxes a bit. He picks Chloe up by her waist and sets her on his lap. Without moving toward the edge, he points to the ground, people, and buildings. He whispers something and then he tickles her. I have waited so long for these moments. To see her with him. To have him in our lives again. So long, that it doesn't seem real, but I'm thrilled. If only her uncle could be here… could share moments like these… He would have loved Chloe. To watch her grow up. It breaks my heart every day, not having Garrett around, not just for me, but for everyone. I will never stop missing him.

The ride stops at the bottom. With Chloe still in Zach's arms, we walk in the direction of the booth, pausing at the cotton candy stand along the way. Chloe twirls a bit in her fingers and Zach takes a chunk out in one big bite. This tattooed man that I used to know so long ago is holding our child like he's spent her whole life knowing her. It's absolutely amazing.

The line at the booth is long—mostly women, each one flirting like school girls when they approach Tank and Throttle. It's amusing to watch. If Zach were standing there, he would definitely be drawing in his own admirers and adding to the crowd of flirtatious women.

The sound of motorcycle engines rumbling fills the background and Zach and I look in that direction. The bikes roar in and park, before two big men walk our way. My heart drops when I see who they are. They swagger in our direction, with the crowd parting like the Red Sea. As they pass, glares are shot their way. They look meaner, scarier, and just overall like pure evil in comparison to The Chains. My stomach is doing summersaults.

I go to grab Chloe out of protective instinct, but Zach has already handed her over to Mags. Maggie guides Chloe away and Zach comes back over to me. "Go with Mags, Jules." Before I can escape, I am trapped by the chains of their boots and the crunching of the stones beneath their heels. The line for the booth disappears as if the crowd is too scared to stick around. Tank and Throttle step up next to us. Zach is already in front of me, shielding nearly my whole body.

"Well, shit. Look at all you wonderful Samaritans doin' your good deeds for the day. You think that'll get you outta the pits of hell, fellas?"

"I don't know, man, but maybe save us a seat, just in case?" Tank crosses his muscled arms over his chest. The President of the Skulls, Scorpion, laughs then pulls out a cigarette. I don't want to, but I take a quick glance over at Venom. He doesn't pay any attention to me yet, but there's no way to avoid this. My heartbeat picks up, and I feel like such a coward behind Zach.

"What the fuck you guys doing here?" Zach's voice is low, gruff, and demanding.

"Just wanted to see for ourselves what kind of business our comrades were doing on *our* turf."

"That's right, *our* turf. Both of our clubs run this territory. And let's get one thing straight, we aren't your fucking comrades."

Scorpion doesn't answer, but takes a puff and exhales, sending the smoke swirling into the air.

"You know, if you boys wanted a taste of Mags's delicious desserts, all you had to do was ask." Angel cocks her hip to the right and blows them both an air kiss from the booth.

"Shit, I want more than those treats, maybe some of you." Venom scrapes his tongue along his lips.

"You wish, pretty boy." Angel snorts.

"Look, we don't give a shit why you came here." Zach takes a step closer to Scorpion, leaving me exposed. That's when Venom notices me. "Just get the fuck out of here."

Venom has me in a staring match, his eyebrows burrowed in. He looks between Zach and me. "Jules…?" he says my name with a question. Zach looks at me as if the earth just fell. He darts his eyes between us.

"You two know each other?" Zach's voice is impatient. Shocked. Angry. Everyone watches silently, including Scorpion, who appears the most amused.

After the shock wears off, Venom smirks. "Oh yeah, we know each other. Isn't that right, Jules?" Everything is muffled, as if I am inside a tunnel or under water. My ears burn and my breathing kicks into overdrive.

"What the fuck is he talking about?" Zach's furious.

I should probably start talking, maybe. "Venom and I…"

"We fucked, that's what we did. For almost a year straight." *Oh my God*. I could not be any more mortified than I am right now. "So, how does it feel to share a pussy, Charger?" Zach ignores him, but his fists clench at his sides, his chest expanding. "It was nice and tight, that is until I jammed my cock into her a few times. Thing stretched out like fucking fabric."

"Fuck," Tank blurts out.

Zach lunges forward at Venom in one quick step, but Tank, with the help of Throttle, wraps his large arms around him, holding Zach back before he can make it. It's like holding back a charging bull. The muscles in his arms and neck are violently trying to break free. Then there's me, unable to speak a damn word since they arrived. But that comment pissed me off. I take in a deep breath and exhale, calming myself before I walk straight to Venom. I don't know where I found the courage, but I cock back my arm and land probably the most girlie punch, straight to his face. He doesn't even move, but his head whips to the side and his lip starts bleeding. *Well, shit, if I'm not proud.* Zach stops trying to break free, and the guys stare in disbelief.

"Don't you *ever* talk about me like that again. And actually, Charger had me first, so technically, you shared *his* pussy." I turn on my heels in one swift motion and walk straight for the booth with a fucking smile on my face. I hear a deep laugh, which I think comes from Tank, and another from Scorpion. I can't believe I did that. But I'm sure happy I did.

Charger

Did that just happen? I watch as Jules walks away after just having punched Venom in his face. I have never been prouder of her than I am right now. I let the leftover anger slip slowly out of my body. Because I wanted to pound his face into the ground myself and if it wasn't for Tank or Throttle, I would have.

CHARGER

"My Vice here can't seem to keep his dick in his pants." Scorpion throws the cigarette to the ground and grinds it with his boot.

"Fuck, she's got a mean right hook. I like them feisty. Turns me on even more." Venom grins.

This fucking asshole.

My anger builds again. Tank grabs the back of my cut. "Lemme go, Tank, now," I growl, the blood rushing to my ears.

"Nope, no can do. Not here."

I look around. We already have a small crowd forming. I turn back to Venom. "You're lucky we are where we are, because I would have fucking killed you by now."

"Sounds like a threat to me, huh, boss?"

Scorpion shrugs. "That it does. Well, gentlemen, it's been fun. Oh, one last thing before we take off. Meet up at Copper Ridge, tomorrow night. We'll give you the details. Two shiny red Mustangs have our names on them. Could sell um for a whole lot of cash."

"You can shove those Mustangs up your asses because we aren't dealing with you." Tank spits at Scorpion's feet. "Also, you guys come near our club or girls again, and it's going to take a lot more than two guys to hold *me* back. And considering you also pissed off my friend here for touching his girl, I'd say you'd be royally fucked because we might not hold him back next time."

"Ha, tell your President to be there." He and Venom walk back to their rides, Venom giving Jules one last look before their both gone.

"Fuckers. You good, man?"

My heart's still pounding, my fists are still balled together, and I've never wanted to spill blood more than I do right now. I look at Tank and Throttle, then to Jules, who is hugging herself at the booth and talking with Angel.

"Yeah, I'm good. Just time to have a chat with my woman."

Both Tank and Throttle laugh, then turn serious. "You know that ain't good, her in bed with the Skulls." Throttle doesn't want to test me right now, and the look I give him lets him know that. "Sorry, just sayin'."

The thought of her and Venom leaves a bad fucking taste in my mouth. It makes me want to murder that fucker. His hands, his dick, touched *my* Jules. Fuck that.

CHAPTER TWENTY-FIVE

Charger

Mags took Chloe with her after the fundraiser so I could have a nice little chat with Jules. It was a long way back to her place and neither one of us tried speaking to the other. I am fuming right now, knowing someone else, someone like Venom, had touched her. The fury inside me is ripping through my veins and clawing its way to the surface.

We get inside and I slam the door behind me. Jules jumps where she stands, with her back to me. She doesn't have to be scared of me. I would never hurt her and she knows that. But the anger inside me needs to be released.

"So, you fucked Venom?" I could have started with something else.

She slowly turns around, her skin glistening against the sun and the leftover moisture from the heat. My dick twitches, like it always fucking does. I look over at her, then up her legs to her daisy duke shorts, and I am powerless.

"For your information, it was a lot more than that. We didn't just *fuck*; we had a relationship."

"Oh, oh good. Yeah, that makes me feel better. *Thanks*." Hearing her tell me they had only fucked each other would have been better.

C.M. Danks

She shakes her head. "Unbelievable. So, let me get this straight. You expected me to what, exactly? Wait for you? Wait, while you were God only knows where. Not have sex with any other men until you came back. Which, by the way…. were you even going to come back? Because the whole seeing you again at my bar was clearly coincidental."

I don't know if I was going to come back, so I can't answer her. I wanted to see her again, and maybe I would have tracked her down and found her one day.

"How could you have had something with that bastard. Venom? Seriously, Jules? What the fuck could you have seen in him? Did he sweep you off your feet like those books you used to read, huh? Because I'm sorry… I'm having a hard time believing he was your Prince fucking Charming."

"Well, for one, he was here!" she yells. I already know she's pissed at me. But I don't care.

"Was that before or after he stuck his dick into another woman, right after fucking you? Because I can promise you, Jules, that's what he did."

Her mouth drops open. "Nice, real nice, Zach. I think you should just go. We're done here."

"Fuck that. I'm not leaving. And you can't possibly think he was loyal to you." I move closer to her. She turns her head to avoid my eyes.

"No, you're right." She drops her arms in defeat. "He was cheating on me. That's why I dumped him. That, and the fact that his club gave me the creeps. I wasn't around them much, but when I was, something didn't settle right. I didn't like them."

"He was around Chloe. Jules tell me he didn't hurt…"

"No! No, he didn't. I would never let him hurt her. He was fine with her." She sighs. "You're the one who rejected me last night, so I'm not sure why you're so upset over me being with someone else."

"I told you why I did what I did last night. You were drunk, Jules. I wasn't gonna fuck my high school girlfriend and the mother of my daughter for the first time in years while she was intoxicated."

"I wasn't even that drunk. Whatever, let's just drop this conversation. I'm tired, I probably need to ice my hand, and I'm just sick of talking about him."

"Let me see."

"What?" She looks at me, confused.

"Your hand, let me see it."

She holds it out and I take it in mine, turning it over to see her already bruising knuckles. "First time punching someone?" I rub the tips of my fingers over the top of her hand and she winces.

"Yeah, how could you tell?" she chuckles sarcastically.

"Well, for one, you never close your fist with your thumb on the outside. You can break something. Secondly, you always throw your body into the punch, not your arm."

"Well, I guess I'll remember that for next time."

Over my dead body will she have to punch someone. *Again*. She shouldn't have been punching anyone in the first place. "Not that I wasn't proud of you back there, but this won't be happening again, Jules. I'll fight every battle you'll ever have. I promise you that. And to be honest, the thought of him with you, touching you." I sigh, then connect eyes. "It makes me want to rip his damn throat out."

"I'm sorry." She tucks a fallen strand of hair behind her ear. "For just… more bullshit. I guess, ugh, I don't know. Everything is just too much." If she cries, I swear on my life…

"Let's go sit down." I guide her to the sofa, sit her down, and go grab a bag of green beans from her freezer. I gently place it on her hand.

"I punch people now, apparently, so that's cool."

I smirk. "You know, green beans are gross. I also remember when you did this for me in your bedroom, except it wasn't with frozen vegetables."

She laughs, which makes my damn heart beat faster. "Your daughter hates them too."

"Well, she's smart."

"She asks about him all the time you know. About Garrett. It breaks my heart."

I force a smile. "He would have been a great uncle." Fuck, there they are, the tears. "Come here." Setting the bag down, I tug her closer. I then scoot her to my chest, wrap my arms around her, and hold on for dear life.

"It doesn't ever get easier, does it?"

"I don't think so, babe, but we do get stronger. We learn to live with the pain and how to cope."

"Want to know why I called my bar the Fallen Star?" Her voice comes out as a muffle against my chest.

"I might have an idea."

She pulls away from me. "My star, the one you held so high for me, was anything but hanging in the sky anymore. My spirit was broken, losing both of you. So, it felt right, calling it that." It tears me up inside, knowing I was part of the reason. I'll never fully be able to forgive myself.

My phone vibrates in my pocket. "Fuck, sorry." I check it and it's a text from Chain. "Shit, I have to go. I'm sorry, Jules."

"No, it's fine. I have to get ready for work anyway."

"Maybe I'll swing by tonight?"

CHARGER

She smiles, then I'm out the door and onto my bike within five minutes. When Chain sends a "be here asap" text, you better be there asap.

I make my way inside the club and head upstairs, because I already know Church is taking place. The smell of smoke fills my nostrils as soon as the door opens. Everyone looks at me. Chain gives me a silent "we need to talk" look.

"Your girl is sleeping with the enemy." It wasn't a question; Chain makes that clear.

"*Was* sleeping with the enemy." Saying that out loud makes me twitch. "She's not anymore. There's a difference."

Bullet clears his throat next to me. "If I might add, how do we know she wasn't hired as a rat, feeding their club shit about us? You never know… They might want to take us out."

I crack my neck, giving him one mean-ass glare. "Wanna say that to me again, fucker?"

Bullet jumps from his chair and I do the same.

"Hey! Sit the fuck down, Jesus Christ." Chain growls from the head of the table. Bullet and I have our stare down, my fists ready to pop him in that smug face of his. "Now!" Chain slams his fist down on the table and it shakes the whole damn thing.

I do as I am told, like a good little boy, but I do it in a pissed off manner. "May *I* add something." I give Bullet a once over. Then turn back to Chain. "In case you dumb fucks forgot, I just recently reconnected with Jules. Therefore, she didn't know who I was or that I'm involved with a motorcycle club. But if she did, she still wouldn't have been a rat, as you called her, which by the fucking way, no one is to talk about her like that again."

C.M. Danks

Bullet surrenders with a hand raised and Chain comments, "Yeah, yeah. We get it. No one was trying to offend your Ol' Lady here, just trying to get to the bottom of shit." Chain said *Ol' Lady* like it was decided. "All right, so Scorpion and his clan of snakes want us to meet up tomorrow night to do some GTA'ing with them. Sounds like a blast, but I'll be honest, I'd rather be home fucking my Ol' Lady. So, I'll take a pass." Sarcasm drips from his lips. It's never a dull moment. "I do want two men there, in hiding, to stake out the place. Get some info on what exactly it is they're doing, because I have a feeling it's not your plain old *Gone in 60 Seconds* shit." He lights a cigar. "Hush and Charger, you're on it."

"Can't, boss. I got the pit tomorrow night."

He grumbles. "Okay then, Tank, Hush, and Bullet." Hush does a silent head nod from the back. "And Tank, you keep that hotheaded shit at bay, got me?"

"Who, me?" Tank laughs, waiting for people to join in but no one follows suit. What Chain really means is no going ape shit and tearing up the meeting. When it comes to Tank, well, dude's got a short fuse just waiting to blow. His laughter disappears. "Yeah, got it."

When Church is over, I change and head to the gym to get a quick workout in before riding over to see Jules at the bar.

CHARGER

CHAPTER TWENTY-SIX

Jules

Despite the drama that went down today with the Skulls and Venom, I have a sense of relief. Having Zach finally know about him, and not having to worry about stepping on any toes, makes me breathe a little easier. I smile to myself like a weirdo and Joe looks at me strangely.

"I'm glad to see you smiling, honey."

"Thanks, Joe, I'm feeling pretty good tonight." I sway my hips to the song playing, "Fire Up the Night" by New Medicine, as requested by Lucy. She loves her music. I do too. He shakes his head, laughs, and drinks his beer. Lucy comes over and shakes her hips while grabbing the tray of drinks. She's so petite she gets lost in the crowd. One of my bartenders comes alongside me. I tie the full trash bag, tugging it free of the can. "I'll be back. I'm taking the trash out." She nods and I head for the side door.

I inhale the summer night air, whipping the bag over the open dumpster. But my newfound happiness is about to end.

Before I can turn around, a rough hand grabs the back of my neck and walks me against the building. First confusion, then panic sets in, bringing me back to reality. My cheek feels like it's getting violently scraped along the hard, uneven brick. No matter how much I want to scream, I can't choke out the words. The air feels like it's kicked out of me.

"So, you're fucking him, huh, Jules?" He spins me around to face him. A surge of terror enters my body, shooting down my spine.

"G-Get off of me, Venom," I manage to choke out, but his hand still holds the front of my throat. "You're hurting me."

He quickly releases his hold, giving the air a chance to return to my lungs. His focus lands on the scrape across my cheek, staring with sadness and regret. If I didn't know better, it looked like he showed a hint of remorse.

His breath brushes against my face as he leans in. "Answer my question. Are. You. Fucking. Him?" I try to move around him, but he's too strong and his body is smashed against mine, making it nearly impossible.

The tears let loose, falling down my cheeks, and the darkness in his eyes lighten.

"He's Chloe's father. I don't owe you an explanation, but he's Chloe's fucking father!" More tears fall as I yell, though I doubt anyone can hear me with the music.

A roar of a motorcycle engine sounds nearby, then it stops. I'm hoping it's not more of his buddies.

"I told you that you're mine, Jules. Remember that?" he sneers at me.

"I am not yours. Now get away from me." I push at his chest. Surprisingly he stumbles back and right into Zach, who then grips Venom by his vest before looking over at me, while I am still rubbing my (probably) bruising throat. Zach's eyes turn menacing; there's an underlying darkness like nothing I have ever seen before.

CHARGER

"Did you fucking touch her?" Venom smirks as Zach brings the son of a bitch up to his face. "You're fucking dead." Zach releases him before cocking a fist back and into his jaw. Venom plummets to the ground.

Why does it look like he's not even trying to defend himself at this point? My money is all on Zach, but it's not like Venom to go down so easily, so why is he not fighting back? Zach throws himself on top of the prone figure, launching punch after punch.

"Zach! Zach, stop!" I pull him back with all the strength I have, but it's like trying to move a wall. "Stop!" He pauses midair before landing just one more blow. "Just stop. Come on." I tug at him and at last, he gets up, standing just above Venom, who is left bloodied and bruised on the ground. He lies there another second before he climbs to his feet, spits out blood, and wipes his face with the back of his hand.

"I ever see you near her again, and I swear on my life… I will kill you." Zach's chest puffs in and out as he points at the battered biker. He doesn't take his eyes off Venom until the creep starts walking back to his own bike.

He turns around, giving us parting words. "You just signed your death warrant, asshole." He laughs and takes off. I'm no genius when it comes to biker lingo, but that wasn't exactly code; the word death certificate was pretty obvious.

"Zach, what did he mean…"

He charges for me and takes my face in his hands, avoiding the open cut. "He hurt you," he whispers, tenderly rubbing his thumb over my neck, in a soothing and comforting way. "I'm going to kill him. I'm going to fucking kill him. And you can't stop me next time, Jules."

I shake my head. "No, no, stop. I'm okay."

C.M. Danks

He runs his hands down both of my arms, stops at my waist, and pulls me to him. My wrists are pressed against his chest and I'm engulfed in his massive embrace.

"You're mine, Jules. Do you understand that? You've always been mine. Every day, for the past six years, you were *still* mine." I pull away, each of us staring at the other like nothing else exists right now. He grips my ass with both hands and lifts me up. I wrap my legs around him, and his lips crash to mine. They feel like home. His lips, his arms, it all feels like home. He walks me backwards until I'm against the uneven wall. His tongue teases mine, reminding me how he tastes. Mint and oranges, that's what he tastes like. Like fucking citrus.

He pulls away, breathing heavily, then slowly starts kissing my neck. I moan from the pleasure soaring through me. My lady bits are screaming for him. "Fuck, I've missed you so fucking much. Your taste, your smell, your body." His breath tickles my ear and he holds me with such strength.

The back door of the bar swings open. "Oh, shit, sorry." We both look at Lucy, who is standing there like a deer in headlights. "Ignore me. I'm not here. Well, I am here but you know what I mean. Just seeing where you went off to and well, I see why, so I'm just going to shut up and walk back inside now." She turns around. "One more thing, we got the bar covered. I don't want to see you for the rest of the night." She winks before closing the door. We turn back to each other, our faces so close and the hot air of his breath on my cheek.

"Chloe staying at your parents?" I nod, my mouth parting. "Good." He walks us off the wall and upstairs to my place. He sets me down, only so I can get the key out of my pocket. As soon as we're inside, he kicks the door shut with his boot and has me against the wall in seconds. He lifts my shirt from the hem, and I raise my arms as he pulls it off. He takes in my breasts, his eyes roaming all over my body. But he's not making me feel insecure; no, he's making me feel like the sexiest woman on the planet.

He closes the gap between us, grabs my face with his hands and crashes his mouth to mine again. I need his hands on me. I want to feel them everywhere.

It's like he can read my mind, because he glides his palms from my hips up, until they're over my breasts.

In one quick motion, I'm spun around, facing the wall with my hands planted to it. His arms are on either side of me, caging me in. He kisses my back and I let out a soft moan. Then he grips a fist full of my hair and gently tugs it toward him until I hit his chest. His breath tickles my ear.

"You're mine. Everything about you is mine." His voice is soft, yet raspy.

He can say it all he wants, because I fully enjoy the way it sounds. He reaches around to unhook the button of my jeans and the ache between my thighs intensifies. He tugs them off my hips and rips my lace thong in the process. His muscled forearm comes around my stomach, holding me to him.

Still holding me, he slides his finger down to my slit and I squeeze my hand around his arm, digging my nails in. "You're fucking soaked." His whisper is soft, so seductive. He lingers around my slit before sliding inside. My head falls back and his other hand moves up, gently forming around my throat. It's completely different from when Venom had his hand around me. Zach's touch is not the same; it's sexy, possessive, letting me know he's in control.

C.M. Danks

I'm his. But there's no sign of anger, or hate. Just lust and heated, passionate aggression. I need more than this inside me. I need him.

"Zach, I need you, all of you," I moan to him. Begging. He pulls his hand away from me, and I hear the ruffled sound of his jeans being removed. He runs a hand seductively down my back, forcing me to bend so I am now almost parallel to the floor. My palms still planted to the wall in front of me, he yanks me toward him so that his length is resting right on my aching, needing, wet clit. I move to gain friction between us. God, it's been so long... What is it like to have Zachary Scott inside me after all these years?

"Let me grab a condom, babe."

"No, no, you don't have to. I'm covered."

That is all the validation he needs. He slowly slides his dick into me and it sets me on fire. I cry out, my head tilting from such pleasure. I could self-combust right here. He gives another small push and he's fully inside me. Jesus, he feels like perfection. After the twinge of pain is gone, my body reacts, needing more.

"Fuck, Jules. You're still so tight." His hands grip my hips. Mine curl into balls on the wall in front of me, searching for something to grab hold of. He drives me forward and back, and I crash into his pelvis with each erotic shove. The sensation picks up with each hard, fast thrust. I scream out his name, not giving a shit if anyone hears me. Let them hear me. Let them hear me cry for him. I've been crying over him for years, so now that I have him, let the world know. He grabs my hair but he still doesn't slow down. It feels amazing. He's fucking me like he's claiming me. I want him to claim me. Possess me like I'm his forever.

CHARGER

My body unfolds, releasing a burst of pleasure. Zach growls with a deep moan. Stars cloud my vision, as every nerve ending tingles throughout my insides. I come down from my high as Zach pulls out of me. Resting my forehead on my arm against the wall, I attempt to catch my breath. He relaxes his arms on either side of me. My jeans are still resting at the bottom of my ankles and so are his. My hair is a tousled mess but I've never felt hotter, sexier. His breathing is heavy from behind me, with his warm breath on my neck.

"You okay?" The heat from his chest hits my back like fire.

"Yes, I'm fine. More than fine actually."

His warmth is gone as he pulls his clothing back on. I'm about to do the same but he stops me. His hand gently rests on mine. With extreme intensity, we exchange looks. "Don't. I want you in that bed with nothing on."

I nod in compliance as he stalks off to the bathroom.

We each take turns doing our thing, cleaning up. When I walk in the bedroom, I take him in. All six-foot-something of him makes me look like a dollhouse toy. His arm is resting behind his head, muscles flexed, while the other is crossed over his stomach. He's lying there naked. My eyes travel everywhere on him. He's so beautiful.

I'm being drawn to him. I crawl into bed and straddle him. We stare deeply into each other's eyes, getting completely lost. He reaches up and strokes my cheek with his thumb. I can't help but lean into his touch. My hands rest on his solid chest. I lean down, flicking my tongue on his piercing. Then I stroke his ribbed ab muscles, exploring because I've missed out on touching him. Feeling him. Feeling his strength.

C.M. Danks

His hand moves behind my neck, pulling me down to him before connecting our mouths together, his soft lips locked with mine.

His hard, thick length is pressing on my bare clit, sending fire through me. I bite my lip from the pleasure. We don't say anything in this moment. We don't need to. He lifts me up by my hips with such ease, guiding all his glory into me. I start moving on him. *In slow, measured motions.* He grabs hold of my breasts, one in each of his hands. Hands that are rough and calloused. But they feel good.

I tilt my head back, letting my body get lost in him. Lost in another moment.

CHARGER

CHAPTER TWENTY-SEVEN

Charger

Her beauty is indescribable and I'm completely mesmerized by her in every way possible. The way her tits feel in my hands, or every time I run my palms down her waist to her hips... Her skin is like silk and she smells like fucking dessert. I watch as she tilts her head and body back as she rides me. Her pussy feels so fucking good. Fuck, I missed this. I missed her.

"Zach, I'm gonna come."

That's right, babe, you come for me. Her moaning is enough to set me off and I release at the same time. "Fuck, babe."

After sharing such a powerful moment, she collapses on top of me, and I stroke her back. "Let's do that all the time."

"No argument here." I mean every bit of it. She rolls off me before laying her head to my chest. I pull her close, needing to hold her, to make sure she's safe. It's the greatest power I have. The only power I have. To keep her in my grasp, keep her away from danger, or at least to keep her safe from it. Her soft breaths have me thinking she's asleep until she reaches for my hand, taking it in hers.

"Do you ever think about high school?" she asks. We both stare up at the ceiling, intertwining our fingers together.

Was she serious? Of course, I do.

"Yeah, but it's always about you. There hasn't been a day since, where you weren't a thought in my mind, Jules."

"Same." She pauses. "You remember that time freshman year... when you and Garrett dumped the whole mac and cheese plate on Rory Evans just because he called me four eyes. He didn't even so much as glance at me after that. Actually, for the rest of high school."

"Yeah, I threatened to beat him up if he so much as coughed your way."

She rises to her elbows. "I knew it." She playfully smacks my chest then lies back down. "Of course, you did. You were always looking out for me."

She is right about that. Since the day I moved next door, I vowed to make it my mission. Jules was sweet, but feisty. And I knew that I had to look out for her. Hell, I *needed* to look out for her. There was something inside me, the possessiveness I held for her. I wanted to always be the one to save her. Keep her close. But in the end, I turned out to be the one to hurt her, the one to leave her broken.

"I was afraid to date anyone because of you two."

"Good, that was our plan." We both laugh.

"I did love watching you with Sam though; it was so fun seeing the boy you were in love with, with someone else." Her sarcasm makes me tense.

Little did she know... "It was equally as hard to be with someone, while being in love with someone else. And you, Jules, fucking owned my heart and soul." She gasps.

CHARGER

"I still have the cheesy card you gave me on my birthday, you know." I can hear the playfulness in her voice.

"Hey, it took me a long time to write that. Shit wasn't easy. It's hard describing how much you like someone in a tiny-ass card." I laugh while poking her shoulder.

"Well, I loved it. It was sweet." Her soft giggles are like a sunny day. "I wonder what ever happened to our little hellcat."

"Who knows? She probably married a sixty-year-old and had like ten babies." We both laugh in unison. It would most definitely not surprise me one bit. It sounded like something Sam would do.

"I still talk to Lisa from time to time. She's doing okay... from what I can tell. Sometimes, she'll call and I can sense that her spark's gone. But I guess we all lost a little spark in us." Her fingers graze my skin, making circles around my tattoos. "Are you ever going to tell me what happened to you, Zach?"

I wanted to leave my past in the past. Bury it. Burn it. Do whatever it was I could do to forget. But I owe it to her to tell her the truth. All of it.

With a sigh, I begin to tell her, "After that phone call from you, it was like someone flicked a switch. I can't explain it. Hearing those words, it did something to me. You have to remember, Jules. I had no one. My dad left us, my mom was a complete train wreck, and your brother was like *my* brother. He was the only one I considered a true friend at that fucking school. Besides you of course, but it's different... having a guy best friend versus... *you*. I wanted to wrap you up in my arms and shield you from everything. With Garrett, it was an unbreakable bond. We were brothers, not just friends." I stopped to see if she wanted me to keep going. I can feel her tears on my chest. When she doesn't say anything, I continue.

"Even though I knew I still had you, I was completely lost. I wanted, needed, to run somewhere, get away from every reminder of him. So, I skipped town, went and stayed with my uncle. I tossed my phone. Got into a bad crowd. We did some shit, bad shit, some drugs here and there. Acid, mostly weed. But I needed something to break me free. Make me forget. And one night when I was twenty-three, we went to this party. Shit got out of hand. I ended up on the side of the road. Didn't know where the fuck I was. Two bikers pulled up to see if I was okay. I don't remember much, but they took me in, got me sober, and here we are. I owe my life to them. I might be dead if they hadn't taken me in."

"Wow, Zach." Her soft sniffle breaks me. I hate seeing, hearing, her cry. Especially for me... She doesn't need to cry for me. I don't deserve it.

"Yeah, they are my family now. You, Chloe, the club. They are all I have, but I'm glad for it. For everything that happened. Made me a better fucking person. So, you see, babe, we ain't the bad guys. Our club's not like those fuckers at the Skulls. And I promise you... Venom ever puts his hands on you again, I will kill him. Don't get me wrong, when I say we aren't the bad guys, I mean it. However, we protect the people we care about and we will do what is necessary. Get me, Jules?"

"Have you ever... you know, killed someone?" The shakiness of her voice cuts me deep. I don't want her to be afraid of me, *or* my club.

CHARGER

"No, I haven't. But I've seen it. Been there for it. We witness some fucked up shit from time to time. But we protect this town, so we do what we have to do."

"What about the pit? Is that illegal?"

I hug her close, my arm pulling her into me. "You ask a lot of questions, woman." I sigh.

"I just want to know about your life. What it all means for us. For Chloe and me."

"There's going to be things I can't tell you. It's just club rules."

"I understand." A couple of seconds pass by. And I hope I didn't scare her with too much *all at once*. "So, um, any relationships? Ha, you know about mine. Venom was a total flop. Can't say I'm proud of that one."

The fact that he had his hands on her, his dick inside her, has me seeing red. But taking note of the marks on her neck starting to form makes me even more insane.

"Pretty girl, you don't want to hear about my relationships. There was nothing ever steady, but I will say that I've been with a lot of women." I feel her wince.

"I'm not surprised. You're even hotter now than you were in high school. I'm sure all the women here are throwing themselves at you."

I blush, like a fucking pussy. I cannot tell her how many women I've slept with. When you're single, without a fuck to give, you don't keep count. And there are women here willing to give you whatever you want. We never force them. We never, ever disrespect women. That being said, if they offer, we take it. But that's all it was for me. I never loved anyone, not since Jules. I probably would never love anyone after her either. I haven't even stuck my dick in another woman since we crossed paths again.

C.M. Danks

When I don't say anything, she changes the subject.

"You know what's funny? You breaking Tommy Stevenson's nose."

Even years later, I still hate that fucker. If I saw him out somewhere, I'd probably break his nose all over again.

"He put his hands on you. He's lucky that's all I fucking did." I laugh, but I'm fuming inside at the memory.

"Yeah, I shouldn't have gone to the party with him. I shouldn't have left the dance."

"Hey." I prop myself up, tilting her face to meet my eyes. "It's not your fault. Do you hear me? None of it was your fault, Jules. We can't change the past, and your brother wouldn't want you to keep beating yourself up about it." A silent tear falls from her eye.

"I know." Her saddened smile breaks me for the second time today. "I don't blame myself anymore. I really don't. I just miss him so much still."

"Me too. Me fucking too." It's true... what I wouldn't give to throw a football with him again, even though I hated the damn game. It was never me; that life wasn't meant for me. "I'm sorry you had to spend those years raising Chloe by yourself."

"I had help. My parents are amazing and really looked after us. Especially when I went to school. Got my bachelors in business."

"I'm fucking proud of you, you know that?" I lean in, giving her a kiss on her head.

"Zach, I still love you. I never stopped." We lie there in silence for what seems like forever before she finally falls asleep.

CHARGER

"I love you too," I whisper softly, knowing she doesn't hear me. My chest still damp from her leftover tears, I stroke her hair like she's a damn kitten. My kitten.

C.M. Danks

Chapter Twenty-Eight

Charger

The bell rings, with the song "Rise Above It" by I Prevail playing in the background. I stare back at my opponent; the smug look on his face makes me want to beat the piss out of him even more than I already do. He's got maybe twenty pounds on me. But it won't matter. I'll win, because I always win.

After getting my shit together, I needed something that would let me release my frustration or temptation, and this was it. I worked my ass off every day. I put on muscle. The gym was my therapy, my escape, and this was the added prize. The high from winning alone was more than what any drug could do.

I crack my neck back and forth, raising my taped fists in front of my face. I don't wear gloves, fuck that. If I pound in someone's face, I want to feel my knuckles hit flesh. Maybe I'm that fucked up, or maybe I just don't care.

He goes in for a low kick, but I saw that coming and I dodge it, hopping backwards in one step. Next, he goes for a high kick—saw that coming too. I grab him by the ankle, spinning him in the air and causing him to fall.

"Come on, fucker, that all you got?" I wink.

CHARGER

He gets up—*now he's pissed*. Yeah, that's right, asshole, get pissed. I want you to fuck up. The crowd in the background is loud, and they get more rowdy with each blow, which has my adrenaline pumping.

He gets impatient, coming at me with two fists. I lean my body to each side of the punch, dodging both. I smirk at him, going in for the jab. My fist collides with his cheek. He backs up and shakes it off. I can tell it makes him a little foggy.

Good.

Come on, buddy, I got all day. His fist connects with the side of my face and I laugh. My eyes water from the blow. That's right—I gave him one to make him tired. And he's looking a little gassed. I rotate my right arm and get back into position. All right, the fucker's mad. He barrels toward me, throwing punch after punch. I block every one, waiting for my moment to charge. He tires and stumbles back. *Here it is.*

I lunge forward in one fast motion. Grabbing him around the waist, I pick him up and slam him down onto the mat. I tower over him and the dude taps out before the ref even starts counting. Well, that was easy.

I wipe the already dried blood off my lip and hop down from the ring. The crowd parts with some hand claps of congratulations to my back. I wipe a towel down my face, attempting to take some of the sweat away. My eyes burn from the salt of my sweat. I sit down on the dingy locker room bench and check my messages. There's one from Chain.

Chain: *My office. Now.*

C.M. Danks

Fuck. The meeting with the Skulls is tonight. Tank, Hush, and Bullet must have found out something.

I throw on my sweats and a t-shirt and strut down the hallway. I make it to Chain's office in less than five minutes. I walk in and he gestures for me to shut the door. I sit and he hands me his phone, displaying an image sent from Bullet. The picture shows the Mustangs they must have stolen and next to them are two vans with no windows. My eyes dart from the phone to Chain. He knows what I'm thinking.

"That picture was taken from behind one of the empty abandoned buildings. I told the guys to hold back. Not to show their faces at the meeting. Which, I know Scorpion is just going to fucking love that. Missing one of his dinner dates again." He leans forward, his elbows on the desk. "But we all know what the fuck those vans are for." If there was any doubt that the Skulls were serious, this just confirmed it. They're going down this path, women trafficking. Fucking dirtbags are actually going to do this. Rage builds inside me. "Hey, snap out of that place. I need you here, focused." Chain points a finger down at his desk.

"Please tell me those vans were empty."

"Yeah, for now. These fuckers just started a war, a war they didn't know they were gonna lose." Chain's eyes hold darkness. These guys were fucked.

"What about the Feds?" I ask, but I already know the answer. We know some guys on the force that keep us in the loop. We have this agreement with them. We keep the peace, keep the town safe; we help each other out. They stay out of our way for the most part and in exchange, we help them too. This situation? It might be better if taken into our own hands.

CHARGER

"We'll keep tabs with them, but this is our war now." The rumble in Chain's voice has the hairs on the back of my neck standing straight up. "Tomorrow, it's time we pay them a long overdue visit. And I want a guy on our women, asap. That includes Angel."

I need to make sure someone is with Jules and Chloe at all times, whenever I can't be. I had a guy tailing her before, but that wasn't all the time. It needs to be all the time.

I get up to leave but Chain stops me. "Tomorrow, don't forget." He thinks I'll forget? Not likely.

"Oh, I'll be ready."

I head upstairs, shower, and take off for Jules's place.

★★★

When I get there, I head straight to the back, up the stairs and knock. The door opens with her gorgeousness staring straight at me, while she wears a smile that could turn me into the biggest pussy.

Her smile fades as soon as she sees my battered face. "What happened to you?" She reaches up, touching my battle wound. Her soft skin makes the pain go away instantly, as if she's my healer. Who was I kidding? She *is* my healer.

"The pit." I take her hand gently before kissing her knuckles, and we share a small moment.

"Daddy!" Chloe comes running at me and I immediately scoop her up in my arms.

"What's up, kid?"

"What happened to your face?"

"Uh, Daddy ran into a door."

C.M. Danks

"You're silly. Oh!" She wiggles, trying to get out of my hold, so I put her down. "I know how to fix your booboo." She runs off and Jules's parents step forward. I didn't even notice they were here. Her mom smiles warmly, but her dad gives me a glare. He looks the same, except his dark Italian hair is more silver at the ends, and the lines around his eyes are more defined. Seeing her dad hurts in a way. He was more of a father to me than my own. I definitely missed them both.

He takes a step, the air tense and heavy. You could hear a pin drop. I reach out, offering a handshake. "Mr. Taccarelli."

He glances down and his eyes burrow in. Maybe a handshake wasn't the best idea. He probably hates my guts for what I did to his daughter. He takes another step in and wraps a warm hug around me, just like Jules's mother had.

He claps me on the back. "Son." He does another clap. "Good to see you, boy." I catch Mrs. T's eyes and she smiles. It takes me a second, but I return the hug. I don't deserve their kindness, but I'll gladly take it. He breaks us apart, holding onto both my shoulders. "You look like you put on some muscle. You look good. Except for *that*." He points to the small swelling of my cheek, followed by the leftover cut.

"Yeah, about that..."

"Here, Daddy! Chloe holds a band-aid up to me, so I kneel down to take a look. It's a pink unicorn band-aid and, I'll be completely honest, it makes my heart melt. If she wants me to wear a pink unicorn band-aid, I'll fucking wear a pink unicorn band-aid.

"You know what? I think this is exactly what I need. Think the unicorn will heal it?" She bobs her head up and down. "Then how about you stick it on me." I point to the cut on my cheek. "Right here." She peels the wrapping away and plants the adhesive to my face with a giggle.

"It's perfect! You'll be healed in no time." She runs off to the dolls on the floor.

Here I am, with a pink unicorn band-aid, and I couldn't be fucking happier.

"It looks good on you, Zach." Jules lets out a laugh.

"Son, let's step outside. There're some things I'd like to talk to you about."

The talk. The talk that I can't get out of, even if I tried, which is fine. I get it. So, without argument or comment, I follow Mr. T outside. I mean, shit, if I was him, I'd like to know who the hell I was too, six years later.

We walk in silence for a few minutes; the only sounds are my boots and chains hitting the pavement. He stops, his hands in his pockets and sadness in his eyes. "Losing a child, a son, isn't easy. Every day is a constant battle. But we move on because we have to. Because we owe it to ourselves, and to Chloe, to be the best. We need to be. But I will tell you… watching Chloe grow up all these years without a father was another stab to the heart." I swallow; never have I been so close to crying in years. But I fight it back. There's no way I'm going to show weakness when her father is nothing but fucking strong right now. "Now, I will say this. We weren't one hundred percent in the right on this either. Could we have tried to contact you better? Sure, but I guess… I guess it needed to happen as fate intended. You two needed to find your way back to each other not by force, but by fate. And I think, for some years now, I was a believer in that."

"Look, sir, I never…"

He raises a hand. "I'm not finished." I nod in acknowledgment. "We want you to know that we didn't only lose one son that night; we lost two." *Fuck.* I didn't realize what I had put everyone through. I guess, in my own mind, I didn't think anyone would really miss me. I was wrong. Dead fucking wrong. "So, with all that said…" He clears his throat. "I don't know what you and Jules have going on, if there is anything going on, but I expect you to be the best damn father I know you can and will be. And as for that…" He points to my leather cut. "From what Jules tells us, sounds like your club isn't the bad guys. We watched Jules get hurt with that other club. Don't be dragging her into the same bullshit and putting them in danger."

"No sir, you have my word on that."

"Good." He sighs. "Let's get back in there before her mother thinks I buried you out here." We laugh and it's every bit sincere. He starts to walk ahead of me.

"Hey, Mr. T. Thanks for being a better father to me than my own for all those years."

He smirks. "You're a good kid, Zach. We all make mistakes from time to time. It's how we bounce back from them that makes us who we are."

He heads upstairs but I fall back, needing a minute for his words to sink in. Can I do this? Be this man everyone expects me to be. I have to. I don't know what's going on between Jules and me, but I do know I fucking love her. I never stopped.

★★★

"Zach, I'll be fine. I don't need someone here watching me twenty-four seven. It's not necessary." After her parents left with Chloe, I tell Jules (with as little detail as possible) why she needs someone to be here keeping eyes on her. Of course, she fights me on it. She's as stubborn as she always has been, thinking she can handle everything herself.

I hold her waist and back her up until she hits the wall. I claim her space, lean in and take in her scent. I watch as she flusters. Her mouth parts.

Wanting.

Needing.

She stares at me with such lust and desire; it's so fucking sexy. The tips of my fingers trace the bare skin on her arms and I grab the back of her neck, bringing her in close to my lips but not quite making the connection. My dick presses against her stomach, ready for her. The little moans she releases are going to make me come right here.

"If I can't be here, you will have someone watching you. It's not a question; it's going to fucking happen, get me?"

She bites her lip as she nods. Then she runs her tongue along her parted mouth. I press my chest and body into her. "Don't do that, pretty girl, because you're gonna make me drop you on this floor and taste that pussy right here." She grips the front of my shirt with her hands.

"I think I might just quit and sell my bar right now if that's a promise." The right side of her mouth turns up.

I huff out air as I laugh. Damn, she's sexy.

I back off, moving a strand of hair away from her face. "Get to work. I'll call you tomorrow." I kiss her cheek. Since when did I become so fucking soft?

"Zach, I, uh, I don't think I can be friends with benefits with you. Like if you want us to see other people or whatever, I won't be able to do it. It'll destroy me." The worry in her eyes tears right through me.

C.M. Danks

"Babe, I can assure you that whatever is going on, it isn't just friends with benefits. And as for seeing other people, I can promise you that won't happen. If another man so much as looks at you, let alone sticks his dick inside you, I'll kill him." I run the pad of my thumb to her chin and walk out. Friends with benefits? Seeing other people? Yeah, that's not fucking happening. Jules is *mine*.

CHARGER

CHAPTER TWENTY-NINE

Jules

I stare into space as I fiddle with the same shirt I've been trying to fold for ten minutes. So, Zach doesn't want to be friends with benefits. Thank God, the only thing is... now what? Obviously not being friends with benefits means we're together, right? And he did say he would basically put any guy into the ground if he touched me... But I need those words to be said out loud. I need the words "yes, we are together" and "yes, we are dating" in order for me to believe it. Call me old school, but it's how my brain operates.

"Fucking men." I whip the shirt clear across the room in frustration. It's not me being needy; no, I just like to have validation. My annoyance is carried over to the knock on my door. I swing it open, practically ripping it from its hinges.

"Woah, chick, who pissed in your Cheerios?" Angel and Tequila are standing with high-heeled pumps, leggings and black skinny jeans while dripping in leather. "Wait, lemme guess. Is it a certain man with dirty blond hair, killer blue eyes, and the type of body that makes you want to do bad things?" Tequila rolls her eyes and I cock my head to the side. "What? He might be your man, but I'm not blind."

My man.

C.M. Danks

She pushes past me with Tequila following close behind.

"Actually…" I want to plead the fifth, but maybe talking about it will help. "You're not wrong."

Tequila sits on the sofa while Angel sits on the armrest, her legs crossed.

"So, tell us why he's got your panties in a wad?"

"Yeah, call us like your therapeutic bitches." Tequila blows a kiss with her red painted lips and chocolate flowing hair.

I fidget with the zipper of my hoodie. "Promise me you two won't think I'm overthinking, or being dumb."

"Nope, we can't make that promise. Sorry." Angel shrugs. "We offer truth and honesty."

"Okay, fine. Zach and I kind of slept together."

I swear I hear the sound of crickets fill the room as Angel raises a brow. "Hang on… one, his name is Zach? Had no idea and two, what do you mean you *kind of* slept together? You did or you didn't."

"Okay, okay, we did… twice."

"Okay, so, what's the question?" Tequila twirls her hair.

"He doesn't want me to see anyone else or sleep with anyone else. But he never said anything about us being, you know, official. I just figured with Chloe and everything, he would be like: yeah, we're dating."

Angel and Tequila laugh at the same time. I feel my cheeks warm. "You guys, don't laugh. I'm serious."

"Sorry." Angel holds her hand up. "You are adorable. But just remember, sweetie, he's not the same boy that you knew back then. He's Charger, part of a biker club. He just found out he has a kid, all about thirty seconds ago. And the love of his life, the one who got away, is now back in it. Give the guy some time. It's a lot for him to process."

CHARGER

God, she was right. All of this was just thrown at him. I'm over here thinking-about whether or not we have a label stamped on us yet, when he just learned about Chloe. Not to mention, I'm back in his life too. Cool it, Jules.

"Yeah, I'm an idiot."

"No, sweetie, you're just in love." Angel winks and I can't help but smile. She's right... I am in love.

"Okay, ladies. How about we remedy this whole depressed vibe with some music, dancing, and drinks?" Tequila gets up and slaps her thigh. "*You*, get dressed. We're going out to a club tonight."

"Wait, I thought you all were going to talk to the Skulls tonight." I look over at Angel, who has a sour expression on her face.

"Sore subject," Tequila whispers.

"Damn right, it's a sore subject. Chain gave me the whole *no girls allowed* bullshit. I think he forgets I have a patch too, and I have just as much a right to be there as they all do."

"See, this is what happens when we get her started." Tequila rolls her eyes and I try to stifle a chuckle. Angel glares at us. "Bitch, I know. You have the right to go all Wonder Woman. Feel the power and all that jazz. But doesn't a dance club sound like so much more fun right now?"

Angel sighs. "Yeah, it does. Jules, go change into something hot."

I look down at my attire. I feel like Angel has impeccable timing when it comes to catching me in the worst outfits.

I fumble through my jeans in my closet, grabbing my black skinny pair. I pick the sexiest tank top I can find, which ends up being my black corset lined with lace. I pull my hair down from its bun, tousle it a bit and run the curling iron through it. I do the fastest makeup job ever and grab my heels. The same heels Angel talked me into getting before.

"Damn, girl, you are hot. Come on, the dance floor is awaiting." Angel leads us downstairs to her Camaro, which is parked in the lot. I crawl in the back while Tequila climbs in the front.

"So, are we planning on bringing the guy who's supposed to be protecting us?"

Angel looks in her rearview. "Oh, you mean the prospect who's tailing us? Yeah, no. In case you haven't noticed, I don't need some protective detail. Watch and learn, sweetie." Angel switches gears and I'm thrown against the back seat. I don't think I can grip the seat belt any more without it digging into my hand.

"What are you doing?"

"She's trying to lose him." Tequila laughs.

"Not trying. I did lose him."

I look back to see if she is right. There was no sign of the guy. She actually lost the prospect. I laugh out loud. "Wow, that was amazing."

"I've got skills." She winks.

After about twenty minutes of driving, we make it downtown to Club Beat. Angel pulls up to the valet, we all get out, and she hands the guy her keys. "Don't scratch him, babe." She runs her finger over the guy's chin and his mouth drops open. He looks to be about nineteen at best, and she probably just made the kid's night.

We walk inside and it's elbow-to-elbow people. "It's been a while since I've been to a club," I yell to them over the music. A while? *Try years.* I don't think I've been out since Chloe was born, unless you count the time at Zach's club's fundraiser party.

CHARGER

"Then we have to make it count," Tequila shouts back.

Angel points to the three empty spots at the bar. We head over, getting mauled by looks from men everywhere. I'll be the first to admit: *we draw attention*. Tequila and Angel are goddesses. They're both tall and long-legged, while their hair flows and hangs down their backs. Let's be honest, they both look like supermodels. Me? I would say I'm pretty, but next to them, I feel like the discounted cereal you get at the dollar store.

Angel leans over the bar, her breasts spilling over. I have no doubt the male bartender notices—in fact, he hasn't stopped noticing.

"What can I get you, darlin'?"

"Three shots to start and then three Sex on the Beaches." She gives him a flirtatious smile.

"Um, actually, I'll just have a water," I yell to him. After the last party, I think I'll stick to water for now.

"Okay, fine, make that two and a water. Thanks, handsome."

She's so good at being fun and seductive, like it's natural for her.

"You're really good at this flirting thing," I tell her.

She shrugs her shoulders. "They're called boobs. You got them. Men notice them." She laughs. But there's something behind her laughter, something almost fake. Her eyes hold some sort of pain or maybe fear. It's weird.

The bartender brings over the shots and drinks. The girls take the shots back in one swig and slam the glasses down.

"So, you and Venom, huh?" Angel catches me off guard with her sudden question. I was hoping that would never get brought up.

C.M. Danks

Tequila practically chokes on her drink. "Wait, what about you and Venom? What am I missing?"

"Nothing." They both look at me, knowing it's not *nothing*. "Okay, we dated for like almost a year. If you can even call it that…"

Tequila doesn't even try to hide the mouth drop. "Woah, I was not expecting that at all." She takes a sip of her drink. "So, um, how was he?"

Now, I almost choke. "How was he what?"

"*You know*. I mean call me sick, but the man is jacked and hot." Angel smacks Tequila on the arm, and I tense. They both notice the vibe shift. "What?"

"He kind of came by the bar the other night and had me by the throat." They both gasp, freezing in their seats. "He threatened me because I'm with Zach. Said I was *his*." An awkward laugh escapes me. The girls are still stunned into silence.

"Shit, girl, I never would have said all of that if I had known. Are you okay?"

"Yeah, I'm okay. Zach beat the shit out of him." I take a sip of my water and the girls laugh. I smirk and laugh along, because Zach did beat the shit out of him. I might have enjoyed it too.

"All right, well, here's to a good night with new friends, being men-free, and all the other stuff." We all clink our glasses together and Angel shakes her hips to the new song that came on. "Okay, let's go dance!" She grabs my arm and I take Tequila's, each of us dragging the other to the dance floor. It's packed, with sweaty bodies bumping into us, but we don't care. Our one and only goal for tonight is to have fun.

CHARGER

I close my eyes and listen to the music. The DJ starts playing "NBK" by Niykee. My hands are swaying up above my head. All three of us girls move our hips in a seductive way, feeling the music, getting lost in it, and not worrying about anything. Angel grinds her ass on some random guy. She throws her one arm around his neck and slowly travels down on him. It's erotic and I can't look away; she's so beautiful. She could have any guy she wants, in a heartbeat. I'm not jealous of her confidence or good looks, just maybe a little envious. But I have to wonder if she's hiding some buried secrets. If her tough act is some sort of front...

Tequila dances against me. We grind our hips together and I throw my head back with a laugh. I love these girls. They're fun, real, and I can be myself with them. It's so good to have girlfriends.

By the time the song switches, we're all a little sweaty and breathless. We disperse from the crowd and head back to the bar.

"Damn, I love dancing." Tequila slouches over the counter, laughing. I agree—there's just something about getting lost in a song and moving to it.

I get ready to say something when a large body bumps into me, sending me flying right into Angel. She catches my arm, but glares at the man behind me. "Um, excuse me. How about you watch what you're doing," she yells over to him, and as soon as I straighten to get a look at the man, my eyes widen. The guy's huge and three of his buddies are just about the same size. They're all wearing motorcycle vests. *Not Good.* The monster of a man turns his head and eyes Angel up and down. But Angel doesn't back down; she stands with her head held high, her hands on her hips.

"What did you say to me?"

C.M. Danks

"I said." She takes a step closer to him. "Watch where the fuck you're going. You almost knocked my friend down. Now apologize."

My jaw is to the floor. I glance at Tequila, who is texting someone before she gives me an "Oh shit" look. "Come on, Angel. It's fine. Let's just go."

He cocks his head to the side and smirks when he reads the patch on her leather jacket. "You're on the wrong turf, honey." Despite his choice of words, his voice is anything but kind. It's growing angrier by the second. His friends are sneering behind him. One of them does an air kiss at me and winks; the gesture makes me shiver. Why can't all the biker clubs be like Zach's?

"I can be in whatever turf I want to be in, buddy."

"Jesus, Angel, let's go." Tequila grabs Angel's hand, dragging her away. I follow close behind them.

We hightail it out of their club, bumping into people along the way. Once we're outside, Angel shrugs out of Tequila's hold. "What the hell, Angel? Did you happen to notice who the hell they were? Not good. You're lucky they didn't follow us out of there. What were you thinking?"

Angel stands with a hip cocked, her arms folded at her chest. "What? The guy was an ass. Jules deserved an apology."

"Oh, come on, Angel, it's about more than some damn apology with you. It's like you're trying to prove yourself *all the time*. Yes, we get it. You are hot shit, and can probably kick any dude's ass. But in there..." She points inside. "Those were *three* very large men, and let's not forget about the patches they were all wearing."

CHARGER

I stand there in silence, watching the argument between them both. I don't feel like it's my place to butt in, so I stay quiet.

Angel runs her tongue over her top teeth and bites the side of her cheek. "Well, whatever. Let's just get my damn car and get the hell out of here."

"Good idea," Tequila agrees. "Where the hell is the damn valet guy?"

The street and sidewalk are pretty much dead. There's not a soul in sight. But the club is still hopping.

The back door of the club swings open and out walks the three large bikers. We all tense, even Angel. My heartbeat picks up as we stare at them, hoping that by some miracle, they don't notice us standing here. It's like we stop breathing, waiting for them to walk by. They're laughing; one of them lights a cigarette, and that's when he spots us. Their laughter dies down and the guys eye us like hungry prey. Should we be worried? Would they try anything? They look scary, and by the way Angel pissed them off, I would say we're fucked.

All three come walking in our direction. Tequila and I exchange worried looks. But Angel, being Angel, steps forward. "I texted Throttle," Tequila whispers to me. Well, that's a relief at least. Now if our guys can only get here in time.

C.M. Danks

Chapter Thirty

Charger

We roll up to the Skulls' clubhouse: me, Chain, Tank, Hush, Throttle, and Bullet. The place just screams *ass twats*. Trash on the grass, people partying in the front yard and parking lot... I shake my head and swing my legs over my bike, stepping forward with the guys. We stalk up to the door in silence, game faces on. Hush twirls his bat in his hand. A big bearded man is standing by the door, his arms crossed and feet spread in a wide stance.

Chain steps up to him, nose to nose, matching his size. "Move the fuck out of our way." The man swallows nervously and steps to the side.

Pussy.

When we walk inside, the music stops playing. The place goes silent instantly. Scorpion steps out from the shadows. "Well, hello, boys. To what do we owe the pleasure of having you raid my clubhouse," he sneers.

Venom pushes a woman off his lap and goes to stand next to his bastard of a President. My hands tighten into fists when I see him. Chain takes a palm to my shoulder as he steps up. He can feel my anger, my rage, growing every second as I stand in the same room as Venom. Breathing the same air as him. He's lucky I don't strangle him right here. I won't forget about him putting his hands on Jules, ever. I'll make him pay, eventually.

Chain and Scorpion square up to each other, Bullet side by side with Chain. "We got a few things to discuss." Chain's words sound threatening with a grind of his teeth.

Scorpion glares, his brows burrowing inward. "Everyone out now!" He and Chain don't take their challenging eyes off each other. The screeching sound of chairs being moved against the floor fill the room and people scurry away. The space empties, leaving just the members from each of our respective clubs. The air is heavy and the tension could be cut with a knife. "All right, buddy, let's talk."

Chain smirks. "First off, I ain't your fuckin' buddy." He points at Scorpion. "Second, we saw your vans parked outside Clover Road. Care to explain?"

Scorpion looks left, then right, before letting out a laugh, like he's mocking our President. "Vans, huh. Boys do you know what *vans* our friend here is talking about?" His club members, including Venom, grin and shake their heads.

"Nah, boss. No idea what he's talking about." Venom laughs.

A loud crash of glasses being shattered, one by one, sounds from behind us. Hush is walking beside the front of the bar top, running his bat along it and taking out each and every one of the glasses sitting there. He doesn't stop until they're all shattered, shards scattered across the floor—expressionless as it's done. Just a blank, cold stare.

"Huh, well, he thinks you're lying." Chain hooks a thumb toward Hush. Scorpion and the rest of the guys look

C.M. Danks

pissed now, the once sneering smiles wiped clean off their faces. "See, here's the thing… We have a hard time ignoring things that concern women. So, I'm going to say this once and only once: whatever it is you got going on with those vans, you so much as breathe that little plan of yours, and we will come for you. Get me, buddy?"

"And here we thought you guys stood us up. Guess you were there after all." Scorpion grins, sending unwelcomed vibes through my veins.

Throttle's phone goes off, breaking only the silence, not the tension. Chain and Scorpion have their stare down, along with Venom and me. This fucker will be dead in minutes if I ever get the chance again.

"Uh, boss, we need to go. It's the girls." My head whips toward him so fast a twinge of pain shoots up my neck.

Chain groans and takes a step forward to Scorpion. "Remember this warning, *buddy*." Chain turns to leave but Scorpion takes one last shot.

"Hey, Chain, how's that woman of yours doing?" It happens so fast… Chain launches straight for Scorpion, but Venom steps forward, as do I. Tank grabs Chain around the chest; he's probably the only one big enough to stop him. He drags our Pres backwards, heading for the door.

"You ever fucking mention her again and I'll snap your ugly neck. You hear me!? I'll break it like a fucking twig." All we hear is laughter as we shove Chain out the door and onto the front lot. "I'm fine. I'm fine. Get the fuck off me." He straightens his shirt and stalks off to the bikes.

I waste no time. If Jules is in trouble, I need to know and I need to know now. "What's going on with the girls?" I ask Throttle as he takes his phone out.

CHARGER

"I got two texts. The first one was from our prospect saying he lost the girls. Angel ditched him. And the second one was from Tequila; she sent an SOS. They're at Club Beat. Jules is with them." He glances at me and my stomach turns.

"Fuck! Of course, Angel ditched her tail. Jesus Christ. Let's move." Chain runs a hand down his face.

My mind is hazy; an SOS was assigned for us to send when we need backup. So, the fact that the girls sent it makes me dizzy. I don't know what's happening. Is she safe?

★★★

It takes us about ten minutes to reach Club Beat. At normal speed, it would take twenty-five, but we weren't wasting any time. Three large guys are standing off against Angel, Tequila, and Jules.

What the fuck is going on, and what the fuck are these bastards doing going against women half their sizes? The pulsation in my ears grows heavy and my breathing is uncontrollable.

We pull up to the front of the club and park; we're all off our bikes in seconds. I don't even think twice. I head straight for Jules. The relief in her eyes when she sees me makes me feel like fucking Superman. I take her face in my hands and look her up and down. "You okay? What the fuck, Jules? You okay?"

She nods frantically then relaxes. I gently kiss her forehead. I'll be back for her but first… I spin to see Tank, Chain and the rest of them step up in front of Angel. Throttle is blocking Tequila, creating a barrier. I beeline it to Tank. Angel's behind him.

C.M. Danks

"You guys, I got this." Angel goes to step around Tank, but Chain shoves her back. Not hard, but enough to get his point across. "*You*, shut the fuck up and stay back."

"Chain, well, shit. It's been a long time." The large dude chucks his cigarette to the side. He's wearing a leather motorcycle vest, all three of them are.

"Pipe." Chain's stern voice echoes through the night air.

"That's quite a mouth your girl has back there. I could put it to better use."

A growl comes from Tank. "You wanna say that again?"

"Jesus Christ." Chain runs his hand down his face. "I'm going to step up and apologize for anything my member might have said. Sometimes her hotheadedness gets the better of her. We're just trying to keep the peace, brother." Chain surrenders with a hand up in the air. "However, with that being said, don't you ever go up against our women again, or I might not be so nice and apologetic next time."

The intensity in the air is thick.

"We'll take care of it." Bullet nods to Pipe. "You and this club are done here."

"All right, fine. I suggest putting a muzzle on her though." With those fine parting words, they walk away. We watch them until they get on their bikes and disappear.

"Can I just say one thing…"

Chain's hand shoots up in Angel's face, closing any gap between them. "You don't talk. You're going to listen and you're going to listen well. I don't know if you knew who those guys were that you single handily pissed the fuck off, but I can guarantee you don't want them as an enemy. And what? You thought having the Skulls on our bad side wasn't enough. You just had to go and piss off another club?" Angel doesn't say anything; she just looks at him, taking it

CHARGER

like she's getting scolded by her father. "Now, I suggest you get your shit together. Take Tequila home and get out of my sight."

A couple of glances are being shared before the girls walk away. I immediately stalk toward Jules. I tug her close to me, wrapping my arms around her and needing to feel her against me. I breathe in her scent and she clenches onto my shirt for dear life. *They* aren't the ones we need to worry about. But that's just for right now.

"I'm sorry I didn't tell you that we were going out tonight." Her voice is muffled in my shirt.

"Anything happens like that again, you immediately call me, no questions, Jules." She nods her pretty little head. "Let's go. I'll take you home." I grab her soft hand in mine, leading her to my bike. Some of the guys left already and Tank looks to me with a head nod.

"You guys good, brother?"

"Yeah, we're good." He nods back before taking off behind Chain and the rest of them.

"Should we be worried about those guys?" Jules is concerned and I don't blame her.

"Not at the moment."

I do mean *not at the moment*. We've never had a problem with them. Not before tonight. Angel needs to learn to cool it.

"I just realized this is going to be my first time on the back of your bike." She smiles with a hint of excitement in her eyes.

"This will be the first time any woman has been on the back of my bike, pretty girl."

Surprise hits her face. "Wait, what? You mean you've never had another woman on the back with you?"

C.M. Danks

"Nope, you're it, babe." I hand her my helmet, helping her with the strap, then I swing over my seat. "We don't let just any woman on the back of our bikes. She needs to be our ride or die. Climb on."

She stares at me intently, and with lust, before climbing on the back and scooting in close. The faint breath of her whisper grazes my ear.

"I have to admit... I'm glad no one else has been on here."

I smirk, squeezing her thigh. "You're gonna want to hang on tight to me, babe."

"I'll never let go," she answers and my dick twitches a little. When did she turn me into such a pining sap?

I start her up and take off into the night. Jules gives a cute little squeal as she hugs my stomach. I feel different with Jules on the back of my bike. I'm used to riding by myself. But her being here with me makes me feel complete. Like I'm whole again—a feeling I haven't had in a long-ass time.

CHARGER

Chapter Thirty-One

Jules

I tighten my hold on Zach as we roar down the side roads. Trees fly by us in blurs. This is the first time I have ever been on the back of a motorcycle and I have to admit, it's an adrenaline rush. Zach's muscular hard back is pressed against my chest. He's the sexiest man to me, and he's even sexier when he's riding. It's like he's calm. Something takes over, as if he's free. His body relaxes, his mind relaxes, and I can't help but smile for him.

Zach turns onto a side dirt road that leads up to an abandoned building. He slows down and parks behind it. I lean back, removing my helmet. He gets off, staring at me without a word.

"Okay, should I be worried?" I smile playfully, but Zach's expression is serious. "Okay, maybe that's a yes."

"You never have to worry with me." He takes my hands in his, pulling me up toward him, and my body obeys by swinging a leg around his bike. His eyes study me like they would art. They move down over every inch of my body. He runs both rough hands from my shoulders, slowly down, his thumbs grazing my breasts. He continues over my waist, stopping at my hips—our breaths both heavy. My panties are already soaked. Because this man sets my body on fire. He jerks me flush against him, my arms trapped, stapled to his chest. He leans into me, his nose grazing my neck.

"You're like my drug, pretty girl."

My eyes slowly close and I rest my forehead on his shoulder. His hands come around my back, skimming over the bare part of my skin, like he needs to touch every single inch of me.

I can feel him grip the lace ties of my corset in the back; he pulls with one tug and it comes apart. I'm not wearing a bra, so when he shifts me away just enough to remove the corset from my body, I'm left standing there with my naked breasts on display. My nipples ache, begging for his mouth to touch them. He must read my mind because he leans his head down, flicking my hard nipple with his tongue. I moan with heavy, hot breaths. He runs his tongue over each of them and the sensation goes straight to my already wet, needy lady parts.

"I'm going to fuck you, right here, on my bike. Is that okay with you?"

I might have just mini orgasmed right here. I bite my bottom lip hard enough it almost bleeds.

He shrugs out of his club leather and sets it across his handlebars. Then, in one *hot as fuck* motion, he pulls the hem of his t-shirt up and over him. His broad shoulders, hard chest, and rippled abs are now on display, like there's spotlights shining down on him. The lust is burning in me, waiting to be released, and I need him to release it. He runs his palms over my breasts then my stomach, before reaching for the button of my jeans; electricity shoots through me and down to my core. He pulls them over my hips then my thighs, slowly exposing my lace G-string. I can feel the strength in each of his hands as he grips both sides of my waist, lifting me onto the seat of his bike. He slips off each of my heels, then finishes pulling off my jeans, our stares never disconnecting from each other. The cool night breeze hits my practically bare body. I feel his soft lips touch my shoulder when he leans in; they trail down my body, and he rips my lace G-string away from me.

"You keep this up, and I'll have to replace all of my lace panties."

"Oh, I plan on ripping them all to shreds, babe." He starts kissing the insides of my thighs. "Hold on, pretty girl." He kneels on the ground, adjusts my legs so they rest on top of his shoulders and he slowly, softly licks my clit. I look for the nearest thing to grip. I close my fist around the handlebar of his bike, trying to clench the seat with my free hand. He swipes his tongue in circular motions and my body ignites. The pressure from his mouth is sending currents zipping through me. I want to grab onto his hair but I know I'll fall backwards. He gently sucks, his open mouth buried between my slit, and I lose my fucking mind. I scream out, not caring if someone hears.

"Fucking Christ, Jules." He rises to his hero height, removing the rest of his clothing, and his thick, large length is resting against my entrance. "You ready to ride with me?"

The skin on my clit is dancing. Yes, yes, I will always be ready for this man. I move down to lick his length like it's a damn ice cream cone. Then I surround it with my lips. "Fuck." He holds my shoulders then takes my hair into his fist. "Yes, baby." He doesn't let me suck him too long before his hands are on my waist again. But this time, he lays me back, my head resting on the tank of his Harley. He swings his leg over and thrusts inside me with ease. I reach above me, gripping the fuck out of his handlebars. He places his hands on top of mine and continues moving inside me. My eyes roll back with a moan. I cry out in pleasure. My back arches and he feels up my breasts. At some point, his bike shakes as if it'll fall from the violent, thunderous thrusts he's wielding. He growls, sending shock after shock. With one more impact, I'm sent over the edge. The world spins, aligns, and my body lets go. My walls close in on him. We pulsate with each other. He leans over me with his muscular outstretched arms, returning his hands to mine, our breaths rapid.

When I look up, I see the stars. My star is back up there somewhere and I can't help but smile. His hands touch my back and lift me until I'm resting in his arms, my cheek against his bare chest.

"I will never be able to be just your friend. It would kill me to not touch you, to not feel you in this way. I want this. I want us, Jules. No one else, ever."

"I want this too." I sigh, my breath on his skin. He pulls me away, cups my face, and gently touches his lips to mine. His smooth, soft, citrus-tasting lips. It's one hell of a passionate kiss. Comfortable, easy, and gentle.

"You just fucked me on your motorcycle." My voice is quiet, as if trying to match the silence of the night around us.

"I did, and we're gonna be doing that a fuck-ton more." He kisses my forehead and my cheeks burn from the cute gesture. He gets off his bike, scooping me up into a cradle position before setting my feet on the grassy dirt ground. "We should probably get dressed and get out of here."

CHARGER

"Zach, you ruined my corset top." I hold up the unmendable black lace top in my hand.

"Uh, yeah, sorry about that. It just couldn't be helped." He winks and I shake my head.

"It's fine, I guess. It was hot as hell. Definitely worth it."

"I think I'm going to like this kinky side of you, babe."

"You might, but my clothes aren't going to. Which, by the way, um, you're going to have to lend me your t-shirt."

He hands me his *way too big for me* shirt and proceeds to get dressed. He ties his boots, shrugging his cut on. *Oh my God.*

Jeans, no shirt. Nothing except his leather cut, tattoos, and muscles. I have to force my mouth shut. "You look so hot it's painful."

He glances over at me with a grin. Oh my God, my ovaries. He saunters over, puts his hands on my hips, then lifts me so my legs hug around his waist. His warm, strong palms grip my ass, and I wrap my arms around his neck. Our foreheads touch in a tender way.

"I will love you until all the stars fall, Julianna Lynn Taccarelli."

"And I will love you until the last one burns out, Zachary William Scott." I collide my lips with his, our tongues dancing with one another slowly.

He breaks the connection and looks into my eyes. "All right, beautiful, let's get out of here."

★★★

We pull up to the Fallen Star and Zach walks his bike around back. We stroll inside with his arm encasing the

C.M. Danks

bend of my waist. "I'm not tired. Stay with me for a bit?" I ask. But let's be honest, I'm practically begging.

"I wasn't planning on leaving, babe."

I smile then flip on the light to the bar. I get two glasses out from behind the counter and set them down in front of us. It must have been a busy night because most of the whiskey bottles are empty.

I pour the remaining alcohol into the glasses, moving around the bar, and we both sit on the stools. I swivel to face him and he rests his warm hand on my thigh.

"I'm proud of you, Jules. Not that I didn't think you could do whatever it was you wanted, but I'm just so fucking proud of you. You never were one to sit back and not put in the work. You're smart, beautiful, and a great fucking mother."

I smile, a little embarrassed by his compliment. "I was driving by one day and saw that this place was up for sale. I don't know… something inside me was screaming *buy*. I worked for years, saving money through college. My parents helped me with the loan, but I've been fine paying it back. I'm sitting comfortable." I sip my whiskey. "So, what about you, biker man. How do you earn your income?"

"Our earnings are shared. The gym, the bike shop. But the pit is where I earn most of it. I never lose. People come there just to watch me fight." He leans back, lost in thought. "I don't know how to describe it, but it makes me feel alive, *high*." Moving back to me, he rubs my cheek with the pad of his thumb. "And let's just say it's been very therapeutic for many reasons."

His thumb parts my lips. I gasp when he grips the ends of the stool, tugging the whole thing closer to him. Warmth fills my skin as his hands caress my thighs.

CHARGER

"I think I'm ready for another round."

"Oh yeah?" I laugh.

"*Oh yeah.*" He picks me up underneath my arms, placing me onto his lap, and I kiss him like I never want to stop.

C.M. Danks

Chapter Thirty-Two

Charger

Sweat drips from my forehead down my face. With every single punch to the bag, my muscles rip apart. Working out, fighting in the pit, and being with my girls—this combination is the greatest high. *And reward.* Nothing else consumes my mind while I'm in this element. Everything right now is simple; it makes sense. For the first time, it makes fucking sense.

I go for the jump rope and complete my normal reps, feeling my calf muscles burn. Then I head over to the weights and rep out some bicep curls, repeating the process several times. Or until my muscles feel like they've had enough.

It's been weeks since we approached The Skulls. Chain assigned a couple of prospects to keep an eye out without the other club knowing. Nothing suspicious or fucked up has gone down. It doesn't mean it won't though. So we have to be prepared. We have guys on our women at all times. I get shit from Jules about it, but ask me if I give a shit?

Tank sits down on the bench beside me, doing shoulder reps with the dumbbells. He makes seventy pounds (in each

CHARGER

hand) look easy. Angel walks in and heads straight for the treadmill. She turns the speed up and sprints like she's on a mission. She seems to be a little less rebellious since the whole thing at the bar went down. The girl is a spitfire and Chain has to remind her daily that she needs to chill the fuck out. She's going to get herself in trouble someday.

A low grunt sounds from Tank as he sets his weights down beside him. "Fuck, that feels good."

"Sounds like you need to get laid, my friend." I squeeze my tumbler, sending splashes of water over my head.

He raises a brow and smirks. "My brother reunites with his *one that got away*, and he's a fuck expert now."

"What can I say? I am a man of wisdom." I laugh and he shakes his head.

"How's that going anyway? Being a family man. Not the fucking Jules part. Although, I wouldn't say no to details."

"One, you ever picture my girl naked, or have any other perverted fucking thoughts, I'll break your neck. Two, it's pretty fucking great, man. Speaking of, got myself a date with them after this."

Tank laughs. "Sounds like it." He gets up, grabbing his water. "Well, have fun, brother. We're all fucking happy for you." He slaps a hand to my shoulder while walking off to the treadmills. Picturing them both, Chloe and Jules, I can't help but smile. At long fucking last.

★★★

As I push my daughter on the tiny swing in the park. *My* daughter, will that ever get old? I glance over at Jules, who's looking at me like I can lasso the moon. That's right, pretty girl. I'll lasso the moon for you, for both of you.

C.M. Danks

I catch some parents giving me weird looks. What, a biker can't have a family? Fuck them and their fucked-up, biased opinions. We struggle every day with having a bad name. We can try, proving ourselves over and over again, but it doesn't seem to matter. The town compares us to the others, like the Skulls, and that will forever have an impact on us.

Every day I may be faced with a new challenge, but being a dad is even more rewarding than I would have thought. As the days go by, it's becoming more and more natural to me. Like this is exactly who I want to be, and where I want to be. With Jules and Chloe. I've wanted this since we were kids, wanted to be with her forever. When I found out the condom broke that night in her bedroom, I wasn't even scared. I was eighteen years old and wasn't even scared at the thought of her having our baby. That's how fucking in love with her I was. *I am.* I didn't even think (when I ran like a coward) that she could have gotten pregnant. I didn't think with such a small chance that it would actually happen.

"Daddy, can I go play with the other kids on the jungle gym?" She looks at me with her big blue eyes. Same as mine.

I pick her up, then kiss her cheek. "Yes, but stay where we can see you. Got it?" She nods her head, then I set her down and she runs to the other kids, her pigtails flying in the air behind her.

I walk back over to Jules, wrapping my arm around her waist before tugging her to me. "We created that," I say as I nod my head in Chloe's direction.

"Pretty cool, huh?" Jules smiles and sets her palm to my chest. I turn, staring deep into her eyes. I run my fingertips along her soft, blushed cheeks.

CHARGER

"Jules, I want to tell you…" I stop when her mouth opens and her eyes widen. I see the fear inside her, which makes me immediately spin back around.

"Zach…" Jules's voice trails off. I hear the nervousness in it. But all I see is fury.

"This fucker." I leave Jules's side, anger coursing through my veins. My fists are clenched and I don't know how I am going to be able to control myself. I continue to stalk toward Venom, who is crouched down in front of Chloe. A lot of parents are walking away with their kids in hand, giving questionable looks. She's not smiling and as soon as she sees me, she runs behind me and grabs hold of my leg.

"Chloe, go over to your mom, now." She waddles over, Jules meeting her halfway as she scoops her up. Once I see that they're both at a good distance, I'm on him. He slowly rises at the same time I meet his face—our noses practically touching as the toes of our boots meet. "You've got some fuckin' nerve," I sneer at him. I'm five seconds from lashing out and losing my shit. I clench my jaw, my fists tight.

"I was out for a nice stroll. Just thought I'd come see them both. I miss them, really. Chloe was like a daughter to me, you know. And I was like a father figure to her. Since, well, you weren't around." He smirks. I grip his shirt in my hands.

"You don't ever, and I mean *ever*, come near Chloe again. You're running out of warnings, Venom. I swear to fuckin' Christ I will bury you." I grind my teeth. "I. Will. Bury. You." I release his shirt, tossing him backwards. "That goes for all your little biker buddies." I turn on my heels, but don't look back. If I do, I might just change my mind and give the onlookers a reason to think they're right about us. I reach Jules, who has Chloe in her arms. "You okay, kid?"

"I don't like that man. He's scary."

"Chloe, listen to me. If he or anyone else who isn't Uncle Chain, Aunt Maggie, or the others I work with ever approaches you, you run, understand?" She nods. "Good, let's go." I wrap my arm around Jules's shoulder and we head back to the car. Our family fun-filled day had to get cut short because of that asshole. My patience is running thin. Very fucking thin.

When we get back to Jules's place, Chloe runs to her room and Jules fishes for glasses in the cabinet. As she reaches up on her tiptoes, her shirt rises enough to show a small part of her bare back. Goddamn, she's beautiful. I stalk toward her like she's my prey, placing both hands on either side of her from behind and trapping her in. My chest presses up against her back, and I get a whiff of lavender and vanilla. I lean in to get a better whiff. She breathes in deeply, laying her head back against me. My hands find her waist and I jerk her ass up against my growing cock.

"I will never let anything happen to you two," I whisper close to her ear.

"I know, but honestly…" She spins, still in my arms. "Venom never hurt Chloe and I don't think he ever would."

I cock my head back like she's slapped me across my face. "What? Are you trying to tell me that man has a fucking soul?"

"No, no, I'm not, trust me. I don't think any of them have much of a soul." She wraps her arms around my neck. "What were you trying to tell me in the park before?"

She's begging me with her eyes. Her gorgeous brown eyes. "I…" A buzzing followed by a ringtone sounds from my pocket. *Damn it.* I want to tell Jules exactly how I feel, that I want them to live with me, to find a home that we can all live and be happy together in. Like something out of a damn chick-flick. But I'll happily admit it.

I crash my mouth to hers and she lets out a small moan. Every time she does that, my dick twitches, ready to come alive for her. But I break us apart to check my cell.

"Church meeting." I touch my forehead to hers. "I'll come back tonight."

"I close the bar tonight."

"Then I'll come by after you close."

She smiles. "Okay."

I kiss her forehead, say goodbye to her and Chloe, then walk out. I hate leaving—it's something I plan on never doing again.

C.M. Danks

Chapter Thirty-Three

Jules

"Hey, girl, care if I take off?" Lucy's at the end of the bar counter, throwing her hair up in a pony. I check the clock on the wall—it's already three fifteen in the morning. Zach said he'd be here by now.

"Yeah, Lucy, of course. I'm just going to do one more sweep, then refill the ketchup bottles."

"Thanks." She unties her waitress apron, tucking it under the bar. "Bye, Joe. You know if I were Jules, I would start putting you to work." She waves and the back door closes. Joe doesn't laugh; in fact, he's been abnormally quiet all night. Not to mention, he hasn't left yet. Beads of sweat glisten his forehead.

I lean my hands on the counter, slouching into my shoulders. "Joe, I'm sorry but I'm gonna have to kick ya out." He doesn't look at me, but his breathing picks up and his chest heaves in and out faster. "Joe…"

"I'm so sorry, Jules." He eventually turns to me. Tears start to form in his eyes. I step away from the counter and straighten.

CHARGER

"What are you talking about?" I can feel my heart beating faster and faster.

"I needed the money. I... they said they would pay me. I just... I'm so, so sorry. But I didn't do it. I couldn't do it. They wanted me to..." Sobs leave him and I can barely make out what he's even saying. He slouches forward, his hands shaking.

I step back, pausing to think. Now I'm panicking; my gut is telling me that something is about to happen. What exactly could he be referring to? Does it have anything to do with the Skulls?

The back door opens at the same time the front one does. Scorpion walks in and through the back, Venom. It's as if the world stops. No one moves. I can hear my breathing, like I'm no longer in my own body, as if I'm floating outside it. I can't move. I can't speak. My stomach turns and tears start to burn my eyes. Utter panic overtakes me. I need to move. Come on, Jules, *move.* I dart to the opposite side of the bar, thinking I'm in the clear, and try to make it upstairs, but I run straight into what feels like a brick wall. One of them grabs my wrists and I start thrashing around violently, trying everything possible in order to get away. I scream but someone behind me pulls a gag over my mouth.

He leans in my ear from behind me. "Shh, I promise if you just give in, this will be so much easier." Scorpion's vile, hot, cigarette-smelling breath grazes my cheek. I start thrashing again, and whoever's holding me spins me around in his arms, hugging me so that I'm trapped and unable to move. Venom's still on the opposite side, his arms crossed and a blank expression on his smug face. Tears are flowing down my cheeks, stopped only by the gag that still covers my mouth. It tastes like dirt and grime. That alone

C.M. Danks

makes me want to dry heave. Scorpion tilts his head to the side, taking his thumbs and wiping the tears as they fall. I shake my head, like it's going to keep him away. I don't want him touching me, which makes my crying even worse. But he holds my face so I can't move.

Joe, who can't even look at me, is crying, sobbing, like a coward. I have so many questions. Like why... why would he do this to me? My sobs pick up and they aren't just for me anymore. I lost the father figure I thought I had. He's dead to me, nothing to me, and I hope he rots in hell. I turn to Venom, as if he's my last hope in having someone come to my rescue, but he doesn't do or say anything. His expression remains emotionless.

Scorpion leans in, licking a tear off my cheek. I wince, screaming against the gag. Bile rises up with a wave of nausea swirling in my stomach. "We're a little disappointed in Joe here. He didn't quite hold up on his end of the deal in bringing you to us. But I have to admit, when we first hired him to watch this place, we didn't realize it was *you* he'd be watching." *Venom never mentioned I worked here?* "This bar is a great place to pick up our... how should I put this... our little employees. We had some outside eyes, but we needed someone from the inside. Didn't know we'd be scoring Venom's little whore too." He laughs. "Actually, guess she's not your little whore anymore, is she, V? Guess she's Charger's plaything now."

Venom's jaw ticks. Maybe that just hit a nerve. Did Venom not like the fact Scorpion just called me his whore? Doubtful, because he quickly returns to being a blank canvas. He didn't like the idea of me being with Zach; that's what it was.

CHARGER

I try again to get out of the man's hold. He smells of body odor and alcohol. But he is too strong. Then I feel a sharp pain on the side of my neck, followed by pressure. The room starts spinning, and the drowsiness hits like a ton of bricks. A blurry, almost distorted version of Scorpion leans in closer to me.

"It'll all be over soon."

I try to shake the cloudiness, but it weighs too heavily and my eyes begin to close. I am completely powerless and the darkness takes over.

★★★

Charger

I back my bike into Jules's parking lot. The lights are still on, which is odd. I figured she'd be done cleaning up by now. I would have been here sooner if I didn't pass the fuck out waiting for her shift to end. It seems my sleepless nights have been a little better since being with Jules again. She makes me feel at ease, at damn peace. And that's something I haven't felt in a long time. She and Chloe make me the happiest fucking man on the planet.

On the ride over tonight, I had time to think and I have every intention of telling her how I feel. I want them to move in with me. I want Jules to be with me, really be with me.

I stalk toward the back of the bar, but stop dead. The front door to the Fallen Star is wide open. I turn to pan the street for the prospect who was supposed to be watching her, but I don't see him. Panic runs through me like ice. I take off sprinting inside.

"Jules!" I run straight upstairs and jiggle the locked handle. *Fuck.* I take a shoulder to the door, knocking it off the hinges in one strong force. My adrenaline is on fire right now. "Jules," I call out again, checking both her and Chloe's rooms. But nothing; the place is empty.

I run back downstairs, skipping two steps at a time and jumping down from the last two. My chest is heavy and my breathing is out of control. I take out my cell and dial her number, but it goes straight to voicemail.

"Fuck!"

I pick up one of the stools in anger, tossing it across the room until it hits the wall; the legs shatter in one blow. Resting my hands on the bar counter, I try to slow down my breathing, try to calm myself, but I can't. I slouch into my shoulders, my thoughts on overdrive. That's when I hear a groan. I follow the sound to the back, and in the corner where the kitchen is at, there's a man slumped on the floor. *Joe.*

"Joe? What the fuck happened?" He's battered, bruised, and his eyes are starting to swell shut. Blood's everywhere. If they wanted to kill him, they almost succeeded. I pick him up gently by the shirt. "Joe. What happened!? Where's Jules?"

He's sobbing and tries to say something, but his jaw is severely fucked up. "I-I'm s-sorry." He winces from the pain.

"Joe, what happened?"

"It's all... it's all m-my fault. I'm so sorry. They took her. I-I don't know where, but they took her."

My stomach drops.

CHARGER

"Who? Who fucking took her!?"

He sobs another sob before saying, "The Skulls," and I drop him to the floor. I run my hands through the top of my hair and fall back onto the tile. My ears are ringing, the blood is pulsing through them, and everything is muffled.

A surge of rage takes over as I slide back over to Joe. Picking him up by his shirt again, I get in his face. "What the fuck did you do?" I grind my teeth.

"They told me if I brought her... if I watched this place, scoped it out, they would pay me in cash, lots of cash." He starts crying again. "I have no one, no family, no money. I needed the money."

"I hope it was worth it, fucker. Because if you don't die here, I will make sure to fucking kill you myself." I toss him back to the ground like fucking trash, and pull out my cell.

The first person I call is Chain. My hands visibly shake. This is the first time in my life I have ever felt scared. Scared of losing her. She's mine. Jules is mine. I will tear apart anyone who tries to stop me from getting to her. Destroy anyone who touches her.

C.M. Danks

Chapter Thirty-Four

Jules

A deep shiver wakens me. My muscles ache immediately when I try to move. Have you ever been hit by a car? Because this might be how it feels. As soon as I get a grip on where I am, I feel the cold, damp cement ground under my cheek. The ache in my head is pulsing, thumping, and the nausea is overpowering. I slowly start to sit up, but it's a bitch, considering my hands are bound together. At least they removed my gag—*that was nice of them.*

I rest my head against the wall behind me, focusing on anything but the musty smell. Sucking in a lungful of stale air, I try my damnedest not to lose it emotionally. I can't cry. I won't cry. I have to be strong. Whatever it is these guys plan on doing to me, it won't break me down. Unless they plan on killing me, then I guess I am royally fucked.

I don't want them to know I'm awake, but the cough I try to suppress releases. My mouth is so dry that it's tempting to lick the puddle on the ground. Just thinking about doing so makes me want to vomit.

Just breathe, Jules. Just breathe.

CHARGER

Zach will come for me. It's only a matter of time. But what if he can't find me? I shut my eyes from the utter exhaustion that has taken over my body. I need sleep, but I also need to get the hell out of here.

There's nothing. No windows, no doors, except for the one at the top of the dark staircase. I let out small breaths to calm my nerves, but my eyes start to burn. No, no, there is no way in hell I'm going to cry, even as I think of Joe. Even as I remember what he did. He couldn't look me in the eye. I don't know what they used him for, but it stung deep inside my chest. They said he was watching me, my bar—keeping tabs on it for what? He was supposed to kidnap me? It doesn't make any sense. Someone I thought I knew wasn't real.

With my head tilted back against the wall, I look up at the grungy ceiling riddled with spider webs. Is this it? Am I going to die here, get killed, raped? And there they are... the tears.

I hear the creak of the door above the stairs. A small cast of light trails down the steps, coinciding with the dull light bulb dangling above in the center of the room. I try to scooch closer to the wall, which is impossible because I am already flush against it. My jeans are covered in dust and dirt. My V-neck t-shirt with my bar's name on it is smeared with a similar layer of grime.

I swallow, waiting nervously for the silhouette to present himself. When he does, I can't say I'm relieved, but at least it's not Scorpion.

"Morning, sunshine." Venom walks over with his usual serpentine grin. He's carrying a water bottle, and I immediately lick my lips with excitement. He crouches down in front of me. The scent of cigarettes fills my nose.

"All right, princess." He holds the bottle out in front of me, and my reaction is like a caged dog. I'm practically salivating.

"You expect me to drink that with my hands tied behind my back?" The attitude drips from my mouth and Venom grins even wider. *Bastard.*

He doesn't say anything as he unscrews the cap, his elbows resting on his knees. "You didn't think I was going to let you go thirsty, did you? Come on, Jules, I'm not the monster you think I am."

I glare at him. "Oh, no? So, kidnapping me and locking me in a basement qualifies you as what? Knight in shining armor status? If I were you, I wouldn't put that on your dating profile."

He throws back his head with a laugh. "Well, I see you haven't lost your sense of humor." He raises a brow and holds the water bottle out, gesturing for me to tilt my head back. Fine, I'm dying of thirst so I couldn't care less about keeping my pride right now. As soon as the water hits my mouth, sliding to my throat, it's like heaven. Venom tugs the bottle away, leaving me wanting to squeal for more.

"All right, can't have you choking. Unless it's on my dick." He laughs and I make a disgusted face. "Oh, come on, you enjoyed it, at one point."

I shake my head. "What am I doing here, Venom? Tell me. What the fuck is going on?"

He sighs, losing his playful side. "Look, we took you to prove a point."

"Huh?" I look around dramatically. "What point is that, exactly?" I cock my head, waiting for a reply.

He leans in and I suddenly don't feel as comfortable with him. My body scrambles to the wall as he takes my chin in

CHARGER

his hand. "The point. The point is to not fuck with us." His eyes stare through me. The only chance I thought I had of making it out of here was him. And my hopes were just tossed to the floor and set on fire. "Your little fuck buddy, along with the rest of the Chains, thought we were kidding. Well, now look who's bluffing."

"Bluffing about what?" It comes out as almost a whisper.

He stands to his full height, which is tall and smirks. His green eyes sparkle with hate. Then with a wink, he turns around back toward the stairs.

"Wait! Venom, where are you going?" I can't believe I'm actually upset to see him leave. "You can't just leave me here! What's going on? What are you guys going to do with me?"

"Get some shut eye, princess." With that, the door slams shut and I fall silent, staring off into the darkness.

I actually feel myself start to drift off—must be the leftover side effects of whatever they drugged me with. I slouch against the wall, letting the exhaustion overtake me.

★★★

"Rise and fucking shine, darling." Someone kicks my leg, jerking me awake.

Panic floods through me and my heart starts beating out of my chest. Scorpion is looking at me with those cold, dead eyes. Eyeing me up like I'm his breakfast. What time is it? Venom is next to him, his arms crossed.

I'm starting to feel extremely weak. I'm not even sure how long I've been down here.

He pulls me to a stand, though I feel like my legs may give way. I haven't stretched them in what seems like forever. The stiff pain in each muscle has me vibrating with fatigue and anxiety.

"We need to get you presentable, darlin'." Scorpion smirks.

"Presentable for w-what?" My voice sounds like I swallowed gravel.

"For your potential buyer."

I swear my heart stops. Venom's head whips in Scorpion's direction. He moves his arms down at his sides, flexing his bicep muscles.

"Wait, Pres. I thought this was just for show. To warn the Chains." He turns a little and Scorpion rakes his eyes up and down my body again.

"I changed my mind. She looks like she could be worth a lot of money, and well, I'm willing to sell."

Oh my God. I'm being used for human trafficking. They're going to sell me off? Is this real? Everything becomes blurry, and I think I might pass out. The sounds around me are muffled and my chest is so tight I have to gasp for oxygen. I back up until I hit the wall, my palms flat against it. I have to find a way to get out of here. I can't lose Chloe. She can't lose me. I try to steady my breathing but it's pointless. It's a losing battle. My vision starts to turn grey.

"Hey, you." Rough hands grip my upper arms. The pain brings me back. "Get your shit together, darling. We can't have you passin' out on us."

"Boss…"

"Shut the fuck up, V. You might be Vice of this club, but don't forget who runs the show," Scorpion snarls then pulls me from the wall, dragging me behind him.

My feet are barely able to keep up. I catch eye contact with Venom. His eyes, which I thought couldn't hold any

CHARGER

emotion, may actually look regretful and apologetic. Worried even. But I won't forget that he was the one who helped bring me here. He helped kidnap me; he took me away from my daughter. So, fuck him and his fake display of empathy.

As soon as we're upstairs, the warmer air hits my body. I welcome it—the basement was so cold.

At least due to the lack of fluids, I haven't had to urinate. And I still have what little pride I have left.

With my arm locked in Scorpion's grip, I'm helpless as he drags me along until he stops in front of the bathroom. "Time to get you cleaned up. Don't want your potential buyer to see you like this. And what better way to get to know each other." The evil in his eyes shoots panic through me. I violently shake my head, feeling the tears form. He pulls me close. I hit his chest and he scrapes his cold, dead fingers down my waist. Bile rises from the pit of my stomach.

"No, no, please. I can't... p-please."

"Come on, boss." Venom smiles as he moves closer to us. "Let me handle this. Besides, you don't wanna sample the merchandise right before it's sold. They can smell that shit. They'll know it's tainted."

I stop thrashing in his arms, but Scorpion studies me one last time before backing off. Relief crashes down on me.

He points in Venom's face. "No touching, but make sure she doesn't do anything stupid." He strides off and Venom's eyes follow him until he's gone. He stalks toward me, grabbing my arm and tossing me into the bathroom like a doll. Then he kicks the door shut.

"What are you doing?"

C.M. Danks

He reaches for the shower nozzle, turning it on. "I just saved you from getting raped, princess. Now undress." He stands, arms crossed over his muscular chest. *Staring*. Is he serious?

"So, what? Am I supposed to thank you?"

He snorts out a chuckle. "Do not mistake what I did for any type of kindness. And whatever happens after this, I have no control over it. Now get the fuck undressed and in the damn shower."

"You're disgusting and I can't believe I ever let you touch me."

Venom's jaw ticks, and a hint of anger flashes through his eyes. He catches the floor with a look then spins around. "Try anything stupid and I'll kill you myself." He whips the bathroom door open then slams it shut.

I run to secure it but of course there's no lock. There's no window either. I look around for something, anything, I might be able to use as a weapon. I open the cabinet door under the sink. Nothing. It's bare. The only things in here are the shampoo package and bar of soap. I can't exactly hurt anyone with those.

I grip the cabinet knobs in frustration and let my body sink to the floor. Is this it? Am I really going to be sold off? Visions of Chloe enter my mind.

Come on, Zach. I need you.

CHAPTER THIRTY-FIVE

Charger

My knuckles burn, throb, but I don't care. With each blow to his face, he grows more and more tired. Dead, it's only a matter of time before he dies at my hand.

"I-I swear," he coughs, blood hitting the ground. "I don't have any idea where they took her." The chains that hold his wrists and body upright are clanking together as he tries to thrash against them.

I can feel the presence of the others behind me. "Son, let us take it from here." Chain sets a hand to my shoulder. Rage is burning through my body, needing to be released and right now, this is the only way I can get it.

I shrug out of his grasp and make my way back to the asshole bound in front of me. I give Joe another punch but this time, it's to his ribs. By the sounds of it, I probably cracked a couple. More blood hits the floor from his mouth. I lean down so he can see my eyes as his head hangs low.

"She trusted you like a fucking father."

"I-I know. They wanted me to kidnap her tonight, drug her, and drop her off on the side of the road off forty-six. Then they would pick her up from there. I told them no.

C.M. Danks

That I changed my mind, and that's when they came in themselves. But I couldn't do it!"

"Well, aren't you a fucking saint. You did nothing to help her. You didn't even warn her. You just sat back and watched while they took her. Am I right?"

"Y-yes, but I was scared."

It's funny. We run from what we're scared of. Or we hide from it, ignoring those important to us because we're afraid.

"I'm going to kill you, you get me?" I grip his chin in my hand and pull back for another blow, but Chain stops me.

"We got this. *Go*. Get some fucking air. And this time, I'm not asking."

My eyes are still focused out in front of me. But I drop my arm and trudge upstairs, leaving the pit. It's where we like to do our interrogations. No one will notice if we get blood on the floor; there's *always* blood on the floor. I slam the door closed, spin on my heel and pound my fist into the brick wall. Did it hurt? Probably, but I can't feel a fucking thing right now. I am numb from head to toe. The thought of Jules with them boils my blood. I have so much anger and hate right now I don't know what to do. I run my hands down my face.

"Hey, killer." Angel's soft voice seems a tad calming. "You're not going to have many functioning bones left if you keep that up."

"Any word from Bullet?"

Bullet's been trying to locate Jules since we found out she was gone. His brainiac tendencies are all we have right now.

She sighs. "He's tapping into every security camera within a five-mile radius. So, if anyone can find her, it'll be him." She places a reassuring hand to my arm. "Hey, we

CHARGER

will get her back. Okay?" I ignore her useless attempt at comfort.

"What about Chloe?"

"She's still with Jules's parents, who, by the way, are begging us to go to the cops, Charger. We're running out of excuses as to why we can't tell the police their daughter was kidnapped. Maggie is with them too. We're hoping it'll help."

"And we're going to keep it that way. Mags better make sure they don't go to the cops." I stalk off past her and into the club, which we closed down to the normal hang-abouts. Tell the cops? Nah, we want to handle it ourselves. And by handle, I mean slaughter every last one of them.

I head straight to the back, where Bullet is sitting with his laptop. "Anything, man?"

He takes his glasses off, tossing them to the side and rubbing his eyes. "Been at this for hours and the only thing I seem to get is a shitty-ass image of a van speeding off from the parking lot. No license plate."

"Fuck!" I run my hands through the longer part of my hair. "Is it one of the vans from the other night?"

"Yeah, but they had no license plates then either." He clears his throat. "The prospect who was supposed to be watching her... they slit his throat, man. Found him next to the dumpster behind her bar."

It should have been me. I should have been watching her. I should have been with her. I should not have been late. The rage slowly turns to panic. I'm scared... I am scared of losing her and I feel absolutely fucking powerless.

"I have to do something other than just waiting around. I'm going to their clubhouse."

"Hush and Tank are already there, brother. They're looking, but they haven't found anything yet. Only a couple of locals hanging around, until they kicked them out." Bullet leans forward, placing his glasses back on. "I'll tap into the cameras from the day before."

I straighten my stance. "I'm driving over to the Skulls' club. I can't stay here." Already walking away, I yell back to Bullet. "Call me if you find out anything."

"Roger that!"

I'm out on my bike and driving away within minutes.

★★★

I head inside their shitty-ass club at the same time Tank walks down from the top floor. "Find anything?"

"Only boxes of condoms and really nasty sex toys. Remind me never to use handcuffs again. A vision I can never unsee." He pretends to shiver as Hush walks over to meet us.

"Nothing." His voice is low, faint.

A thump sounds from directly above us and we exchange glances. Then I bolt it upstairs. If there was any hope left, I feel like whoever is hiding up here may be it.

I kick open every door until I find him. "Well, hello, prospect. We're gonna have a little chat." I pick him up from his huddled position in the closet. Fucking pussy, hiding like a bitch. I grip his shirt and toss him to the wall. He holds his hands up, shaking and looking like he's about to piss himself.

"This fucker wasn't in here before." Tank folds his arms over his chest.

CHARGER

"P-please, please don't kill me." He starts sobbing frantically. All cowards cry. Joe cried.

"What kind of prospect are you, huh?" I grip the front of his shirt and pull him to my face. My bicep muscles burn. "Where are they?"

He shakes his head. "They'll kill me if I tell you."

"Oh yeah? I think my friend here will kill you if you *don't*," Tank tells the kid, and then snickers from beside me. The prospect's eyes dart nervously back and forth between mine.

"T-they said they were bringing her to some cabin-looking place on the outskirts. Off route ten. I swear that's all I know and I don't know an address."

I toss him to the floor and Tank already has Bullet on speakerphone. "Aw, man, fucker stole my spotlight." I can hear him typing. "Ahh, yes got it. I'm sending you guys the address. Chain and I will meet you there."

Tank picks up the prospect (who barely looks legal) by his shirt and drags him outside. "Listen to me, kid. We're giving you this one and only chance to get the fuck out while you can. You leave and you never come back. If we see you, then you'll give us no other option but to chop your balls off, kill you, and feed you to the Ohio River. Got it?" The kid sniffles, nods his head, and scurries away.

We don't waste any time. Tank, Hush, and I run to our bikes. I answer the call from Chain before we take off. "You guys *wait*. If you get there first, you fucking wait. That's an order, Charger." I hear him. I'm listening, but asking me to wait… to give them more time with her. More time for them to hurt her. It's just not possible. "Throttle is staying here with the girls. Bullet and I are already on the way." I hang up. It should take us maybe an hour to get there. Fuck, that's

C.M. Danks

way too much time. We start up our bikes and take off for the address. Hang on, pretty girl. I'm coming for you.

CHAPTER THIRTY-SIX

Jules

I clench the towel to my body as I sit on the edge of the tub. The heat from the shower is still lingering in the air.

The red lace-up dress they want me to wear is tiny. I stare at it, wishing desperately that by some chance, a miracle will happen and I won't have to put it on. The tears leave me and my body shakes.

I don't know if I can be strong anymore. Burying my face into my hands, I think how this doesn't seem real, doesn't seem possible.

I practically jump out of my skin at the sound of a bang on the other end of the door. "You've got five more minutes or I'm coming in there." Venom's growl has me wanting to shoot daggers through my eyes. I hate him and all the Skulls—even if he did save me from Scorpion earlier, if saving is what you would even call it.

I take in a deep breath, letting the towel hit the floor. Then I shimmy into the lace dress and run my fingers through my hair. I zip the side of it with my unsteady hands. Looking in the mirror, I see that my eyes are red and swollen from crying. I swipe the still flowing tears with my forefingers.

C.M. Danks

Venom walks in, staring at me. His eyes move slowly. "Let's go." He yanks me out of the bathroom and into a room full of Skulls members, where I feel utterly exposed. I tug down the bottom of my dress and hug my middle. They're all undressing me with their eyes and I want to throw up.

"Doesn't someone look mighty tasty?" Scorpion sneers and subconsciously I move closer to Venom, like he's going to protect me. What a joke. Scorpion stands in front of me, scraping his tongue across his bottom lip and making me wince in disgust. "I see you're a natural beauty. Mr. Galiente is going to appreciate that." His rough, cold thumb rakes across my cheek. I jerk my head away, but really all I want to do is throw a punch right into his ugly face.

Venom guides me over then pushes me down to the seat in the middle of the gathering room. I get a good look at the place for the first time. It's some sort of cabin, or cottage. So, they took me to some place buried in the woods. Great.

I focus on my breathing, keeping it slow and steady. I can't lose my shit. I need to stay calm. When I look up, all the Skulls are staring at me. It's like being on display. I feel completely vulnerable. A shiver runs through me.

The sound of gravel and tires outside breaks the uncomfortable silence. It's not the sound of motorcycles so my excitement dies down immediately. I'm still holding onto the hope that Zach and his club are going to come save me.

"All right, everyone, scatter. I want men on the back doors, side and front. Now." They all scatter like ants and my hands fidget in my lap.

"Please, please, don't do this. I beg you." The fear inside me is enough to urge me to beg and plead. But Scorpion just sneers at me, not giving two shits about what's going to happen.

Three men walk inside; they're wearing suits and two of them look like security for the one in the middle. He's tall, well built, and if he wasn't here looking to buy me for sex, then I would even say he's somewhat attractive. He's dressed like a business man—maybe even involved with the mafia in some way. He takes his sunglasses off and stares right at me. I tense and a trickle of a tear falls down my left cheek.

The man stalks slowly to me with such evil in his eyes. Evil that's even stronger than Scorpion's. He tilts my head up, so I'm forced to stare at him, slowly moving it from side to side. "Her cheekbones are impeccable. And her skin is that of an angel's. Just heavenly." He does another look over, stepping back. "Stand up, girl." My heart skips a beat and the room spins. "Stand. Up. Now." His voice is stern but still eerily calm. I rise without any confidence because, well, what's one to do, when this sort of man is glaring at you like this? Sizing you up like his property. A man who might be buying you off as a sex slave.

He takes a step closer to me and my body freezes. Venom and Scorpion are watching like it's a free movie showing. "Her body is exquisite. Maybe I'll use her as one of my private dancers." He leans his head into my neck, breathing in deeply. "Lavender, it's such a delicate scent." His fingers graze my skin as they travel down my shoulder, skimming my breast before trailing over my waist.

"Would you like to sample the goods before purchasing?" Scorpion's voice carries over the shoulder of the man who is standing about three inches away from me.

C.M. Danks

No. Please say no. I won't be able to survive this *mentally*. I am not that strong. I'm not.

The man grins. "Is there a private room we can go to?"

My stomach twists, bile rising up in my throat—sheer panic at its best. I step back, hitting the chair with the underside of my legs, but the guy grabs hold of my waist while locking my arms behind me. Tears stream down my face and I want to scream. But what good is it? We're in the middle of the woods. Who would hear me anyway?

"There's a bedroom down the hall." Scorpion smirks.

I'm numb; my body is numb. There's nothing I can do. Nothing. I look at Venom, who seems to have all the color drained from his face. But I lose any hope when he walks away, following Scorpion. The door closes behind them, leaving me, the mafia guy and his two lackeys.

"All right, sweetheart, it's time for a little fun."

"Y-you don't have to do this. Is it money you want? I have it. I own a bar, so I make pretty decent money. I promise I'm good for it." That last part squeaks out as a hiccup of sobs escape me.

He brushes a strand of hair away from my tear-soaked face. "Shh, sweetheart. I don't do this for the money. If you knew who I was, you would know I already have all the money in the world." He spins me around so fast my back is flush against his front, and I can feel his hard-on pressed into me.

He walks us forward down the hall, but I try with all my might to fight him. He's just too strong. I'm practically skidding across the floor, burying the weight of my heels into the hardwood. As he pushes me into the bedroom, I'm tossed so hard that I land face down on the bed. He shuts the door, locks it, and starts undoing his tie.

CHARGER

"No, no, p-please, don't." My voice is unrecognizable. The sobs are uncontrollable.

He walks closer, stalking me like prey, then shrugs his suit jacket off and climbs on top of me. Holding onto my wrists and raising them above my head, he leans down and takes a long whiff, like he's smelling roses. Fucking psycho. I twist my head to the side, burying my cheek into the bedsheet that smells like mildew.

"I'll make this very enjoyable for you."

I start kicking, thrashing. "No! Get off me!" I move with panic in his grip, cry, scream, kick. He holds my wrists together with just one hand and grabs my breasts with his other. He then pulls the zipper down on the side of my dress. "He's going to fucking murder you. Do you hear me? He's going to fucking kill you!" I scream in his face and he smirks.

"I don't know who you're referring to, sweetheart. But *he* isn't here, now is he?"

He's right... he's not. My Zach, my Charger. He isn't here.

He continues to tug at my dress, slipping it down to my ankles. He studies every inch of my almost naked body and it makes me nauseous. I refuse to give up. I can't give up.

Just as I'm about to fight more, I hear the sounds of motorcycles outside and my body (despite this current situation) roars with excitement. Is it them? Gunshots echo back, followed by shouting.

It has to be them.

His attention goes straight to the chaos outside and I take this as my chance. In one quick motion, I jerk my knee up, striking him in the only proof of manhood he has left.

C.M. Danks

"Fucking bitch." He doubles over breathless before releasing a cry of pain.

I dart toward the door, unlock it, and whip it open. I walk slowly against the wall, making sure no one is there. I still hear a lot of commotion outside, yelling, more gunshots. *God, I hope it's them.* When I see that I'm in the clear, I open the back door, cautiously lurking around each corner. I hear Chain's voice and then Zach's. My heart stills. His voice is pure comfort so I follow it. There are some bodies (unrecognizable Skulls members) lying motionless on the ground. I step over them and, in the distance, I see Zach. He's shouting something—*likely threats.* The sound is muffled and my vision blurs from the tears.

I call out to him, but he doesn't hear me. My voice is still too faint. Then I start walking in his direction and yell one more time. "Zach!"

The men still, and Zach drops the guy he's holding by the shirt. "Jules!" I start to run, only now realizing I'm in my lace bra and thong panties. But I don't care. I just run. As I make it to the front of the house, someone jumps out in front of me, spins me around, and locks my arms behind my back. A knife is held to my throat, the sharp tip piercing into my skin.

I was so close.

"Drop the guns or I fucking slice her throat." It's the asshole who tried to rape me. He's shirtless, his hair disheveled with sweat beading down his face. "She's mine! No one else's."

"She's not fucking yours. Let her go." Zach inches closer.

Chain and the others lower their weapons. Venom is pinned against a tree by Tank, but Scorpion is nowhere to be found. I blink the tears away, letting them stream down my face. My body is exhausted, *I'm* exhausted, and I just want this to be over.

I jump when the sound of flesh being punctured fills my ears. Then a gargle emits from my captor as he hits the floor. Blood seeps from the bullet hole in the man's neck. It all happens so fast.

"Now that! That is why they call me Bullet."

I'm stunned, looking from the body to Bullet. Damn, he's a good shot. Thank fucking God.

"Jules, pretty girl."

My head whips to Zach, who's already stalking toward me. I unglue my feet from the ground and start running to him. Closer and closer, we lessen the distance between us. When I make it to him, I throw my body into his. It crashes hard and I bury myself in his chest. His strong arms tighten around my back, securing me against the beat of his heart and exactly where I belong. All the fear, the terror, vanishes from my body. His arms are my safety net.

"Jesus, Jules, I'm so sorry. I'm so fucking sorry." He breaks us apart, tugs his cut off and pulls his t-shirt over his head. "Put this on."

His shirt comes below my waist, stopping just above my knees and covering my undergarments. It's warm and smells like him. I wipe the tears from my cheeks and he tugs me back to him.

"Please tell me they didn't hurt you." His hand cups the back of my head; his other arm closes around my waist. My cheek is pressing onto his hard, bare chest and I relax into him, closing my eyes and finding comfort in listening to his heartbeat.

"No, they didn't. You got here just in time."

I feel his body loosen underneath mine.

C.M. Danks

"Fuck, man, at least take me out first." I tilt my head to the opposite side, enough to see Venom being manhandled by Tank. He's shoving him toward one of the cars.

"Come on, pretty girl, we have to get out of here. The guys will take care of all of this." He dips down, securing an arm under my knees. He picks me up in an effortless swoop. I lock my wrists around his neck while he carries me off.

"Hey, son, we got this. Get your girl home. One of the guys will drive your bike back." Chain tells Zach.

"I'll drive you both." Bullet nods our way.

Zach agrees, lowers me to the back seat of the Traverse, then scoots in beside me. He pulls me over so that I'm cradled in his lap. I curl up in his arms until I drift off.

CHAPTER THIRTY-SEVEN

Charger

I glance down at the most beautiful woman I have ever seen. She's strong, powerful, and she's mine.

She's lying motionless in my arms. Arms that were supposed to protect her, but couldn't. I failed. I've never been so scared of losing someone, and the thought of her being... For what it's worth, that's one thing I am happy about. They didn't touch her in that way. Thank fucking Christ.

Her small breaths hit my naked chest. I lean down, kissing her forehead, and she stirs at my touch.

"Hey." Her gorgeous eyes look up at me.

"Hey, pretty girl. We're almost back home. You slept the whole way." Her exhausted, saddened eyes make my smile fade. "Jules, I..." Her finger presses to my lips.

"You, Zachary Scott, will always be my everything. And today was not your fault. I can see it in your eyes—*that you're blaming yourself*. Don't you dare. It was going to happen regardless. So, you being in my life just saved me from a miserable, painful future. I love you, Zach. I love you until every star in the sky burns out. I've loved you since we were kids."

"I love you too. With every last fucking breath I take, I will always love you."

Her eyes, her smile, everything about her turns my world upright. It just makes sense. *She* makes sense. *We* make sense. I've waited for her for so long, and now I have her in my arms. But what if something like this happens again? Being in my world, the risks are always high. What if I can't protect her and Chloe? What if something worse were to happen, and I'm not able to save them?

Bullet pulls up to the clubhouse and I open the door, tucking Jules into my chest while scooping her up again. "You know, Zach, I promise you I can walk." She smirks and I grin back. "Yeah, babe, I know. But I would rather have you in my arms, if that's okay?"

She shrugs. "I don't mind."

I walk inside, carrying her up to my club bedroom. Setting her down, I take out a pair of sweatpants. "Angel called your parents. They'll bring Chloe back tomorrow when we know shit is safe."

"I'm sure they were a frantic mess." Jules hugs her midsection.

"Yeah, I'm probably back on the shit list with your father. At least, I would guess."

"Zach, I told you it's not your fault. You got me back." She steps closer, cupping my face. "This is where I want to be. With you. *Us*. Chloe, you, and me." She steps up on the tips of her feet and touches her lips to mine. I groan as she teases me with her tongue, the sensation shooting straight down to my dick. God, I want her. What kind of sick man wants to fuck his girl after she was kidnapped? "Zach, I want you to make love to me."

CHARGER

Those words send my manhood dancing. I squeeze her waist, jerking her to me until she hits my chest. I look down into her beautiful eyes. "Jules, maybe we shouldn't. You've been through a lot."

"I need this. I need to wash away the memories of those men and you're the only one who can do that." She grabs onto my shoulders. "I want you inside me, Charger."

Fuck. I love it when she calls me Zach, but goddamn, if hearing my club name like that wasn't the sexiest thing. I lift her up until she wraps her legs around my waist. Grabbing her ass, I walk us backwards until I hit the chair. I crash my mouth onto hers and sit while she straddles me. She pulls my shirt off her, throwing it across the room. We violently lock our lips together, tongue fucking like it's our dying wish.

My hands trace every inch of her body, feeling her silky soft skin under my touch. She leans forward and flicks her tongue on my piercing. "Fuck." I lay my head back as she starts grinding her soaked pussy on my dick. I can feel how wet she is even between our clothing. She unzips the top of my jeans and I lift my ass off the seat. Clutching her against my lap, I pull them down along with the hem of my boxers. We share an intense moment, before I tug her panties to the side, sliding my dick right into her.

"Fucking Christ, babe. You feel so good." I moan while unhooking her bra. She tilts her head back, her eyes closed, while I gently play at her *hard for me* nipples.

Then she starts moving on me, slow and steady at first, then faster. I fist her hair and tug her head back even more—sucking, kissing, grazing my teeth on her neck. There's a twinge of pain on my scalp when she pulls my hair at the top. And it turns me the fuck on even more. Each movement of her riding my dick has me closer to coming right inside her. My hands dig into her hips and I pump harder with each forward motion.

"Oh my God, Charger." She runs her fingers down her tits, then over her stomach. And I fucking lose it. I feel myself starting to let go.

So close.

As soon as she screams out in pleasure, I release. Stars blur my vision and I can feel her pussy pulsate around me.

When she comes down from her high, she rests her head on my shoulder.

"Damn, pretty girl. I'm never going to get enough of that."

She chuckles. "And I will never get enough of this." She wiggles her eyebrows as her fingertips skim down my chest to my abs. I give her a subtle kiss on the nose and she falls into me. I feel her soft skin as I rub my hands up and down her bare back.

"Move in with me, Jules. I've been trying to ask you that for a while now."

Her body tenses and slowly she straightens herself on top of me. "Really?"

Shit. Her face is telling me that might have been the wrong thing to say. Too fast, did she think I was moving too fast?

"Sorry, that was way too fast."

"No, I mean yes. I mean no, it's not too fast and yes, I want to live with you."

I relax, but my heart is still beating like it wants to jump out of my chest. "Yeah?" I smile and she smiles back.

"Yeah, I've been away from you for too long and I want to be with you always."

CHARGER

"Same, Jules." I tuck a lose strand of hair behind her ear. "We can get a house. Somewhere close to both your bar and my club. Guess I'm turning you into my Ol' Lady."

"Sounds perfect." She smiles.

"Does it scare you?"

She moves back so I can see her whole face. "Are you kidding? I want you to claim me. Own me. Possess every part of me, Charger."

I let out a growl, because what man doesn't want to hear that? "I plan on it, babe."

I lift her off me. "Let's get cleaned up. Shall we?"

★★★

Jules and I spend most of the day in bed together, talking, having sex, talking again, and more sex. I can't seem to get enough. No matter how many times my dick is inside her, it's never enough. I reassure her, over and over again, that tonight is a prime example of what my life could be like, but she doesn't seem to care. She wants us all to be a family, as do I. Nothing can stop that.

We talked about Joe for a little. She cried on my chest over the betrayal. She must be hurting and I can see why. She trusted someone, someone who she thought was like another father figure to her. But since the Skulls promised him a hefty share of cash, the fucker took it. They had Joe keep watch on any activity at the Fallen Star, and wanted him to kidnap her. Then, when he chickened out, they almost beat him to death. And now, now he wants a pass for it. A pass for not going through with it. Yeah, right. Scorpion

C.M. Danks

also found it amusing when everyone turned out to be connected. Jules, me, Venom. *Rat bastard.* Wherever their former Pres is, we'll find him. As for Joe? Yeah, deep down, Jules knows what happened to that piece of shit. However, I saved her the gory details. There's certain things we don't tell our Ol' Ladies and there's a reason for that.

I walk downstairs hand in hand with Jules, to where the guys are waiting. There's nothing but silence when they see us. I get a look from Chain, telling me it's time for that meeting. Jules, being the amazing woman that she is, already knows.

"I think I'll go help Mags with dinner." She turns, slowly letting go of my hand, but she comes back to stand close to me. "Charger, whatever it is you plan on doing with Venom, I just want you to know that he did save me from Scorpion at one point. Just remember that."

Jules, my kind-hearted woman, always finding the glimmer of good in people when she can. But Venom, he doesn't have one decent bone inside his body. Not one. So, whatever we end up doing to him, in the long run, it will never be enough. I run my thumb across her soft cheek and plant a kiss on her forehead.

"Don't worry about him, babe, okay?"

She hesitates, then slowly nods before turning and leaving us. I wait until I hear the clunking of pots and pans.

"Where is he?" I ask them, grinding my teeth together. My fists are aching to feel his face, to break some goddamn bones.

"Hang on." Chain walks over, hands in the air. "We got him in the pit's basement, but listen to me. We need him alive. That bastard Scorpion took off before we got there,

CHARGER

and no one knows where the fuck he's at. And our best chance at finding him is in that pit." He points out back.

I look at the rest of the guys: Tank, Hush, Bullet, Throttle. They're all giving me the same look. The look that says, "Sorry, man, but he's right."

"Chain, Pres. He kidnapped my Ol' Lady. He helped Scorpion almost sell her off to a fucking mob boss. So, what you're asking of me, not to touch him, not to crush his skull with my bare hands, I cannot, and will not do." I'm quick on my feet, heading for the back door. But the loud thunderous voice behind me stops me dead in my tracks.

"I'm not asking you. Everyone seems to think I'm asking people to do things. No." He chuckles. "No, son, I'm fucking telling you right now. You are not to touch him." By this time, I've already turned around, looking him straight in the eyes. Eyes that drip with authority, with rage, with fury. The same emotions mine held at the cottage. He steps closer, a nose hair from my face, and we're toe-to-toe. "You think your girl is the only one? You think she's the only one they planned on taking, on fucking selling? Believe me, son, I fucking get it. I would want to destroy whoever touched, whoever hurt, my Ol' Lady too, but let me tell you something. Do you want to be responsible for another woman getting hurt because you can't control your fucking anger?"

Thinking of being *that* guy, of being someone who could be responsible for taking away another life, makes me sick.

"Fuck," I sigh and Chain smirks.

"You'll get your chance. This just isn't it."

I nod, but really… I want to punch something.

"Okay, but can we all acknowledge the fact that our boy Charger here just called Jules his Ol' Lady." Tank laughs, everyone else joining in.

My fury softens. My Jules. My Ol' Lady.

"Well, shit." Bullet gets off his stool and walks to me, slapping me on the shoulder. "Guess a fucking congratulations is in order."

"I mean, it's about damn time you claimed that shit," Throttle chimes in, then gives me the same slap to the shoulder, followed by another—this one from Hush.

"Uh, there is one more thing." We all go silent as we look at Chain. "That mob boss who Bullet shot… Turns out he has a brother. A very powerful brother. And I have a feeling once he finds out about us sending his sibling six feet under, we're going to have a real fucking shit show on our hands."

The mood shifts almost immediately, all laughter stifled.

"Fuck, ain't that a bitch."

Tank rubs his chin before Chain replies, "Which is why the faster we find Scorpion, the better."

"So, what do you plan on doing with Venom, boss? Leaving him down there with his thoughts and feelings?" Tank asks the question we were all thinking.

"I might have an idea."

We all exchange looks. This could be interesting.

CHARGER

CHAPTER THIRTY-EIGHT

Jules

The smile on my face only grows bigger watching Chloe with Charger. I decided to call him Charger from here on out. The man before me, bouncing his five-year-old daughter on his knee, is not the boy I used to know. Sure, the kind, strong-willed, protective boy is still in there. But he's different. He's not the football-type jock who would make out with Sam in the hallways. Or, I guess you could say, he never was that boy to begin with. He never wanted to play football as a career. Hell, he never even wanted to go to college. He always wanted to be himself. And *that* was never him. He was the guy who wanted to be free, who wanted to own his own motorcycle, wanted to rebel in the most honest way he knew how. Somehow, whatever hardships he had to face along the way brought him to exactly where he needed and wanted to be.

"Uncle Chain, do you and Aunt Maggie have any cookies?"

Charger tugs me to him. Maggie makes a dramatically playful face. "Do we have any cookies? What kind of place do you think we're running here, young lady? Of course, we have cookies."

C.M. Danks

"Yeah, dontcha know, squirt, your Aunt Mags here makes the best dam-dang chocolate chip cookies around," Tank says to Chloe.

"Yay!"

"Only a couple. You'll spoil your appetite, little bug."

"Aw, come on, Mommy."

"Yeah, come on, Mommy. You're no fun." I smack Charger on his chest and he laughs while rubbing it. Maggie smiles then looks over at Chain.

"How about us girls go see what we can find, huh?" Maggie takes Chloe and I catch the hint. I follow Mags and Chloe to the back.

★★★

Charger

"So, anyone else find it strangely eerie that we're all hanging out, while Venom is chained to the pit floor like a rabid dog? I mean, let me just quickly say I'm not complaining. Guy's a bastard. I'm just saying... it's sort of a buzzkill," Tank directs his statement to Chain.

It's been a couple of days since everything went down, and all of us have been keeping close watch on the women, including Angel. Although she likes to venture off to God only knows where from time to time.

There's still no word on Scorpion. It's like he just up and ran. His club is going about their everyday business, but without their President, which leads us to believe that they're somehow communicating with him. Let's not forget about the fact that Venom, who we still have locked away in the pit's basement, is cramping my fucking style.

"Yeah, yeah, I know. I'm workin' on it. He's fine. Last time one of the prospects checked, he was enjoying his little getaway to the Steel Valley Chains' pit." Chain grunts. "And what do you know, our guest of honor, the girl I needed to speak to just walked the fuck in." I give Chain a questionable look as he waves Angel over. "Girl's been on my shit list ever since the bar incident."

Angel comes strutting over in her high-heeled boots and leather pants. Tank whistles under his breath. "Damn, girl, where you going tonight? Or should I ask where did you come from?"

She plucks the lime out of Tank's drink and sucks on it. Then she drops it back into the glass. "What? I need an excuse to look this good? And I see you guys started the party without me. What are we celebrating? I mean, besides Charger here finally sealing the deal with his woman?" She elbows me playfully in the side while Chain stares at her blankly.

"Well, since you've been a pain in my ass lately, I came up with the perfect job for you."

Angel's playfully flirty smile fades. "Chain, you know I've apologized like over and over to you. I know I fucked up that night."

"Broken promises, sweetheart." He crosses his arms over his broad chest. "You know a certain person of interest in the pit out back, yeah?"

Watching Chain talk to Angel is like watching a father scold his daughter. The arm she had draped across Tank's shoulder falls to her side as she straightens from her relaxed position.

"Please, please, tell me that whatever it is you want to punish me with, it has nothing to do with Venom?"

Chain smiles and swigs back his whiskey. "See, you got beauty and brains. Meet me in my office first thing in the a.m. Got me, girl?"

She stares for a moment, then grabs the rest of Tank's drink, downing it in one take back. "Needs more lime." She winks and struts off.

I stare at my girls from afar. We closed the bar to outside visitors until we get shit straight with Venom. And tonight, it's just a small gathering with my club, Jules, and Chloe.

She looks fucking happy and so am I. I rub my chest where the aching pain likes to resurface from time to time. Garrett would have been the best fucking uncle to our daughter. But I no longer hold onto that guilt. *I can't*. Today is the day I let go. Let go and let myself be happy.

I kiss my two fingers and point them up to the sky. "Miss you, my brother."

Jules shoots me a smile and I wink back at her.

This is it. My girls. Their protector. My everything.

CHARGER

EPILOGUE

One Month Later

Jules

"Mommy, Daddy! They have a swing set!" Chloe runs to Charger, grabbing hold of his hand and dragging him as best she can to the backyard. I can't help but laugh. I mean, who wouldn't? Although I do feel like I could cry too. Happy tears, not sad ones.

This was the second house we looked at today. It feels more like home than the first one, and it's closer to both his club and the Fallen Star.

The realtor walks out, but stops dead when Charger stands to greet her from the sandbox. I can see her mouth salivating from over here. Since high school, women have swooned over him. He has this power to make every girl's panties wet. And now, shit, now, he is every bit of six foot three and lean muscle. And you can't forget about the tattoos, piercing blue eyes, and one hell of an ass. I shake my head and roll my eyes as I move beside him, placing a hand to his chest.

"Hi, I'm Julianna and this here is Charger, and our daughter Chloe." Chloe waves from the sandbox.

C.M. Danks

The woman flashes an apologetic smile. "I am so sorry. I didn't mean to stare. It's just, um…"

"Oh, it's okay. I get it. I'm used to it actually."

Charger laughs and the realtor chuckles uncomfortably. "Right, I'm not surprised." Anyway, this home has just been newly renovated. The cabinets and flooring were just redone so if you want, we can start the tour inside."

Chloe comes between Charger and me. We each take one of her hands as we walk inside the two-story dream home. Our (soon-to-be) future home. Given the circumstances, my life couldn't be more perfect. I glance over. My Charger. Our protector. My everything.

The End.
But only until next time…

CHARGER

STAY TUNED

For Angel and Venom's story!

Enjoyed *Charger*? Check out another novel by the author: *Dance For Me*

C.M. Danks

ACKNOWLEDGEMENTS

Always chase your dreams.

Thank you so much for reading *Charger*! My love for a good MC romance made writing this one so much fun! Living in Ohio, I wanted to create a world that existed, yet is still fictional. The reason I chose the name Steel Valley Chains MC? My hometown is known as: The Steel Valley. So, what better way to include my hometown in a book that's so important to me?

I need to thank my husband first because he is, and will always be, my biggest supporter. No matter what, he's behind me every step of the way. He fully understands all the "research" that goes into making good teasers. Wink, wink.

I want to thank my family, because I wouldn't be who I am today without them. Not to mention, my mom: my best friend, my Barnes and Noble, book-obsessed shopping buddy. Thanks for letting me swoon over book boyfriends with you. Also, thanks for saying that my books are *the best ever*! But I feel like you might be a tad biased (Lol).

Thank you to my first author friend, Michelle B. I would have been a lost mess without you! You're such a fun, genuine person, and I can't thank you enough for everything you have done and still do for me! Also, thanks for suggesting this stellar line in my Chapter 14: "…leave

CHARGER

my thoughts, my head, my mind, my body." P.S. I will never get over Antonio! Your books are on fire!

Tempest, you are truly one of the kindest, sweetest people I know. You were one of the first people on Instagram I talked to. You have created wonderful edits for my books and supported me every step of the way! Thank you for rearranging my words and making the blurb for *Charger* even better. Thanks for chatting with me about music, books, and just random things like chocolate. Lol. You are a beautiful person. Keep shining bright. Your book *Damien, Forever* will always be close to my heart. "Kisses and Bites."

Kat Pagan, who is not only a kind soul, but my amazing editor for *Charger*! Thank you for turning my mistakes and mess of words into a readable novel! Also, your support means the world.

Daria, you created my first author logo and I still can't believe how stunning it is. It fits me perfectly. I love it so much! You made me some awesome graphics along the way too. Thanks for all the support you have shown me.

Nola Marie, girl. Your *Men of River City* are hot! Thanks for writing them and thanks for all the support you show me every day!

Anita, you are amazing to all of us authors every day in the social media world. Your kindness outshines the darkest rain cloud. Thank you!

Garry, you are such a fabulous, down to earth person, who has shown me nothing but love and support. Thanks for loving Jack and Vanessa in *Dance For Me* as much as I do! Your book *Break Point* is a hit!

C.M. Danks

Dahlia, your support means the world. I love your books, but you already know that. Apollo and Sienna broke my heart and I loved every minute of it.

Finn, your super cool personality makes Instagram more fun. Thanks for all your support!

Thank you to these lovely people as well: Marla, Sebrero Sisters, RC, Felsi, Nikki, Michelle, Andrea, Nybooklover, Melissa, Lorelei, Anna, Cali girl, Patricia, Renee, and so many others! Thank you so much!

And to all my readers: Thank you for reading and sharing this journey with me! This series is going to be one heck of a ride!

With love… until every last star burns out, C.M. Danks.

About the Author

Author C.M. Danks is a proud wife and small-town girl, turned dreamer. She is a caring Medical Assistant, who graduated from her local college in 2014. Her love for reading romance turned into a passionate hobby of writing.

She has an obsession with Starbucks, video games, anime, coffee, and anything sweet.

Feel free to stalk!

Instagram
https://www.instagram.com/c.m.danks/

Facebook
https://www.facebook.com/profile.php?id=100063706299757

Facebook Author Page
https://www.facebook.com/cmdanksbooks/

Goodreads
https://www.goodreads.com/author/show/20959445.C_M_Danks

Amazon

C.M. Danks

https://www.amazon.com/C.M.-Danks/e/B08Q3X8SBD

BookBub
https://www.bookbub.com/profile/c-m-danks

Twitter
https://mobile.twitter.com/CMDanks1